"I understand you've... declined all your potential husbands."

Tibi froze. Aware that her inability to secure a husband had not only enraged her father but had made her a joke, she was mortified to think of Alexius laughing about her behind her back. "Are you mocking me?"

"No. If anything, I admire your unwillingness to accept just any man for a husband."

"I haven't declined all of them," she admitted, enraptured by his nearness and the intensity of his silver eyes enough to speak without subterfuge. "They don't want me."

Tibi tugged free of his grasp, regretting the loss of contact the same instant. To her chagrin, his easy release of her hand when moments before he'd insisted on holding her smacked of rejection.

"Then they must have been deaf and blind, as well as ignorant."

Startled by the unexpected compliment, she reminded herself that Alexius charmed women with the ease of a cobra mesmerizing prey. And he was just as dangerous. To her, perhaps more so.

Books by Carla Capshaw

Love Inspired Historical

The Gladiator
The Duke's Redemption
The Protector
The Champion

CARLA CAPSHAW

Florida native Carla Capshaw is a preacher's kid who grew up grateful for her Christian home and loving family. Always dreaming of being a writer and world traveler, she followed her wanderlust around the globe, including a year spent in the People's Republic of China, before beginning work on her first novel.

A two-time RWA Golden Heart Award winner, Carla loves passionate stories with compelling, nearly impossible conflicts. She's found inspirational historical romance is the perfect vehicle to combine lush settings, vivid characters and a Christian worldview. Currently at work on her next manuscript for Love Inspired Historical, she still lives in Florida, but is always planning her next trip…and plotting her next story.

Carla loves to hear from readers. To contact her, visit www.carlacapshaw.com or write to Carla@carlacapshaw.com.

Carla Capshaw

THE CHAMPION

Love Inspired

Recycling programs for this product may not exist in your area.

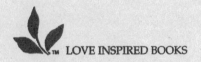 LOVE INSPIRED BOOKS

ISBN-13: 978-0-373-82879-1

THE CHAMPION

www.LoveInspiredBooks.com

Printed in U.S.A.

Blessed are those who hear the word of God,
and keep it.
—*Luke* 11:28

My parents, Kenneth and Patricia Hughes.

Everyone should be as blessed
to have parents like you!

Your fifty plus years of marriage and decades
of ministerial service have shown me true love
and true faith do exist in a world that constantly
questions both. I love you with all my heart.

Chapter One

Rome, AD 84

"You're useless, Tibi. You've been nothing but a disappointment since the day you were born."

Numb to her father's constant condemnation, Tibi stared out the open window of her family's Palatine home. Except for a few distant cook fires dotting the nearby hills, darkness covered Rome like a thick, heavy blanket. The night was still and silent as though it waited to learn Tibi's fate.

"Lepidus was the last man of good family willing to wed you," Tiberius continued to rant. "If he wanted to sample you before the wedding, who are you to object? Instead of welcoming his advances, as you should have done, you reaffirmed your willful reputation and denied him at every turn. Little wonder he stormed from here with no wish to see you again. No man wants a disobedient wife. Not even when her father is willing to pay a fortune to be rid of her."

Tibi winced, but remained silent. She'd stopped defending herself years ago when she realized that her father always sided against her.

"Why the gods cursed me with *two* daughters and took my adopted son is beyond my ken, but at least your sister over there had the decency to bring political connections to this house when she wed Senator Tacitus three years ago. As for you, you're a disgrace."

In the face of her father's condemnation, she'd forgotten that Tiberia, her elder, more winsome sister, sat in an alcove near the inner courtyard. Closing her eyes, Tibi breathed in deep to ward off an onslaught of total humiliation. The sweetness of her perfume mocked her earlier decision to forgo the formless linen tunics and comfortable shoes she preferred in favor of feminine silks and the bejeweled sandals now pinching her toes. Despite her father's belief that she went out of her way to foil all his plans for her, she'd prepared for tonight with care in an effort to please her family and make a good impression on her intended groom.

Shivering from the cool night air, she rubbed the tender spot on her upper arm where Lepidus had grabbed her. He'd cornered her in the shadows of one of the garden columns, then tried to force himself on her while the other guests cheered the gladiatorial contest her father had arranged for their entertainment. She'd narrowly escaped Lepidus's mauling by biting his lip and refusing to let go until he released her. Neither he nor her father had considered her self-defense justified. Lepidus had stormed from the house, vowing revenge on her shameless behavior and leaving her to bear the brunt of her father's wrath.

"Four broken betrothals, Tibi. *Four.* I'm at the end of my patience with you."

Tibi tightened her jaw to keep from scoffing. When had he ever been patient with her? As a child she'd wondered why he tolerated her elder sister, Tiberia, yet ignored *her*. She'd tried to gain his love by being quiet and obedient, two traits her mother assured her would lead to his affection, but he continued to regard her as less important than the rugs he trod upon.

As she'd grown older, she realized that she disappointed her father simply by being a girl. The knowledge killed any hope of winning his affection. Instead, she'd worked to earn his respect and shone in areas traditionally reserved for boys. She'd studied history, astronomy and philosophy. She knew how to read and write Latin, as well as speak Greek. She excelled at archery and practiced athletics at the bath's gymnasium. But she remained a failure in his eyes.

"Look at me," Tiberius demanded sharply.

Tibi forced her feet to comply and turned around to face him. Aware of the bitterness oozing from her soul, she avoided looking at him directly and studied the lantern-lit room beyond his shoulder. A whiff of incense was the last trace of the disastrous banquet held earlier. Slaves had cleared the colorful room of dishes and swept the mosaic tiles clean. The low couches the diners reclined on while eating had been restored to their proper places against the frescoed walls.

"Your mother coddled you, insisting I waste coin on tutors that gave you the mistaken impression that your opinion counts the same as a man's," he sneered. "However, if you were *wise,* you'd understand that at eighteen years old, you're well past a ripe marriage age. A girl is a drain on her family if she doesn't marry for connections. Since no acceptable man will have you, I'm taking you to the temple of Opis tomorrow—"

Both girls gasped in unison. Tibi's heart kicked with alarm. Her appalled gaze darted to her father's angry visage. As she expected, his narrowed eyes radiated his antipathy.

"Father, please." Tiberia, silent until now, rose elegantly from a bench placed beneath one of the archways leading to the garden. "Isn't that a bit extreme? Perhaps Antonius—"

"Quiet! If I want your counsel I'll ask for it, daughter. Your husband has already done all I can expect of him by arranging this gathering tonight. Even with his far-flung and lofty contacts, Tibi's reputation for humiliating men precedes her. It was no simple task for him to snare Lepidus's interest."

Like Jupiter condemning mankind from the summit of Olympus, Tiberius jabbed his index finger in Tibi's direction. "That…that *girl* has embarrassed me for the last time. If she won't bring honor to this house through marriage, I'll see that she fulfills her duty to this family another way and buy her a position as a priestess. Who better for her to serve than the goddess of abundance and fertility? She can attempt to garner blessings for all of us. Who knows? She might even be able to correct your failure as a wife and wrangle a child for you in the bargain."

Tibi's stomach churned. The threat of having to perform fertility rites caused her palms to begin to sweat. The room seemed to swirl. "No—"

"Cease." Tiberius pinned her with a livid glare, his full cheeks bright red with fury. "How dare you presume to say no to me? I'm your *father*. Not some wretch you can chase off with your contrary ways."

Horrified, Tibi watched him stalk toward her, an unnatural gleam in his eyes.

"Get to your room before I club you," he ordered, his lips almost purple in his rage. "And don't come down until you're sent for. I can't bear to look at you a moment longer."

Brimming with resentment, she forced herself to keep silent before glancing toward the front door and the freedom beyond the heavy stone portal.

Tiberius lunged toward her, his fist clenched. She sped past him and up the stairs to her room. A servant had lit a fat candle on the dressing table in the far corner. Careful not to slam the door for fear of invoking more of her father's ire, she closed the wood panel behind her and collapsed against it. Her heart was racing as much from her father's threats as from her own anger. At times like this she missed her mother most. Not that Cornelia would have gone against her husband's dictates, but she would have been a shoulder to lean on until Tibi's punishment was carried out.

Despondent, she crossed to the dressing table and removed the diadem of sapphires and gold pins from her blond hair before braiding the long tresses into a single plait that hung to the small of her back. The candlelight illuminated the polished metal mirror hanging on the wall in front of her. She studied the distorted reflection of herself.

Unlike her dark, classically beautiful sister, she was an oddity, not only in looks with her light hair and pale skin, but in her thoughts and deeds as well. A proper woman was meant to be meek, to thrive only in the shadow of her husband and accept his opinions as her own. Little wonder no man had been willing to put up with her when what she longed for most was to be appreciated for herself.

A knock sounded on the door. "Open," Tiberia called. "Father ordered me to stay with you until morning."

Tibi gritted her teeth. She flung the door wide and glared at her sister. "From senator's wife to prison guard all in one evening, Tiberia? How proud you must be."

Tiberia rolled her dark brown eyes. "By the gods, Tibi, you cause your own misery." Her regal sister strolled into the room. The glitter of her jewels and the opulence of her red silk *stola* declared her status as a woman of wealth and social importance. "I've been telling you for years if you'd guard your tongue and do what's expected, life would flow more smoothly for you."

"You believe I should have allowed Lepidus to molest me?" Tibi asked sharply.

"I think it would have made no difference." Tiberia drifted across the room to Tibi's dressing table and began to straighten the perfume bottles and jars of cosmetics into a line. "The marriage contract was ready to be signed. Once you were wed, you would have belonged to him to do with as he liked anyway."

Tibi bristled with indignation. She'd expected as much from her sister, who was a firm believer in the established order, but it hurt that her own flesh and blood couldn't be counted on to side with her.

"However, it seems that the matter is neither here nor there," Tiberia continued. "Your chance to marry walked out the door along with Lepidus. Father was serious about offering you to the temple tomorrow."

"I was just as serious about *not* going," Tibi said, her spine taut. "He doesn't believe it, but I want very much to wed and have children of my own someday."

"One would never know by the way you cast off suitors."

She considered the long list of fortune hunters, old

men and toads like Lepidus her father had wooed on her behalf. "I realize I'm no prize," Tibi said. "But surely there's at least one man in the province who will want to wed me for *me* and not Father's wealth or *your* husband's social rank."

"You speak of love?" Tiberia's tone mocked her. "How did you become so fanciful?"

"I'm talking about respect." Tiberia's attitude annoyed her, especially when her sister's marriage had been celebrated as a rare love match. "When did you become a cynic?"

"I'm not cynical. I'm realistic enough to accept the world for what it is. I was fortunate to marry a highly acceptable man who returned my affections, but even if I'd despised him, I'd have wed him. Marriage is for personal and familial honor…social position…security…legitimate children. Much more serious issues than simple emotion."

"That's easily said when you have all that you hope for."

"No one has all they hope for. Why should you be different? Father has no son. I have yet to give my husband his longed-for heir. My husband's desired advancement within the Senate is far from certain." Tiberia's jaw tightened. "Listen to me. Respect can be earned and love is fleeting, Tibi. Men who fall in love can fall out again just as quickly. If lasting love and respect are what you want, join the temple. Do your duty to your family, bask in the affections of the goddess's patrons, then seek your passions later wherever you happen to find them."

Caught between the reality of her choices and her heart's desire, Tibi shook her head emphatically. "How can I enter the temple when I'm not even certain I believe in the gods—"

"Say no more!" Tiberia fumbled the glass bottle she held, but caught it before it crashed to the floor. "It's bad enough you've disgraced us all tonight, but do you want to invoke the displeasure of our ancestors and the deities as well?"

Tibi stood from the bed and began to pace the rectangular room. The floor tiles were almost as cold as her father's heart toward her. The walls seemed to be closing in like a trap.

"Please don't tell me you've followed Pelonia's bad example and become one of those Christians." Tiberia shuddered delicately. "You know I love Pelonia with all my heart. I can't wait to see her when she arrives in Rome tomorrow, but her choice of religion and husband leaves *much* to be desired."

Tibi stopped by the window. The cool night air ruffled the flaxen curls framing her face as she looked blindly into the night. Hope flickered inside her like the candle on the dressing table. In the chaos of the banquet preparations and the ensuing catastrophe she'd forgotten about their cousin's visit. The reminder helped lessen her gloom. At last she began to see a twinkle of light in the darkness. If anyone might help her, Pelonia and her husband, Caros, might. Like her, they understood what it was to live on the edge of acceptability.

"I disagree," Tibi murmured. "You and Father may see them as mismatched, but Pelonia adores Caros while he practically worships her and their sons. As for their religion, at least they believe in a God of love—"

"Enough." Tiberia shook her head and eyed Tibi with exasperation. "Why do you have to be so blunt and disagreeable? Not everything has to be a contest of opinions. I realize that Pelonia leads a life charmed by Fortune, but she married a lowly *gladiator*. Those men are animals—foreigners and criminals who deserve to die in the sand."

"Tiberia—!"

"And," Tiberia continued undaunted, "if she doesn't keep her choice of religion a secret she might find herself sentenced to the arena *again*. Is that what *you* want? To shame your family more than you already have? To be pitied everywhere you go because you threw yourself away on an ex-slave?"

Although she'd known Tiberia hated Caros for once enslaving their cousin three years earlier, she was stunned by Tiberia's vehemence. The former *lanista* had repented of his ways long ago and proven to be a marvelous husband. No one outside their own family pitied Pelonia. If anything, women from Rome to Umbria secretly envied her.

"Better an ex-slave who's handsome, rich and adores me," Tibi said, "than to sacrifice my life serving a goddess I don't believe in. As for shaming my family, didn't you hear Father? I've been a disappointment since the day I was born. Truly, I'm certain he considers it a shame that I *was* ever born."

The silence lingered. Tiberia couldn't refute a fact they both knew to be true. She turned sharply on her heel and sought out the cushioned chair near the door. Her thoughts in a tumble, Tibi renewed her pacing. Certain she was beyond the reaches of prayer, she fully believed her father planned to be free of her one way or the other.

Somehow she had to escape to the *Ludus Maximus* before sunrise or her father would have a chance to carry out his threat. Caros had sold the *ludus* two years earlier to Alexius of Iolcos, but he and Pelonia stayed there when they returned from Umbria for several weeks each spring.

Tibi only hoped her cousin's plans hadn't changed without warning. If they had made other arrangements, she'd find herself facing Alexius and the mortification that would smother her if he learned the reason behind her current predicament.

A vision of piercing eyes the color of liquid silver formed in her mind's eye. She slowed to a stop in the center of the bedchamber. Ever since she'd first met Alexius three years ago, she'd steered clear of the Greek as much as possible when she visited her cousins to avoid the peculiar way he affected her senses. Just the sound of his softly accented voice infused her with warmth.

She shook her head, determined not to dwell on the darkly handsome *lanista* or the way his quick smile seemed to melt her bones. Although he could have retired from the games when he took over the *Ludus Maximus*, Alexius preferred to fight. He remained Rome's premier gladiatorial champion, a titan who stirred rumors as much for his womanizing as for his bloodlust and lack of pity in the arena.

And I'd be a fool to let myself become enamored with a man as callous as Father.

Not that Alexius had ever made the slightest overture toward her, she mused as she exchanged the silk she wore for a tunic of dark gray wool. In truth, the Greek seemed just as intent on evading her as she was determined to avoid him. Which didn't surprise her, since females all over Rome vied for his attention and she was a woman *no* man wanted.

At the basin, she cleansed her face, wishing she

could wash away the knowledge that she was a failure both to her family and as a woman as easily as she removed the kohl and rouge from her pale skin.

Once Tiberia fell asleep, Tibi quietly packed a small pouch of coins, three fresh tunics, several pieces of jewelry to sell if need be and a few other necessities into a leather satchel. Wondering if her plan to escape was brave or foolhardy, she reminded herself that she had no other option unless she wished to join the temple.

Icy fingers of disgust crept across the back of her neck. She made haste and secured a sheathed knife to her belt for protection before making her way into the dimly lit hall. Downstairs, she slipped past the guard who'd fallen asleep in the courtyard and silently out the door.

Taking a deep breath of crisp night air, she brushed off her fear of the eerily deserted streets and kept to the shadows as she hurried in the direction of the gladiator school.

Alexius of Iolcos set down his chalice of wine, rattled the dice in his hand and cast the ivory pieces onto the scarred wooden table. Seeing the winning roll, the bevy of beauties surrounding him clapped and shrieked like inebriated water nymphs. His opponents' agonized groans competed with the revelry of his many guests and the wandering musicians whose bawdy songs filled the public rooms of the *domus*.

Alexius laughed and taunted the other players good-naturedly, although he was less than satisfied with his win. Of late, boredom trailed him without mercy. The endless stream of wine, women and work no longer muted the monstrous rage he constantly fought to keep caged within him. Known for his congenial nature outside the ring, he found it more and more difficult to smile and pretend that his meaningless existence was any more useful than a dry well in a desert.

As *lanista* of the *Ludus Maximus* and Rome's current gladiator champion, he ruled over a kingdom of vice and violence. He had a comfortable life, a better life than a foreigner and once-condemned man had any right to hope for, but he'd known for months that he needed a change for his sanity's sake.

"Master," his steward, Velus, said over the music and grousing of the other players, "there's a woman here to see you."

"Who is it?" he tossed over his shoulder distractedly as he scooped up his winnings.

The steward's fidgeting drew Alexius's full attention. Velus didn't usually hesitate when he announced the steady stream of female admirers who visited the gladiators on a regular basis. The older man, a dwarf Alexius had saved from certain death as lion fodder in the arena, motioned to come closer and whispered for only his master to hear, "Mistress Pelonia's cousin, Tiberia the Younger."

Tibi? Alexius tensed. His smile faltered. He forgot the remaining coins on the tabletop even as his heart began to echo the drums' frenzied beat. Perhaps—hopefully—he'd misheard.

"Who brought her here?"

"She's alone."

He scowled. He usually admired the girl's untamed spirit, but not when it led her to wander Rome's dangerous streets at all hours of the night. There was no acceptable reason for a well-born woman to venture out alone a few hours after midnight unless...

"Has there been an accident?" he demanded. "Is she hurt?"

"Not that I know of, master, but she's adamant to speak with you."

"Where is she?" Alexius's gaze circled the smoky room on a quest to find Tibi's splendid golden hair. He didn't want her here. The evening may have started out as a *coena libera,* the solemn last meal for the gladiators scheduled to fight the next afternoon, but had rapidly unraveled into a raucous affair of dancing, games of chance and other debauchery he didn't want to be responsible for an innocent girl like Tibi to witnessing.

"She's waiting in your office," Velus said.

Alexius sent the steward to fetch Tibi something to eat and drink from the banquet table overflowing with fresh fruit, breads, roasted fowl and a variety of fish.

Several of the men and women playing dice with him had wandered over to the food during his exchange with Velus, but a few vultures waited expectantly for any scrap of gossip. Gossip he wasn't about to feed them. Tibi's reputation was colorful enough as it was. If she were tattled on for venturing to the gladiator school at this hour, she was bound to suffer trouble with her overbearing father.

Confident that Tibi would go unnoticed in his office, Alexius excused himself from the table as eager to find out the reason for her appearance as to send her safely on her way. As he cut through the maze of revelers, across the central garden and down the long, lantern-lit corridor that separated the house's public rooms from his private sanctuary, he forced his feet to a slow pace, careful not to betray his interest in the night's newest development. The girl's arrival was the first thing to spark any excitement in him in…he couldn't remember how long.

The thought of Tibi made him smile. Both beautiful, yet unaware of the fact, and classically feminine, but audacious, she was as unique as a sunrise—pleasantly different each time he saw her.

Unfortunately, as the cousin of his friends, Caros and Pelonia, Tibi was one of only a handful of females in all of Rome off-limits to him. Caros had made certain of that when he made Alexius swear to stay away from the girl.

Still…something unfortunate must have happened for her to seek him out. If she needed him, it might prove entertaining for a while to offer his help.

Alexius entered his office to find Tibi pacing in front of the long row of arched windows overlooking the gladiators' training field. Stars sparkled in the black sky behind her, a serene contrast to her obvious agitation.

He watched her for a long moment, suddenly unable to breathe. In the six months since he'd last seen her, she'd grown even lovelier than he remembered. Candlelight caused her golden braid to shimmer as she walked from one side of the room to the other and her fair skin was as smooth and creamy as a perfect cameo. For a man who enjoyed women of all shapes, sizes and looks, it was a new experience for him to be knocked breathless by the sight of one.

Shaking off her spell, he leaned against the door frame, crossed his arms over his chest and adopted a nonchalant tone. "Hello, Tibi."

Tibi stilled, then spun to face Rome's champion. "Hello…Alexius."

"Why are you here?" he asked. "It's a bit late—or early—in the day for you to drop by, no?"

Her cheeks burned under the heat of Alexius's warm regard. Her heart fluttered wildly. Finding herself in his company was even more disconcerting than she remembered. Tall and muscular, he was a vibrant man who filled the room with energy and sent her senses reeling.

She dragged in a deep breath to calm her jangled nerves and swallowed thickly. "I understand Caros and Pelonia are coming to Rome for a visit. I'd hoped they were already here. I need to speak with them."

Without taking his eyes off her, Alexius left the doorway and crossed the tiled floor to his desk. "I expect them some time today. Tomorrow at the latest."

"Ah…" Tibi worried at her bottom lip as she struggled to hide her rising desperation. "I'm wasting your time then. I apologize for taking you from your guests."

"No need to apologize." He sounded sincere. "I'd much rather be here with you."

His Greek accent whispered across her skin like the softest caress. Her eyes rounded with surprise before she quickly glanced away. How was it possible for him to touch her without actually *touching* her? "I must be going. I'll come back later."

"Where will you go?" he asked, easing toward her. "It's the middle of the night. I suspect you can't go home. You must be in serious trouble to risk the danger of wandering the streets like a common *pornai*."

She breathed in his scent of smoke and the heady mix of exotic spices. "It's nothing. I wished to speak with Pelonia. I…I've missed her this past year—that's all."

"I can tell you lie as plainly as I can see you're trembling." His calloused palms engulfed her cold hands, refusing to release her when she tried to pull away. "Tell me the truth and I'll free you."

She stopped struggling. It was no use to fight a man famous for his success in battle. "My father…"

"Go on," he invited when she fell into silence. "What's the old dragon done this time?"

Her gaze darted to the shadows dancing on the wall behind him. "He wishes me to wed."

"No surprise there. He'd already prepared you for sacrifice on the marriage altar when I first met you three years ago. I understand you've…declined all your potential husbands."

She froze. Aware that her inability to secure a husband had not only enraged her father but had made her a joke among the females of her social class, she was mortified to think of Alexius laughing about her with his women behind her back. "Are you mocking me?"

"No. If anything, I respect your unwillingness to accept just any man as a husband."

"I haven't declined all of them," she admitted, disturbed by his nearness and the incandescence of his silver eyes enough to speak without subterfuge. "They don't want me."

She tugged free of his grasp, regretting the loss of contact the same instant. To her chagrin, his easy release of her hand when moments before he'd insisted on holding her smacked of rejection.

"Then they must have been deaf and blind as well as ignorant."

Startled by the unexpected compliment, she reminded herself that Alexius charmed women with the ease of a cobra mesmerizing prey. And he was just as dangerous. To her, perhaps more so. "Now who's the liar?"

He reached out and tucked a loose strand of hair behind her ear. "I've no need for falsehoods when it's easier to speak the truth." His warm fingertips brushed her cheek and trailed down the sensitive line of her jaw. Gripped by the too-pleasant sensation of his touch, she prayed the dim candlelight disguised her response.

She eased out of his reach and nearly fell backward when she bumped into a table behind her. He reached to steady her, but she righted herself in time to escape his help. Hot-cheeked and mortified by her lack of grace, she was appalled to realize what a challenge it was to string coherent thoughts together when he touched her.

Outside, a rooster crowed. Morning was nearly upon them. Awareness grew between them until a slow smile curved Alexius's full lips. "Shall we spend the day admiring one another or will you tell me more about why you're here?"

"I wasn't admiring you," she denied. His smirk told her he knew otherwise. Grappling for control of her wayward nerves, she backed away another step and forced herself to concentrate. "As I said, my father wishes me to marry. Last night, he held a banquet."

"Yes, he hired several of my gladiators for his guests' entertainment. He sent the largest number of them back untried. Knowing him, he'll demand I reimburse his fee. He'll be disappointed."

"It's my fault the evening was a failure. The banquet was held in celebration of signing my betrothal contract. Before it was signed, I…I displeased Lepidus, my intended husband. He left amid a storm of indignation. Needless to say, I'm doubtful the agreement will be mended."

"What did you do?"

"I'd rather not say. It's…embarrassing."

Alexius shrugged, not pressing her. "So your father finds a new man. Surely, Tiberius doesn't want a son-in-law who's too weak to harness a spirited girl like you anyway, does he?"

Her left eyebrow arched. "I'm not a horse, Alexius."

He chuckled. "Of course not. But most men want a wife for breeding purposes, so in that regard you're similar to one, are you not?"

"I see your point. Most men are arrogant barbarians. In that regard I can see *you're* sim—"

He laughed, a deep throaty sound that should have annoyed her, but lightened the mood and tempted her to smile instead.

"I've always enjoyed your quick mind, Tibi, but go on. I'm intrigued. You were saying that your spineless intended broke the contract."

Scowling, she continued under duress, her humiliation rising along with the first rays of the sun outside the window. Her father would awaken soon and wonder where she was.

And be murderous when he doesn't find me.

"Father claims there are no acceptable men left in Rome who will bother with me. He's decided if I'm to be of any use to my family, he'll have to buy me a position as a temple priestess in the hope of garnering a blessing on his house."

"Which order?"

She hesitated. "Opis."

All humor left Alexius with a swiftness that shocked Tibi. Except for the arena where Alexius was purported to be as solemn as the grave he fought to avoid, he was known for his carefree manner and unique ability to laugh off almost any situation. "Why a priestess?" he asked with deadly calm. "There must be a legion of men in Rome willing to marry a girl with your dowry and family's connections to Senator Tacitus."

"He wants to be rid of me." A lump formed in her throat, but she swallowed the pain.

"You think Caros and Pelonia will protect you." It wasn't a question. His mood had not lightened. If anything he'd grown more intent, more furious beneath his inscrutable veneer.

"Yes…no." Her head throbbed with tension. She began to pace the tiles again. Why was Alexius angry? Did he think she'd implicated him in her scheme by coming here? "I don't know what I thought exactly, just that I had nowhere else to go. My friends will never defy my father. My sister agrees with him as well."

"I'd expect no less from her," he scoffed under his breath.

She paused. It was no secret that Tiberia disliked the lower classes, especially gladiators and their trade, but as far as Tibi knew no one ever found fault with her sister. Tiberia was the epitome of what a Roman woman should be—beautiful, graceful and well-connected in her happy marriage. For the first time she noticed Alexius was aware of her sister's prejudice and that he bore Tiberia no fondness, either. "I suppose I hoped Pelonia and Caros might have a way to hide me or suggest a safe place for me to go outside of Rome until my father forgives me. I realize now that I was—"

"Desperate?"

"Imprudent."

A half smile curved his lips, but failed to hide the flintiness of his gaze. "I'll keep you until they return. Then the three of you can decide what to do."

"No. My father might make trouble for you if he learns you've helped me thwart him."

"You don't worry he'll cause problems for Caros and Pelonia if they do the same? They're Christians—easy targets for anyone who knows their secret and wishes to take aim at them."

"I'm certain they're safe or I'd never have come here. Father wants to punish me. He has no wish to shame anyone else in the family—or his good name by association."

"Good. I'd hate to have to kill your father for harming my friends." Alexius sat on the edge of his desk and gripped the carved edge on either side of his narrow hips.

"You wouldn't really murder him, would you?" she asked, frightened by the depth of his calm, yet aware that he was entirely capable of killing and with great ease.

"I'm very protective of my loved ones."

She thought she saw a flash of pain in his eyes, but it might have been a flicker of the candlelight. "I didn't intend to cause trouble for you by coming here. I think it's best that I go."

"No. Stay until Caros and Pelonia arrive. They'd never forgive me if I allowed you to leave and harm came to you."

"My family knows they're on the way. What if my father or sister suspects that I've sought them out and comes to search for me here?"

"I won't let them find you."

She bit her lower lip, confused by his willingness to help her. The sound of servants performing their morning chores filtered in from the hallway. She was running out of time. If her circumstances were any less dire, she'd never contemplate his offer. As it was… "My family can be very adamant."

"I'm very convincing."

She caught her breath, momentarily stunned by his smile, yet encouraged by his confidence. "They may insist on searching the *ludus* for me."

He shrugged. "Let them. I'll enjoy holding them off. I'm in need of a challenge."

She frowned. "You don't find battling for your life in the arena enough of a challenge?"

His silver eyes glittered with dangerous amusement. "It's adequate, but not half as much fun as toying with your unreasonable relatives."

Chapter Two

Alexius woke to a fist pounding on his chamber door. "Who is it?" He rubbed his eyes and swung his legs over the edge of his sleeping couch. Usually up before first light, he noted the angle of the sun outside his window and judged it to be midmorning. He and his men were expected at the amphitheater within hours.

"Velus, master."

"Come in," he said, pulling a fresh tunic over his head.

The steward entered carrying a tray of food that filled the large room with the aroma of fresh bread and roasted pork. The dwarf kicked the door shut behind him with more force than necessary.

"What ails you, Velus? You look as though you've downed a bucket of vinegar."

"Tiberia the Elder is downstairs."

Alexius frowned. "The shrew has arrived already?"

"She asked to see master Caros's wife. When I told her Pelonia wasn't here, she demanded to speak with you."

"*Demanded?*" Few people rubbed his skin raw the

way Tibi's self-important sister did. "Have her wait in the entryway."

"She won't like that, *dominus*."

"I don't like her," he said simply.

Velus grunted and set the tray on a side table. "The lady wishes to see her sister."

"How should I know where Tibi is?" he asked, filling a basin with hot water from an *amphora*. "I haven't seen her for—"

"Hours?"

He grinned. "I don't remember when."

Velus's weathered features pinched with confusion. "She's down the hall—"

"Even if I did know where to find Tibi, I wouldn't tell Tiberia—or anyone else for that matter. I promised the girl I'd keep her hidden until Caros and Pelonia arrive later today."

"I understand," Velus said. "But if you lie to his wife, senator Tacitus might take offense on her behalf and strive to make trouble for you."

"I'll take my chances," he replied, unconcerned. Conditioning his face with a mixture of oils and herbs, he picked up a small, straight-edged razor and began to scrape the bristles from his cheeks.

The *Ludus Maximus* supplied the games with the best gladiators and the senator's popularity was down. Tacitus was too canny to risk his reelection by tampering with the mob's favorite source of entertainment. "It's not as though he can force me to close my doors because his wife is in a snit."

"Yes, but if someone took Tibi away without your knowledge you'd be telling the truth when you said you didn't know her whereabouts."

"True." Alexius finished shaving and rinsed the

razor in the basin. A slow smile spread across his face as he dried his throat with a square of linen. "Tibi seems to think her sister will insist on searching the *ludus* for her. If she's not here, I'll have no trouble allowing the shrew to look until her heart's content. When Tibi's nowhere to be found, Tiberia will look elsewhere and we'll have bought some time and peace for a while."

"I'll find a safe place to take her and report to you once the sister is gone," Velus assured him.

Alexius laced up his sandals and slid on a pair of silver wristbands before heading toward the door. "Wherever you take Tibi, make certain she's well-guarded and dressed to go unnoticed. I imagine all that blond hair and creamy skin attracts admirers by the score."

Velus nodded and followed Alexius into the corridor. The shutters had been folded back from the row of arched windows to allow a bird's-eye view of the peach orchard. Clear morning light filled the vaulted path to the stairwell. On the first floor, the two men parted company.

Alexius took his time walking to the reception hall. In order to give Velus more of an opportunity to leave with Tibi by way of the back door, he meandered along the inner peristyle, surrounded by the soothing cascade of the fountains and the sweet fragrance of orange blossoms.

"So you've finally deigned to arrive," Tiberia screeched the moment he entered the brightly painted room. "You took long enough, gladiator."

"I saw no reason to hurry."

Tiberia's dark eyes narrowed. She rose from the plush blue cushions of her chair, the voluminous folds of her white *stola* pooling at her feet. "Your dwarf informed me that my cousin hasn't yet returned to Rome. However, I believe my sister, Tibi, came here to look for her last night. Fetch her for me. My father insists I bring her home."

Hackles rose on the back of Alexius's neck. His gaze slid to the display of weapons hanging on the wall above the hearth. He didn't take orders well, but he controlled his irritation and maintained a tolerant expression. "Then why didn't he bother to come here himself?"

"I offered, in hopes that he'd calm down before we returned. He's furious enough to do her serious bodily harm."

"Then she was wise to leave."

"It's no concern of yours, gladiator."

"That may be. Either way, you've wasted your time. Your sister isn't here, mistress. If I see her, I'll convey the message."

"You lie. I know she's here. Only Pelonia is kindhearted enough to take her in."

"It seems to me a sister should be just as kind."

Her expression soured. "Why would I risk my father's good opinion of me for a bumbler like Tibi?"

"A bumbler?" Raised with a gaggle of close but competitive sisters, Alexius recognized the jealous comment for what it was. Few women were as graceful as Tibi. "How so?"

"What I mean is…she's brought the situation upon herself."

"What situation?" Alexius asked, pretending ignorance in an attempt to learn the details Tibi declined to confide in him. "Does it have anything to do with the reason my men were sent home untested last night?"

Tiberia flushed, but said no more to enlighten him. A citrus-scented breeze carried in from the central garden, rustling the potted palms near the open doorway. "You'll have to discuss the use of your men with my father. Now, call Tibi for me. You've delayed me long enough."

"I told you she isn't here. And I suggest you tread lightly before calling me a liar again."

Tiberia had the wit to put distance between them. "You do grasp that my husband has the power to order a search of this villainous den?"

"There's no need for the senator to trouble himself. Ask nicely and you're free to look for your sister now as long as you wish."

Tiberia moved behind the chair and glared at him. With her haughty expression—as hard as one of the marble columns supporting the painted ceiling—she made it clear that she considered him less than human. To ask him for anything was an affront to her kind's belief in her own superiority. He recognized the signs well. Other than his loving family, people had always looked down on him. First for being a poor farmer's son, then for his life as a slave-turned-gladiator. He waited, his expression placid and betraying none of his desire to toss her into the street. If not for his esteem for her cousins, he wouldn't hesitate.

"What will it be?" he asked, losing patience when she remained silent. "I'm expected at the arena. I have business to attend to."

She raised her chin and attempted to look down her sharp nose at him. "I have several trusted slaves waiting for me outside. I'll have them search the house and grounds."

"I'll inform my steward," he said, pleased she'd

taken the bait. Once she left to gather her people, Velus appeared in the doorway, his round face flushed, his breathing labored. "Is all well with you, Velus? You look as though you've run the marathon."

The steward ambled into the room and closed the door behind him. "Everything is as it should be, master."

"Excellent. Where did you take Tibi?"

"I've sent her to the arena."

Alexius's heart stopped. "You did *what*?"

Velus blanched, obviously realizing he'd made a rare misstep. "I thought she'd be well-protected with your men. I gave her slave's garb and made Darius responsible for keeping her safe. No one in her family will suspect she's there."

"How could you possibly think that beautiful girl would be safe surrounded by men who plan to face death within hours?" Alexius grabbed a *gladius* from the display of weapons on the far wall and ran for the back of the house. He was shaking with fury and a sickening, unfamiliar sensation he could only equate to fear.

Outside in the courtyard, he called for his horse and vaulted into the saddle the moment his slave delivered the gray stallion.

Velus arrived on the doorstep, wringing his stubby hands.

"See to the shrew," Alexius ordered over his shoulder as he spurred the horse through the gates. *And if the gods have any mercy, I'll see to her sister before my men do.*

"Don't be afraid," said Darius, the young, ginger-haired gladiator trainer Velus had charged to ensure

Tibi's protection. Rather than calming her, Darius's warning served to raise her anxiety as she followed Alexius's troupe through the torch-lit path leading into the dank underbelly of the Coliseum.

"The competitors from the other *ludi* are slaves for the most part," Darius continued. "They're shackled and weaponless until moments before they're armed and released to fight in the arena. If one of them escapes and *happens* to notice you're a woman he wishes to molest, we'll keep you safe."

His dubious tone suggested such an event was as likely as the arena crumbling around them. Convinced that any slave given the option of running for freedom or ravishing her meager charms would choose freedom every time, Tibi tried to relax and reminded herself that she was here by choice. Although the circumstances were less than ideal, a few hours in the protective custody of gladiators were preferable to a lifetime of servitude to a goddess she didn't believe in.

Unable to see through the wall of burly warriors encircling her, Tibi tugged the cowl of her dark wool cloak more tightly around her face. The distant roar of lions and the clang of metal against metal echoed in the passageway, competing with the thunderous din of the crowd that bled down the stairwells from the upper levels.

In the staging area, pandemonium reigned. The noise of hundreds of men and beasts reverberated through the cavernous space. Air whooshed through huge bellows, stoking fires used not only for light but for blacksmiths forging hasty repairs on a variety of iron weapons. Big cats—lions, tigers, spotted leopards—prowled in cages stacked against the pitted concrete walls. Bears, horses, boars with huge twisted tusks and even elephants awaited the ring in iron-barred stalls.

Sickened by the sharp stench of fetid hay and human degradation, Tibi watched the maelstrom of activity in awe. Life beneath the amphitheater spun like a well-oiled mechanism. Guards shouted orders to various troupes. Pulleys groaned as multiple lifts filled with dead warriors and animals were lowered from the arena's sandy floor above them. Tibi cringed when the bodies were kicked aside. Just as Darius had said, trainers from the various gladiator schools unshackled their men. The fresh combatants lined up and traded their wooden practice weapons for polished shields, swords and tridents made of iron before being loaded onto the platforms that were raised back to the field.

"We'll wait in here." Darius waved her into a side room divided from the staging area by a low wall. Flanked by stone benches, the converted game pen held a large, chipped ceramic pot filled with water at the far end. The bulk of Alexius's gladiators filed in behind her, while the rest remained beyond the wall to practice their battle stances.

Tibi tugged her cloak around her and buried her nose in a clean patch of itchy wool. The frenzied cheers of the mob blended with the tempest of activity clashing all around her. Doing her best to fade into a darkened corner, she studied the scarred, fierce-looking men. Some of them laughed and joked as though they were boys awaiting a romp while they played dice on the hay-strewn floor. Others were solemn, melancholy even. She wondered at the difference. Unlike most gladiators who were sold or sentenced into the profession, the men of the *Ludus Maximus* were volunteers who'd sworn their loyalty to Alexius, a tradition Caros began a few years earlier when, she suspected, he became a Christian and no longer wished to keep slaves.

The crowd's muffled chant of *"iugula, iugula,"* demanding a fallen man's death, chilled her. The gladiator games were a pillar of the Empire, but she'd never been allowed this close to the carnage before. Nausea swirled in the pit of her stomach. "How many men do you expect to lose today?" she asked Darius when he sat down beside her.

The edges of his mouth turned downward as he mentally took a head count. "Ten. Maybe twenty," he answered prosaically. "The sponsor arranged battle re-enactments instead of a single man-against-man. The group fights are more expensive in lives and coin, but priceless in terms of buying the mob's goodwill."

Cringing, Tibi nodded. Everyone knew authority in the capital depended on keeping the public amused and satisfied. The emperor and other rich men who wished to influence or keep power did so by providing food and sponsoring an endless array of entertainments. The chariot races and gladiator games—the bloodier the better—were by far Rome's favorite sports.

"What drew you to this life, Darius? Why did you volunteer?"

His dark eyes questioned her sanity. "The money's good. So is the acclaim. Where else can slaves, foreigners, the condemned or poverty-stricken men like me go to earn freedom or fortune if not in the arena? We gladiators embody Romans' worst fears. Because of that fear, most people look on us with a mix of repugnance and awe. But train a man with weapons, teach him how to entertain the crowd and in return the mob will give him a godlike reverence few men can ever hope to attain."

"I know, but—" Another loud cheer signaled that the fallen gladiator was dead. She swallowed and wiped the sheen of perspiration from her upper lip with a shaky hand. "Some of you have wives and children. What good is fame and fortune if you're dead? Why not be farmers or blacksmiths or—"

"It takes coin to set up a farm or a shop, mistress. Except for a few men like the master who fight their own rage in the arena, a volunteer does so because his plans require funds to prosper."

Tibi frowned. She'd always sensed an underlying danger in Alexius and assumed his hardened life was the cause, but his charming smiles and easy humor made it difficult to imagine he possessed true menace in his heart. Now, she saw that her instincts had been correct. She'd been right to keep her distance from a man filled with anger.

"What are your plans, Darius?" she said, realizing she'd allowed the conversation to dwindle.

The hard angles of his narrow face softened. "My son is two years old and my wife is with child again. We want to leave Rome, to give our children a better life."

"Where do you plan to go?" she asked, touched by the gladiator's affection for his family.

"The master has a farm in Umbria."

"Umbria? My cousins and their friends live there also."

He nodded. "When Alexius speaks of the place with its green hills and rich soil, it's as though he's gone to Elysium. We want our children to grow up in such a place."

She fiddled with the muddied edge of her cloak, unable to imagine a battle-hardened killer like Alex-

ius enraptured by any type of earth except the sand of
the arena. "I can't see your *lanista* as a farmer," she admitted. "The image of him trailing a beast of burden
with a plow is too foreign to contemplate."

"He does like his comforts." Darius chuckled. "I'm
certain he'll have plenty of slaves to do his bidding, but
you might be surprised. He's the son of a farmer and I
believe Alexius is still a farmer at heart."

Intrigued by the idea of Alexius as a farmer, his chiseled features softened by talk of his land, she suddenly
regretted the differences between them that made it impossible for her to know him better.

Without warning, Darius launched to his feet. "Wait
here, my lady. I see the *editor*. I have to speak with him
about today's roster."

Tibi watched the young trainer go, uncomfortably
aware of the eyes of the other men upon her. Trying to
appear nonchalant, she turned on the bench to watch
the mock fights in the staging area. From the corner of
her eye, she noticed a huge gladiator stoop and rum-
mage through a small pile of hay near an empty cage.
The giant laughed as he straightened and lifted something small, black and squirming in one hand above his
head. He pitched the bundle to one of his practice part-
ners who then tossed it to a third man close enough to
her position for her to see it was a tiny panther cub.

"Toss the runt over here," the first man ordered in
a thick accent as he lifted his sword. "I'll wager five
sesterii I can skewer it in one go."

Tibi surged from the bench. Thanks to the violence
going on above them, she'd had her fill of brutality for
one afternoon. Unable to digest their cruel play, she
dashed to the low dividing wall and planted her palms
on the rough concrete. "No!" she shouted. "Wait!"

The outburst silenced the talk within the small area encircling her, but worked to draw the trio's attention. Three sets of fearsome eyes locked on her like arrows seeking a target. She froze, her mind registering the long, jagged scar that ran across the leader's blunt nose and weathered left cheek.

Clearly undaunted by her command, the gladiator swaggered toward her, inciting her entire body to tremble from fear. He swiped the cub from his comrade and stopped a sword's length away from Tibi. Too proud to do the intelligent thing and turn coward, she lifted her chin and met his sharp gaze.

"Who's going to stop me, little girl?" He dangled the frightened cub by the scruff of the neck, its tiny paws clawing the air. "You? I think not."

Chapter Three

His blood pumping, Alexius raced down the steps of the Coliseum, his sole concern to find Tibi. The frantic ride from the *ludus* had been a torment. The potential dangers of the arena were legion. Imagining all the ways Tibi might be harmed—wild animal attack, rogue gladiators, an accident with any number of weapons—had his mind playing tricks on him. Memories of his last weeks in Greece a decade ago merged with the present, pitching up images of the beloved sister who'd died because he'd failed to protect her.

If it took his last breath to keep her from harm, he refused to allow Tibi to suffer the same fate.

Used to the noise and stench in the staging area, Alexius stormed past stacked cages and gladiators from the other *ludi* donning helmets in preparation for battle. He looked forward to his own fight later in the afternoon when he'd have the chance to release some of the pent-up aggression churning in his gut.

His relief began to rise once he located the familiar faces of his men beyond the central system of lifts, then quickly plummeted when he saw Tibi's trim, cloaked figure engaged in what appeared to be a disagreement with his champion, Gerlach, an ill-tempered *Germanian* who loved nothing more than to wager and brawl.

He picked up his pace.

Gerlach cast a small object to one of his cohorts, Kester. He leaned over Tibi and placed his thick hands on her slim shoulders. The way he leered at her and his mistaken belief that he was allowed to touch the girl in *any* way infuriated Alexius. The fear shining in Tibi's face before she was able to hide it filled his vision with a red haze. The monster inside him rattled its cage. Hay crunched under his sandals just as he imagined how Gerlach's jaw would do beneath the force of his fist.

The cheers and greetings of his men faded to murmurs and questions of concern the closer he drew near. Ignoring them all, he swept past the game pen that housed the majority of his troupe and continued on his course toward Gerlach.

Alexius's presence drew the *Germanian*'s attention. Seeing him, Gerlach switched focus. His arrogance fled. His hands dropped away from Tibi, the bully's game of intimidation forgotten in light of his *lanista*'s arrival.

"Greetings, mas—"

Alexius swung. The satisfying sound of a bone cracking rent the air at the same time a bolt of pain traveled through Alexius's hand and up his arm. Gerlach hit the ground. His cohorts, Laelius and Kester, jumped back. Breathing heavily, he ignored the men's harried explanations, his main concern to comfort Tibi.

"Are you all right?" he asked. That she appeared unharmed soothed some of the bloodlust coursing through his veins.

Wide-eyed and pale, she nodded. "Are *you?*"

The breathy quality of her voice rippled over his skin like the finest silk. With trembling fingers she reached out to take his hand in hers. The knuckles were bloodied, but unbroken.

"It's no more than a scratch." Resisting the urge to take her in his arms and carry her back to the *ludus*, he slipped his hand from hers. His men were close by and watching them with interest. She was scandal-ridden enough. He didn't want to add to her woes.

"It doesn't look like a scratch."

A rapid tattoo at the base of her throat snagged his attention and a sudden, irrational need to brush his thumb over the creamy spot consumed him. Frowning, he clenched his fists at his sides, confused by her singular effect on his self-control.

"What happened here? Where's Darius?" he demanded more roughly than he intended. "Why aren't you in his care as you ought to be?"

"He's speaking with the *editor*. These men—"

"We were going through today's stances," Laelius interrupted in a quick bid to gain Alexius's notice. "Gerlach found this runt and thought to have a little fun before we make for the ring. The girl interrupted."

"They were torturing the poor cub." Tibi moved to Alexius's side. "Throwing it in the air and laughing at its cries of terror…"

He looked down only to find her pleading eyes were twin pools of misery. His heart twisted. Whatever it took, he'd see her made happy.

"When…when Gerlach told this other man to toss him the cub with the intent to skewer the poor animal, I could take no more. I realize we're surrounded by cruelty in this place, that you gladiators are numb to barbarity, but that cub, it's so small…so defenseless."

Gerlach groaned. The hay rustled as he struggled to sit up. Alexius ignored him. He ignored everything except Tibi. She'd always had an unfair hold on him. He'd promised Caros to keep his distance from her, but that didn't make him blind to her beauty or immune to her innate charm. She was kind and lively, intelligent without being crafty. But in this instance her earnest concern and deep well of compassion impressed him most. She had serious worries of her own to mull over, yet she possessed the rare ability to look beyond herself, to *care* for something as insignificant as a panther's runt.

"Give her the cub," he ordered Laelius without taking his eyes off Tibi.

Her relief evident, Tibi reached for the quivering animal. Cooing softly to calm its mewling cries, she cuddled the black ball of fur close to her chest and stroked its sleek head. "It's not a runt," she said, lifting her gaze to meet his. "It's newly born. Its eyes have yet to open. Where do you think his mother is? This little one will starve without her."

"She was killed in the *venatio* this morning. By now, the beast is on the butcher block with the street orphans already waiting in line for the carcass," Laelius sneered as he extended a hand to help Gerlach to his feet.

"How do you know?" Alexius demanded.

"The cub was found half-covered by hay near those empty cages over there."

Alexius watched Tibi's face leech of color as she realized the empty cages had housed the animals killed in the game hunts earlier that morning. "I didn't consider… What can we do?"

Hearing the *we,* Alexius groaned inwardly. The catch in her voice was his undoing. The only way to save the wretch was to buy it. He'd have to look for the *editor* and work out an acceptable price. He smiled ruefully to himself. If the negotiations went as well as the day had gone thus far, it was going to cost him a fortune to a save a worthless animal he didn't want or need. To his surprise, he was willing to pay almost any price to ease Tibi's distress.

As he watched Laelius help Gerlach toward the underground tunnel that linked the Coliseum to the gladiator hospital, he caught sight of Darius and Spurius, the *editor* of the games, walking toward him. He reached for the cub, but Tibi held firm. "What are you going to do?" she asked suspiciously. "You won't hurt him, will you?"

Alexius almost laughed. She seemed to think she could stop him from taking the little beast if he chose. "I won't hurt him. I'm going to buy him for you."

"For me? But—"

"You want him, no?"

"Of course, but that isn't the issue. I have nowhere to keep him. I only wanted your gladiators to stop hurting him."

The hopeful light in her eyes encouraged him. "We'll work out the arrangements later. For now, the *editor* is coming this way. Let me negotiate with him while I have the chance. He's a cur who's quick to take advantage of any situation. If you want to help this animal and keep your identity a secret, hide your face and stand behind me. Try not to draw undue attention to yourself."

Tibi's mouth twisted with unasked questions, but she hurried to hand him the cub. Her cowl had slipped and she made quick work of readjusting the gray wool to completely conceal her distinctive hair and features.

"Greetings, Alexius," Spurius called, his legendary girth making for slow progress down the hay-strewn path. "I've gone over the day's proceedings with Darius. Your troupe is scheduled for battle within the hour. I'll leave it to him to fill you in on the details."

"They're ready," he said with a confidence born from experience.

"They always are," agreed Spurius, as he came to a stop an arm's length away. "Of course, it's you the mob comes to see. What do you have there?"

"A runt Gerlach found in the hay. Apparently, its mother died in the ring this morning. How much do you want for it?"

"No," Spurius said, gasping to catch his breath. "I mean, *who* do you have there?" He pointed a knobby finger over Alexius's shoulder.

Alexius grinned to hide his rising tension. "No one of importance."

"What a pity. She's tall enough to be an *Amazone*. I let myself hope you'd trained a gladiatrix to fight as a gift for the crowd."

"No, but I might consider it," he said, careful to sound intrigued, since women were a favored spectacle in the arena, although they were few and far between. "About the runt—"

"If she's not here to fight, is she your new woman or just a slave…or both? From what I saw of her at a distance, she's a beauty. Let me have a better look."

"There's no need for that," he said amicably. The whoosh of the bellows nearby filled Spurius's surprised silence.

"Come now," the *editor* cajoled. "Perhaps we can make a bargain. I'll trade you the runt for the girl."

"Another day and I might take you up on the offer."

Tibi gasped and thumped him on the back. He coughed to smother his laugh at her reaction, pleased that she wasn't cowed by the situation. "Unfortunately, she's not mine to trade. Besides, you wouldn't want this particular wench. She's nothing but sass and vinegar."

"A saucy one, eh? That's often the best kind." The *editor* eyed him. "If she's not yours, then who does she belong to?"

"She's a freewoman brought here by mistake."

"Her father?"

Alexius shrugged.

"Let me guess," continued Spurius. "You've convinced the poor girl you'll protect her honor."

Alexius's eyes narrowed at the underlying insinuation that no woman was safe with him. "Indeed I have. How perceptive of you."

The *editor* burst out laughing, as though the idea was one of pure comedy. "She must be a foreigner and unaware of your…colorful reputation, then." He strained sideways as though to speak directly to Tibi. "Be warned, girl. If the gossips see you with this great Greek bull, they'll make certain you have no honor left to worry about."

Bitterness welled up inside Alexius. His free hand clenched into a fist at his side. Tibi gripped the back of his tunic between his shoulder blades. "Don't," she whispered for his ears only. "Please don't. He's not worth your anger."

"Perhaps I'm such a prize she doesn't care," he said, his tone rich with irony. He reached into the leather pouch attached to his belt and tossed Spurius a handful of copper *as*. "For the cub."

The *editor*'s laughter subsided as he did a quick count of the coins. "I didn't name a price."

"I chose it for you." He gripped Tibi's wrist behind him, eager to leave when each moment added to the chance of her discovery. "Darius will lead the men of the *Ludus Maximus* this afternoon. I have business elsewhere."

"What do you mean Darius will lead the men?" Spurius sobered in an instant. "You're on the roster. You *never* miss a fight. The mob comes to see *you*. They'll riot if you don't appear."

Alexius shrugged. All of Rome could be sacked today and he wouldn't leave Tibi's side again. "Then let them." His full lips quirked. "I have a new...cub to look after."

Tibi resisted the impulse to glance over her shoulder as Alexius propelled her toward the exit. Amazed that he'd left as important a man as the *editor* to sputter like a clogged drain, she kept her head down and shielded the cub that squirmed in her hand and licked her thumb with its rough tongue.

"Where are we going?" she asked as they entered a torch-lit corridor that had been chiseled from the earth and edged with flat stones.

"To the stables to fetch my horse."

"And then?"

"Back to the *ludus*."

"What if Tiberia is still looking for me?"

"It's doubtful. Velus views strangers as though they're hornets come to sting. I expect he's sent the whole lot of them on their way by now."

His lack of complete certainty renewed her anxiety, but she accepted the situation without further comment. She'd done all she could to buy herself time when she fled her father's home. Either Tiberia was at the *ludus* or she was not, but given her sister's tenacity, it wouldn't surprise her if Tiberia decided to wait at the *Ludus Maximus* all afternoon. There was no way to know until they arrived and learned the truth one way or the other. Her future belonged to the Fates.

Considering the circumstances, the fact that she'd enjoyed even the smallest respite from her worries was a wonder due entirely to Alexius, she acknowledged with a frown. Whenever he was near, she had difficulty thinking of anything but him. Troubled by such an unwelcome reality, she took a deep breath to clear her head.

The mustiness of the tunnel mixed with the faint smell of hay the closer they climbed to the surface and the stable at ground level. "If I were to guess," she said, trying to lighten the atmosphere between them. "I'd say you have a black stallion—maybe one of Caros's Iberian champions—with a gleaming saddle and—"

"Wings?"

"You *are* Greek." She laughed. "Wouldn't it be a delight to have a *pterippus* like the Pegasus?" she added fancifully. "If I had a winged horse to do my bidding, I'd have it take me far from Rome."

"Rome? Or just your father?"

She stroked the top of the cub's smooth head and pretended a keen interest in the path's dirt-packed floor. "Mostly my father. Although, I must admit, a fresh start far from the city's gossips and expectations holds almost as much appeal."

"You must visit your cousins in Umbria someday," he said, leading her up the final stretch of stairs.

"I have. Once, two years ago I was invited to join the party when Tiberia and her husband sojourned with them in *Iguvium* for the summer. Truthfully, I've never seen a more beauteous place. It's no surprise their friends Quintus and Adiona bought their own villa and vineyards nearby. I understand you have a farm there as well."

He nodded.

"Your trainer, Darius, said your description of the area has given him the hope of settling his family there someday."

"Yes, on its worst day *Iguvium* is far better than Rome on its best."

"Then why do you stay here when it's clear your heart is elsewhere?"

He opened the door without answering and waited for her to precede him through what appeared to be the back entrance of the busy stable. The strong odors of horseflesh and leather overpowered the rectangular space constructed of stone and rough-hewn timbers. Stable hands filled troughs with buckets of water. Horses, crowded into stalls lining both walls and the center of the long hay-covered floor, ate from feed bags or flipped their tails to clear the air of flies.

"Wait here," Alexius said tersely.

As she idly petted the drowsing panther cub in her arms, she watched Alexius from beneath lowered lashes while he conversed with one of the Egyptian stable hands. It was widely known that women flocked to Alexius and after less than a day with him she understood why. Tall and broad-shouldered, he was not only physically arresting but possessed an inborn strength that was both undeniable and irresistible.

She leaned against the wall of the tack room and closed her tired eyes. Judging by his sharp tone when he left to seek out the groom, she'd somehow offended him with her chatter. Leave it to her to annoy a male renowned for his tolerance and good humor—at least outside of a fight. Unfortunately, it wouldn't be the first time she was deemed too inquisitive when she was simply trying to make conversation, but it *was* the first time she wished she'd learned the art of acting serene and mysterious like her sister. If her experience with men held true, Alexius would want nothing else to do with her or, as it must seem to him, her talent for asking inappropriate questions.

In all likelihood, he regretted his decision to help her. Who wouldn't? In less than a day, he'd been forced to deceive her family, fight his own men to protect her, spend coin on an animal he considered useless and break a contract to fight in the arena. Once Pelonia and Caros returned to Rome, he'd hand her over, glad to be finished with her and the trouble that constantly plagued her.

Unexpectedly bereft, she cursed the foolish delight she experienced only in Alexius's presence. Somehow she had to resist the numerous ways she found him appealing. Her father would never accept a gladiator for a son-in-law, nor would Alexius ever consent to marry her. His respect for Caros had prompted him to assist her, nothing more. There could be no other reason. Alexius was a wealthy, handsome man of the world known to have any woman he wanted, whereas she was a reviled second daughter without even beauty to offer.

A horse in the closest stall whinnied near her ear, startling her out of her musings. Alexius paid the stable boy then motioned for her to join him halfway up the aisle.

"Is all well?" she asked.

He reached out and ran a gentle index finger along

the cub's silky back. "We're to meet Ptah near the entrance. If the need arises we'll have to share my mount, Calisto. I sought to hire a mare for you, but the games' crowd is considerable today and there are no extra horses on hand."

"Thank you," she murmured, aware that most of the reason for the large show of spectators was due to Alexius's place on the roster. And now he wouldn't be there because of her. "Please don't think your kindness to me has gone unnoticed. I plan to repay—"

He held up a bronzed, battle-scarred hand to quiet her. "I seek no repayment, except your goodwill. I told you this morning, I *like* being with you."

Tibi's heart danced in her chest. A strange weakness entered her knees, challenging her ability to walk as she fell into step beside him. "I assumed you were being polite—"

"Polite?" He laughed.

"Yes, polite." She frowned up at him. "I realize you're helping me because of your friendship with Caros. After what you've endured...and lost because of me today, you deserve compensation."

"What exactly have I lost?"

"Your place on the field for one."

"Maybe I consider today a gain." He gave her a wolfish smile that was wholly unfamiliar to her experience. "What would you say then?"

Her face heated and her mouth ran dry. "I...I have money in my satchel back at the *ludus*."

His burst of laughter startled a trio of tethered horses. "Keep your coin, my lady. I have no need of it. Nor do I want it."

"But—"

"Cease or you'll offend me."

She glanced at him covertly. "I thought I already had."

"Already had what?"

"Offended you," she said over the rising babble of patrons gathered around the arched entranceway.

"How so? Nothing you do bothers me."

She blinked in disbelief. Since the day of her birth she'd been told in word and deed that she was an unwanted irritant. If not for his earnest expression, she might have thought he was teasing with her again. "Before... When I asked why you stay in Rome."

His expression soured. "That has nothing to do with you. Let's not speak of the matter."

She let the subject drop, although her curiosity gnawed at her. It was obvious that she'd struck upon at least *one* topic that vexed him.

"There's Calisto."

Hearing the pride in his voice, she turned her head to see Ptah leading a magnificent gray stallion, its flowing mane and tail the color of glossy obsidian. Like his master, Calisto walked tall, his head held high, clearly used to being admired by all who saw him.

"He's spectacular, Alexius. Perfect."

"Yes, you barely miss the wings."

The humor in his silver eyes was infectious. "Don't be concerned. I won't hold that against him."

Alexius collected the reins from Ptah and stroked Calisto's silken muzzle and forehead. In his native Greek, he greeted the horse like an old friend.

"Let's be on our way." He tugged Tibi's cowl forward. The feather-soft touch of his fingers along her cheek as he tucked a fallen strand of hair beneath the garment sent pleasant sparks across her skin. Her pulse spiked and her startled gaze locked with the liquid silver of his. All the noise and activity swirling through the stable faded away until only Alexius existed.

"Master…?" Ptah approached, breaking their connection. "Is there a problem? Can I help you?"

Alexius groaned and closed his eyes before turning around to address the boy. Released from her stasis, Tibi spun away, grateful for Calisto's tall form to lean against for support. Trembling, her entire body felt feverish, despite the cool spring breeze blowing through the open windows.

The cub whimpered and squirmed in her grasp. Appalled that she'd forgotten not only herself, but the little animal in her care, she loosened her hold, murmuring words of comfort in an effort to soothe him while she gathered her scattered wits.

What was wrong with her? Had she contracted some sort of sickness?

Alexius moved behind her. She held her breath in anticipation of his touch. When his large hands finally settled on her shoulders, she almost collapsed from relief. His warm breath feathered across the sensitive shell of her ear. "You're not alone, little one. I feel the madness, too."

Her head fell forward to rest on Calisto's saddle blanket. She closed her eyes, desperate to understand her wildly off-kilter emotions and her even more foolish wish to believe the madness he spoke of was something as special as what she felt for him. "You do?"

"Yes…but I should know better." He eased her back against his broad chest. His lips pressed a soft kiss on the top of her head. "Gods help me. What am I going to do with you?"

Chapter Four

Still reeling from Alexius's confession, Tibi allowed him to lead her and Calisto from the stable without another word. The design of his saddle, with a pommel at each of the four corners, made riding two people an uncomfortable prospect. Tibi didn't mind walking. She desperately needed a bit of space between her and Alexius to clear her head. The thought of clinging to him for balance while she held the cub and rode in full view above the crowd seemed disasterous.

Outside, the day's aromas and sounds assaulted her senses. The bright sun of midafternoon nearly blinded her after the many hours of dim light in the amphitheater's lower levels. Heavy aromas of smoked fish, roasted nuts and fresh bread woke her hungry stomach.

The thick flow of people coming and going from the entrances of the gleaming white Coliseum surrounded them like a river, threatening to sweep them away. Alexius tightened his grip on her hand and navigated the shifting current with a single-minded purpose that must serve him well in the arena, Tibi acknowledged.

Careful to keep her face concealed, but her view unobstructed lest she trip or knock someone over, she adjusted her woolen hood. A row of makeshift stalls lined the busy circuit around the amphitheater. Hawkers did their best to tempt customers to stop and look at their wares—everything from leather goods to the freshest produce the season had to offer.

However, it wasn't the food and supplies that drew the most notice. It was Alexius. All bronzed skin and sinewy muscle, he stood head and shoulders above the crowd, as perfect to look upon as a masterwork of Greek statuary. Young and old alike stopped to stare at him. Some watched slack-jawed while others jabbed their friends with their elbows and pointed with various levels of discretion. It wasn't long before a path cleared, sidelined by an inquisitive horde that obviously held a gladiator of his skill in high regard. Alexius used the opportunity to move quickly, his only acknowledgment of the attention a quick wave or nod when someone bold enough called his name.

Several streets away, Rome's central region gave way to one of the city's more peaceful areas. Narrow alleyways led to wide-open squares where the elderly chatted around sculpted fountains and energetic children played knucklebones, chased one another or tossed sticks for their dogs to fetch.

The smoke from cooking fires and the aroma of roasted meats tinged the air. Not for the first time, Tibi's stomach growled. Hoping Alexius didn't hear its protests, she raised her face to soak in the warmth of the sun peeking through the rainbow of laundry strung between multistory apartment blocks. She inhaled the fresh scent of herbs growing in clay pots on each side of the footpath and listened to the even gait of Calisto's hooves on the pavers.

"I've never been to this part of the city before," she

said. "Is this a new way back to the *ludus* or can I assume that you're abducting me?"

Alexius sent her a sidelong glance. "If I were going to kidnap a woman, I promise she'd take much less effort than you do."

She tensed. "I told you, you deserve compensation for your inconvenience—"

He sighed. "Don't start that again. I wasn't serious. Did no one in your family ever joke with you?"

There'd been very little laughter in her home, none since the year before when her mother crossed the Styx. "The mood in our *domus* follows my father's lead. Since I've known him, he's been somber, angry or outright dreary."

"Then it's a miracle you have any sense of fun in you at all. I suppose I'll have to make allowances for your shabby upbringing and try to be patient with you."

"Thank you *so* much for understanding." She narrowed her eyes at him, but he merely chuckled when she tried to look threatening. "What of *your* family?" she asked as they passed a hunchbacked woman sweeping a flight of steps. "Judging by your disposition, they must have been a troupe of jesters."

He grinned. "Actually, no. My father was a poor, illiterate farmer who loved the land second only to my mother. My mama was as beautiful as springtime. They said their first meeting was a lightning strike. Within days they married."

"What a wonderful story. Were they always happy?"

"With each other, yes, but for a time my grandfather caused them endless grief. He was a rich merchant who despised the thought of his daughter married to a man so far beneath her."

"What did he do?"

"He disowned her. She was made dead to him and everyone in his house."

"How terrible!" she said, thinking her own father would do the same.

Alexius frowned at her. "Not so terrible at all. My *abba* adored her. They had little coin, but there was always a fire in the hearth and our table was never empty. My six older sisters were—"

"*You* had six older sisters? That explains much."

"How so?"

"You Greeks are worse for want of sons than even we Romans. After half a dozen girls, I can only imagine how much your parents must have spoiled you."

He laughed. "Yes, my sisters used to claim they could smell the stench of my rotten hide for miles."

"I don't doubt it." Her smile faded. What must have happened for Alexius to lose his loving home and become a gladiator? "They must have been distressed when you left them."

His manner shifted imperceptibly. His smile stayed in place, but the light left his eyes. "I hope not, but I imagine so. I never saw them again after I was sold to the slave trader and taken from Iolcos."

A band of sadness squeezed her chest. No wonder she'd sensed such turmoil beneath his smooth facade. He'd been stripped from the home and family he adored. The pain must fester within him like an open wound. Aching for his loss, she wanted to wrap him in her arms and hold him until every drop of grief drained away. "What did you do? I mean…why were you sold into slavery?"

She felt his gaze on her profile as they walked down the shadowed street. She wished she'd kept her mouth shut. Men who were sold into the gladiatorial trade were usually murderers, traitors or the worst sort of thieves. She didn't want to think of Alexius in those terms. He owed her nothing, not his patience or protection, but he'd been more than generous with both. True, she'd seen glimpses of the darker side of his nature, but he was also kind. He'd treated her with more respect in a few hours than she'd been shown in a lifetime. Perhaps it was madness to trust a gladiator, but no one made her feel safer or more confident about herself than Alexius did.

Deciding that the few hours she'd been granted with him were a gift that she loathed to waste, she pushed her doubts to the back of her mind. Tomorrow might find her in the temple, banished to spend the rest of her days serving a goddess who meant the same to her as a block of wood. So far, she'd had few moments worth remembering in her life, but she knew instinctively this day spent with her handsome Greek would be a time to cherish.

"You don't want to know," he said, seeming to read her thoughts.

She didn't argue. Instead, they walked in companionable silence until her stomach growled again. A quick glance at Alexius suggested he hadn't heard.

"Since I'm not worthy of being kidnapped," she said, "and I'm fairly sure the *ludus* is in the opposite direction, where are we going?"

"I'm taking you to get something to eat. Your stomach makes a great disturbance when it's hungry."

She gasped. "How rude of you to mention it."

He laughed. "I'm a lowly gladiator. I can't be expected to know decent manners."

"I don't think you're lowly," she said, her voice infused with sincerity. "Neither did all those other people we left near the amphitheater."

His brow furrowed as he studied her with an intensity that made her squirm. She couldn't think of anything inappropriate she'd said, but then maybe she'd been too forward. Two of her betrothals had been broken because she'd dared to give her opinion. She'd offered Alexius a compliment, but the male mind was a strange thing. On more than one occasion she'd been under the impression that a particular conversation had gone well, only to learn later she'd caused some offense worthy of shaking her already precarious social position.

"Is the way much farther?" she asked, nervous she'd hit upon yet another one of the subjects that soured his usually pleasant demeanor.

"Not much."

"Do you think we might be able to find some milk there to feed this cub? I'm worried. He must be hungry."

"Possibly. My friends who own the *thermopolium* where we'll eat have a cat that gave birth a few weeks ago. Maybe she'll be generous."

Relieved and hopeful, Tibi marched on with renewed purpose.

"It's this way," Alexius said. They made a sharp right turn and crossed a small bridge before following yet another winding alley.

Tibi switched the cub to her right arm and shook the stiffness from her left. "You'd best not leave me. I'll never find my way out of this maze."

"A safe return is your incentive to be good. Your reputation does precede you."

"Does it?" She cringed. "Did you learn of my misdeeds from your many admirers? My sister delights in informing me that I'm the cause of much debate and laughter behind closed doors."

"It pains me to agree with the shrew, but in this case Tiberia is correct."

"What...what have you heard?" she asked, forcing the words through a stranglehold of humiliation.

"Little I can credit."

"No?"

"From what I can gather, you turn into Medusa once the sun sets."

She glared at him, unable to find the smallest kernel of humor in a subject that had caused her years of grief. "Medusa is dead."

"Her great-granddaughter then."

Her lips tightened into a thin line. "Perhaps I'm innocent of all I'm accused of, and the stories about me have been exaggerated until no matter what I do I'm in the wrong."

"That I can believe. The excuses I've heard for your ended betrothals are shallow at best. You're in no way repellent, aloof *or* argumentative, but there is *something* about you that scares those spineless Romans to the soles of their sandals. If, as you claim, you're not Medusa's progeny, why are you such a pariah?"

The question made her fidget, completely stealing the pleasure she received from discovering that Alexius didn't find her ugly or disagreeable. She wanted to tell him the truth, but what if he reacted like other men and labeled her unnatural? To her chagrin, she found his opinion of her mattered more than she cared to admit.

"You don't have to tell me, Tibi. We all have secrets to keep."

"It's not that," she said, instantly consumed with curiosity about the secrets *he* kept buried. No doubt she and half of Rome would be scandalized if the full truth of his deeds were ever discovered. As for the other half of the city, they were probably participants in his exploits. Her shoulders slumped. She must be a terrible bore after all the excitement he was accustomed to.

"The source of my downfall has a fixed starting point. As you can imagine, it's rather embarrassing. I did something when I was too young to realize the consequences of my actions or how unforgiving people can be."

"How old were you?"

"Twelve."

One silky black eyebrow arched. "You Romans are a strange lot."

"No worse than you Greeks."

"At least we don't hold our young responsible for their transgressions for the rest of their lives."

"I've yet to tell you what I did. Once you know you may agree with the others."

"Did you kill someone?"

"No!"

"Then I can promise you I won't agree with them. But I would like to hear the rest of your story."

"All right. I'll tell you, but only because I know you'll harp on me until I do." She waited for a denial, but none came. Her lips twitched at his expression of patient innocence. "As a child I wanted the love of my father more than anything. I failed time and time again to gain his notice unless he wished to berate me for not being the son he wanted. Being unable to change my gender, I decided that if his love was out of reach, perhaps I could earn his respect if I proved that I was as intelligent and able-bodied as any boy. To that end I excelled at my studies and took up sports. Archery was my favorite."

"I can see you with a bow and arrow."

"You can?" Alexius was an expert with weapons. His insight into the subject intrigued her. "How so?"

"The bow is an elegant weapon. It suits you. Continue."

Flattered that he found her elegant, she forgave him for his high-handed command and went on. "Those efforts were also to no avail. Father despised me still. After all I'd done to please him, his continued coldness angered and frustrated me."

"I'm not surprised. I'd be angry, too."

He agreed with her? The notion struck her as incredible when everyone else believed that only her father's feelings held merit. They entered a large, sun-drenched square. People had gone indoors to avoid the heat of the day, leaving only the splash of the fountain to fill the stillness.

They stopped to let Calisto drink water from a trough in the corner of the square. Alexius relieved her of the cub, but with the pain of her past pressing down on her, she hardly noticed the missing weight.

"What happened next?"

She blinked. "Sorry?"

"You were angry at your father," he said, his attention diverted to the tiny cub in his huge brown hand.

Amazed that such a large, fierce man possessed gentleness, she watched him dip his long, battle-scarred fingers into the fountain. He shook off the excess moisture and pressed a single drop of water to the cub's tiny mouth. He repeated the action twice more until the panther's small tongue darted out and licked his fingertip.

"Go on." Silver eyes, fringed with thick black lashes,

caught her staring at him. Her face heated and her lungs locked. A slow, gratified smile curved his sculpted lips, exposing straight white teeth. "What did you do?"

Fearing that he understood the havoc coursing through her veins better than she did, she cleared her throat and took a deep breath. "The next year an archery contest was called for all the boys of the best families to show off their skills. Once again Father complained of his useless daughters and berated my mother for denying him a son to bring honor to the family. I wanted to prove him wrong so I sent one of our stable hands to secure a place for me under a false name. On the day of the event, I donned a short tunic and wore a cloak with a hood to cover my hair and keep my face shadowed. I was terrified of being caught at first, but I soon realized people see what they want to see. Everyone accepted my disguise without a qualm and assumed that I was just another one of the male archers."

Alexius muttered something in Greek under his breath. "What happened next? You were discovered, no?"

"Yes, but not until after I'd bested every last boy. I felt triumphant, I assure you."

He snickered. "I can imagine."

"Yes, yes, I'm sure you can. When you win in the arena, do you feel a rush of invincibility? Is that why you continue to fight when you don't have to?"

"I fight for reasons of my own."

"One of those secrets you spoke of?" She ignored his glare. "Darius mentioned that you need to fight in the arena to battle your own rage."

"The boy speaks too much," he snapped. "He's not paid to have or give an opinion of me."

She backed away, a habit from never knowing when her father might turn violent. For the third time today, Alexius's easy manner had evaporated, reminding her of the volatile side of his nature she didn't dare trust.

He gathered Calisto's reins. "We'd best be on our way."

They left the square with no further words between them. Sunlight filtered through the olive trees, creating a dappled effect on the path in front of them.

"I'm sorry," he muttered.

"No," she said. "I'm the one who's sor—"

"Don't. You did nothing."

"My mouth always runs away from me. I pressed too much for something that is none of my business."

"I didn't mean to frighten you," he said.

"You didn't—"

"Yes." He stopped in the center of the walkway. "I did." Still clutching the reins, his strong fingers gripped her upper arm and turned her gently to face him. "You don't have to deny it. I saw you flinch away from me. I know you live in fear of your father, but I swear I'm not like him. Rest assured, even if I act like a barbarian at times, I promise you have no cause to be afraid of me."

"I don't think you're a barbarian and I'm not frightened of you," she assured him, sensing again that painful struggle inside him she wished she could ease.

"Good, because I'll *never* hurt you, Tibi."

His sincerity was palpable. From out of nowhere, hot tears welled in her eyes. No one ever worried about hurting her. On the contrary, she often thought her family looked for ways to cause her pain. Caught off guard by the force of her reaction, she turned back to the path and hurried to wipe the moisture from her cheeks.

"Tibi? Are you crying?"

"No, there's a speck of dust in my eye. I'm fine."

Alexius allowed her to walk a short distance ahead. He despised the air of sorrow that surrounded her slim, cloaked figure. Worse, he hated that something he'd said or done was responsible for her melancholy.

Usually blessed with the ability to charm even the most hard-shelled of women, he cursed his lack of finesse with the one woman he wanted most to impress. Judging by the way she'd backed away from him as though she expected some form of violence, she either thought of him as a monster or her father's treatment was even worse than the gossips suggested.

Unwilling to squander the few remaining hours he had left to enjoy her fresh-faced beauty and good nature, he followed her up the path. The fact that he had to relinquish Tibi at all maddened him. From the moment he'd promised Caros to keep his distance three years ago, he'd regretted the foolhardy pact. He wanted her. He always had. The longer he spent with Tibi, the more he knew he always would. He was acutely aware that he was too far beneath her to be considered worthy of anything more than assisting her for an afternoon, but if she belonged to him, he'd cherish her as she deserved.

"The *thermopolium* is around the corner," he said, catching up to her in a few long strides. "Over there. The one with the blue door."

Inside the smoky establishment, the aroma of fresh herbs, garlic and roasted fowl made Alexius's mouth water for a good Greek meal. A gladiator's typical diet of barley gruel kept him full when he was training, but never satisfied.

The small room was dimly lit and empty except for the proprietor, his friend, Marcellus, a short, boney man with gray hair at his temples, a hawkish nose and deep-set brown eyes.

Certain he could trust the older man not to spread news of him or his companion, Alexius introduced Marcellus to Tibi before telling her, "His wife, Aldora, is a fine cook. She prepares all the food here."

"My Dora is Greek, like Alexius," said Marcellus who welcomed Tibi with an elaborate wave of his arm. "He says she cooks like his mama used to do."

"Yes, her delicious meals are renowned throughout the city. Where is she?"

"At the market." Marcellus cast his gaze toward Tibi's hooded figure. "She'll be sorry she missed you and your guest. Do you want your usual table in the garden?"

"Yes, but first we need to visit Iris." Alexius indicated the sleeping cub straddled along his forearm. "If she is willing to take in an orphan, we need her help."

Marcellus grinned and fussed over the panther cub before fetching an oil lamp and leading them down a narrow flight of steps into the domed cellar. A continuous chorus of meows filled the damp space. In the far corner stood a large wooden crate padded with hay. "Dora made a spot down here when she found Iris birthing her litter. She's a placid cat. I doubt she'll object to feeding one more."

Thankfully, Marcellus was right. Iris, a gray-and-white ball of fluff, welcomed the cub without fanfare. She sniffed the panther, licked his head and ears, then nudged the little black body into the pile of her own white kittens.

Alexius watched Tibi. Once Marcellus returned to the main room upstairs, she slipped the cowl off her head, revealing a long braid that appeared a burnished gold in the lantern light. She sank to her knees, her soft hands clenched into anxious fists against her thighs. While she focused on the cub, he concentrated on the delicate shell of her ear and the long, slender curve of her throat. He could still feel the sparks of awareness in his fingertips where he'd touched the creamy smoothness of her cheek. If Ptah hadn't interrupted, he'd have taken her in his arms and kissed her breathless.

"There you go, little one," Tibi encouraged, once the snuffling cub rooted its way to Iris's warm body and began to nurse. "That's a good boy."

She glanced up at Alexius. Relief lit her large brown eyes. "It's presumptuous, I know, but do you think we might ask your friends to keep him for a few weeks? Iris seems to have welcomed him. I can offer them coin—"

He wondered at her constant offers of money, as if no one ever did her a kindness for free. "I'll pay them if it comes to that, although I doubt they'll accept it."

The panther cub safe and secure with Iris and her brood, Tibi replaced the cowl to cover her hair and followed him up the stairs. Marcellus led them past the half-dozen tripod tables and stools that took up most of the small room. The worn brick floor joined a back wall studded with shelves containing an array of ceramic plates, bowls and platters. A slave pushed aside the curtain concealing the doorway to the kitchen. He took his place on a small stool near the hearth and began to turn a spit laden with chickens over the fire.

Careful not to bump his head on the low door frame, Alexius followed Marcellus and Tibi outside where a high brick wall, dripping with colorful bougainvillea and wisteria, provided privacy from the adjacent businesses and apartment blocks. Lifelike, plaster statues of satyrs and centaurs guarded the square perimeter.

Alexius showed Tibi to a table in a secluded corner. Years before, the *thermopolium*'s water supply had been diverted to create a Grecian fountain in the center of the courtyard. Pots of varied sizes and shapes overflowed with herbs, miniature fruit trees, and a profusion of colorful flowers lent the cool breeze the sweetened scent of spring.

Like the interior room, the area was empty except for a few slaves sweeping the bricks and scrubbing the tables. He'd timed their arrival well to coincide with the afternoon lull. They had several hours before the rush of evening patrons, limiting the risk of Tibi being discovered in his company.

"What a lovely place," Tibi said, leaning in to smell the vase of purple wisteria adorning their table. "Judging by the front door, I never would have guessed there was such an oasis to be found here."

A slave poured a mug of water for each of them. "Aldora misses our homeland. She tries to re-create a piece of it here for herself."

"Has she succeeded?"

He nodded. "It's as close to the glory of Greece as I've found in this latrine of a city."

She started to speak, but appeared to change course. "Rome is the capital of the world, Alexius. People of every tribe and tongue wish to live here. There must be *something* about it you consider worthwhile. The training school, your men—?"

"You."

"*All* of your women," she added, ignoring him.

Savoring the sound of his name on her lips, he hoped the tinge of bitterness in her voice stemmed from jealousy. "I wouldn't want any of them if I had you."

Her forehead pleated with disbelief. "For a little while, possibly, though I doubt it. What about after? Once the novelty value of an unsophisticated girl wore off."

He sat back in his chair. She doubted his honesty and why *should* she trust him? He was reputed to be many things, but faithful to any one particular woman wasn't one of them. He lived on the edge of death at all times. He was surrounded by it, threatened by it and controlled by the reality that his life and fortune were a commodity to be bought and sold for the amusement of the mob. Years ago, he'd stopped planning for a future—or even hoping for one. He lived in the moment, chasing whatever fleeting pleasure he might find. But that hadn't always been his way.

"You don't understand your appeal, Tibi."

"No," she scoffed. "It's my lack of appeal that I understand quite well."

"*Lack* of appeal?" Her low opinion of herself sparked his irritation. "Nonsense."

"You're right. The reason my father intends to send me to a temple in disgrace is because I'm so fascinating I have an array of suitors clamoring to wed me."

"Which brings us back to the story you didn't finish earlier." He hooked his arm on the back of his chair and studied her tense face over the fragrant wisteria blooms. "We have time and I'm curious. What happened after the archery contest to ruin you for marriage?"

Chapter Five

Tibi took a long drink of water before setting her ceramic mug aside. "I learned a lesson in the evils of pride."

Alexius waited. She glanced away while another slave brought them a loaf of fresh bread. "As I told you, I was elated that I'd won," she continued once they were alone again. "The boys were well-trained and represented the best families in society. Had I gone home and kept the victory between me and my father, all might have been different. Instead, I let my childish impulses run away with me. When I was called forward to collect the laurel diadem that proclaimed me the victor, I convinced myself I needed it as proof for my father. The judge insisted I push back my hood and reveal my identity. By then, I'd begun to regret the decision to go in front of the multitude who'd come to witness the contest. I tried to leave, but it was too late. One of our neighbors, my father's fiercest rival, recognized me."

"He called you out in front of your father?"

"Worse. He understood what I did not and sought to humiliate my entire family by using me. He made a great show of exposing my identity to everyone in attendance and declared that I was a hoyden whose father wasn't man enough to control her."

Alexius's jaw clenched tight from the effort to remain seated and listen.

"After that day, the gossip about me spread like an infection. At best, I was called unfeminine. At worst, they considered me wild and unnatural for wanting to compete with the males. The taint of that day followed me and grew out of proportion. By the time I reached a marriageable age a few years later, no acceptable family wanted to risk teaming their son with a supposed troublemaker who might seek to best him. As for older men and widowers, they want a placid wife, not a woman with a muddied history like mine."

"What of your broken engagements?" he asked, disgusted by her ill treatment. "Correct me if I'm wrong, but you've had, what…three?"

"Four," she despaired to admit. "My suitors were the dregs of the acceptable families with more status than coin. They considered marriage to any woman with a decent dowry. Unfortunately for my father, the first two broke off with me when I disagreed with them on several political issues. The third took offense for reasons I have yet to fully understand. I took offense at the other."

"Last night?" he prompted, unable to imagine Tibi capable of offending him in any way.

"Yes." He heard the mix of pain, embarrassment and bitterness in the whispered word. Her eyes downcast, she shredded a chunk of bread as she spoke. "Lepidus—"

"Catulus Lepidus?"

She nodded. "He accosted me in the garden while the

other guests watched the games. He claimed I should be grateful for his willingness to try me since I'm a...a worthless girl no one wants."

Alexius burned with white-hot rage. His chair scraped back on the bricks. "I'm going to break the fool's neck."

"No!" Tibi lunged forward in her seat and clutched his wrist from across the narrow table. "The betrothal was ended and I'm free of him. You mustn't involve yourself or resort to violence on my account."

Her pleading eyes knocked the fire out of him. He sank back into his seat, his breathing heavy. What had he been about to do? Leave her while he followed his anger in pursuit of a vendetta? Shame replaced his rage. Had the monster claimed more of him than he realized?

She held his hand until his breathing returned to normal and he allowed the contact because even that small connection was addictive. "You need someone to champion you, *agape mou*."

The slight flare of her eyes was the sole indication she'd heard his endearment. "My cousins—"

"Are not here. They might not arrive for days. Besides, they'll want to pray about the situation. Who knows how long *that* will take."

She bit her lower lip. "You don't approve of their ways?"

"I don't disapprove." He chose his words with care. "In the past three years, I've seen too many miraculous changes in both Caros *and* the lady Adiona to doubt their God exists, but I've yet to count myself among His followers."

"Why is that? Do you need no miracles of your own?"

He flicked a stray bloom off the polished wooden

tabletop. He needed more than a miracle. He needed a cure. For now, fighting was his medicine. His fury was an insidious disease he kept under control by the sheer force of his will. Without the arena and the release of rage the games provided, he feared the disease would soon overpower him. "I'd have to give up too much to be a Christian. I saw what Caros sacrificed because of his convictions. He lost a fortune when he left the gladiatorial trade."

"Yes, but he already had more wealth than he could spend in a lifetime and look what he gained. A wife who adores him. Fine, healthy sons. A beautiful property in Umbria—"

"And the constant threat of death because of his religion."

"He faced death anyway, just as you do. At least now he has something worthwhile to die for—or so I've heard him claim."

Alexius grunted, conceding the argument just as he always had to do when he discussed the same topic with Caros. "You plead his case well. Am I to take it you're a follower of the Nazarene? Is that why you find the prospect of serving in a temple abhorrent?"

Before Tibi had a chance to answer, Marcellus entered the garden, a platter of herb-crusted lamb and roasted vegetables in his hands. Steam rose from the hot food, filling the air with the scents of smoked meat, rosemary and mint.

"Dora prepared this meal before she left for the market," Marcellus said, serving them each a portion of lamb. "I won't promise it will be her best since our slave, Carminea, put on the finishing touches."

Impatient to continue his conversation with Tibi, Alexius thanked his friend and assured him that all was well. As Marcellus left, Alexius's gaze swung back to his companion. Her eyes were closed and the sublime expression on her beautiful face as she ate a bite of lamb brought a smile to his lips. Unlike other women of her class who came to him and the other gladiators seeking to add excitement to their mundane lives, Tibi had managed to stay unspoiled. It pleased him that she found satisfaction in simple things. "You like the food?"

"Mmm…it's perfection." Tibi opened her eyes and flushed when she found Alexius's eyes focused on her. "Why haven't you tried your own?"

"I was watching you. No food can be as delectable as the expression of joy on your face."

"I was hungry," she said defensively.

"I know. Your growling stomach proclaimed that fact, remember?"

She narrowed her eyes in mock annoyance. "How good that you find yourself amusing."

"One of us has to."

She took another bite of lamb to stem her laughter. His perverse sense of humor needed no encouragement from her. The tender meat was some of the best she'd ever tasted. The fresh combination of lemon and rosemary complemented both the lamb and root vegetables.

Alexius nudged a light green, odd-shaped ball to the side of his plate. "Have you tried the fennel?"

She did a swift inspection of her plate. "I don't have any."

"Here." He broke the ball in two and handed her one of the pieces.

"I've never seen this." She sniffed the section he'd given her and took a bite. "It's good. Crunchy and a tad sweet."

"I notice you're not eating the cucumbers," he said.

"I'm sorry, I don't care for them. The vinegar is too much for my taste."

"That's the best part."

"Would you like mine?"

"Why don't we trade? Your cucumbers for my fennel."

"You drive a hard bargain, *lanista*." Handing over her plate, she found herself ensnared by the male beauty of his face and the unbridled energy he exuded. His startling eyes were a light metallic silver, made brighter by the darkness of his skin and hair as black as polished obsidian. The ease that settled between them was new to her experience. He didn't sit in judgment of her or take offense when she admitted her true thoughts and feelings. Indeed, he seemed to approve of them.

The unexpected melody of a pan flute drifted across the courtyard from the direction of the fountain. Alexius glanced over his shoulder before returning his attention to his food. "Apparently, Marcellus thinks I need help wooing you."

Tibi choked on an olive. Alexius thrust her cup toward her. "Are you all right?"

She swallowed some water. Her throat and her surprise back under control, she nodded. "Does your friend always offer assistance when you bring a woman here?"

"What makes you think I've brought other women here?"

"Haven't you?"

He shrugged. "Only the most special ones."

Her food lost all its appeal. She could only imagine how many "special ones" there'd been in his life. She wished she was special to him, but didn't delude herself into thinking he'd brought her here for any reason other than he'd needed a place to hide her *and* feed the cub while they waited to return to the *ludus*. "If we're counting just the special ones, I assume there have been a hundred at the very least."

He eyed her thoughtfully. "I don't keep count."

"You mean you've *lost* count."

"If you believe so."

Her brow pleated with indecision. She didn't know what to believe about Alexius of Iolcos. He was an enigma who confused and fascinated her in equal measure.

Marcellus returned to collect the dirty crockery. She complimented him on the food, then felt inadequate with her praise when Alexius raved about the lamb and even the fennel, which she was sure he'd had no taste for.

"I'll bring you some figs and more water," Marcellus said happily, on his way back indoors.

With her stomach full and her view of Alexius unhindered, she listened to the gentle splash of the fountain and the chirping of a pair of birds nesting on top of the wall. When she'd run to the *ludus* before sunrise, she could never have imagined the day turning out as well as it had. Whatever consequences she faced for her actions, at least she'd had these few precious hours of respite with her handsome Greek.

"What are you thinking?" Alexius leaned forward and crossed his arms on the tabletop in front of him.

"That I'm thankful I had this day with you."

His expression softened. "I'm thankful, too."

The air became cooler as late afternoon turned to early evening. "I suppose we have to go back soon. I have to face my fate."

He frowned in apparent rejection of the idea. "We have time. I'm not finished with you."

"Not finished with me?" Her heart quickened. "How so?"

"I want to know more about you. Before the food arrived, you were telling me your opinion of the Nazarene's religion. Now that I can hear you over the growl of your stomach—"

"You exaggerate—"

"Tell me your thoughts on the matter. Have you decided to become one of His followers?"

Chapter Six

"I want to believe in Him. I do." She'd never admitted that particular truth to anyone in the past. She found it liberating, as though the very air was lighter. "As a small child I always envied Pelonia. My uncle Pelonius doted on her. She was the jewel in his crown while I was viewed as a piece of broken glass." She disliked the pity in his eyes. She cleared her throat and sought to sound more matter-of-fact. "When I was seven I asked Uncle why he found Pelonia special— Even then I sought answers to questions that were none of my concern."

"A child should ask as many questions as she wants."

"My family disagrees with you. A daughter isn't supposed to ask questions. She's meant to follow and obey." She reached for a wisteria bloom and breathed in the floral notes. "Uncle was the kindest, most patient of men. He told me Pelonia was a gift to him from his God. That God loved me as well. It was the first time anyone told me I was cared for. That was the moment I began to wish I knew his God."

"And now? What keeps you from following Him? The authorities?"

She shook her head. "I have no wish for death, but I've seen my cousins and their friends face the same threat and thrive."

"Then what is it?"

She hesitated. He was asking for her deepest thoughts. Truths she found far from easy to admit after all the years she'd sought to be indifferent to her family's dissatisfaction with her. "It's foolish, I know, but as hard as I've tried not to care about my father's good opinion of me, there's a part of my heart that continues to wish for his acceptance. I hate that it's so, but I long for his approval. Becoming one of the Christians..." She shook her head. "I think my father would cart me off to the Coliseum and push me into the lions' den himself."

Alexius's square jaw tightened and his lips compressed into a harsh line. "Tiberius is the foolish one, Tibi, not you. Whether you were given from the Christian God or Hera, the queen of heaven, you *are* a gift. It pains me that your father's lies have blinded you to the truth."

Tibi regarded him in speechless amazement, unable to fathom where his declaration had come from. As far as she knew, he'd never given her a second thought after the previous occasions they'd met. She suspected that he was being kind out of loyalty to her cousins because, try as she might, she wasn't able to see anything remotely special about herself.

"You don't believe me, do you?"

"No," she whispered. "I don't."

Marcellus brought the figs he'd promised. He sat a shallow bowl of the wine-poached fruit on the table, apparently unaware of the renewed tension between them. "This year's crop will make your mouth rejoice. Shall I order more music? More water?"

Several of the tables had been filled as the dinner hour drew near. The murmur of voices and bursts of laughter vied with the splash of the fountain. As she drank from her refilled cup, she noticed Alexius frowning at something or someone behind her. "What is the matter?"

"Don't turn around," he warned in a low tone that sent a shiver of apprehension down her spine. "Galerius Basilius just arrived."

A wave of panic crashed over her. Basilius was her brother-in-law's fiercest competition in his bid for advancement within the Senate. Tiberia had already warned that Antonius's bid for consul wasn't going well. Tibi had no doubt that Basilius, a cunning and manipulative rival, would recognize her on sight. Their two families had mingled socially on many occasions in the three years since her sister's marriage. If Basilius saw her with Alexius, she doubted that he'd hesitate to use the meeting to his advantage. The emperor appointed the candidates for consul who were later elected by their peers in the Senate. Much damage could be inflicted by questioning the morals of a candidate's family and she was already considered a liability by her relatives.

Lies were spun in Rome like the webs of a thousand spiders, but deceit wasn't needed to poison her name. Indeed, gossip might be kinder than the truth in her case today. Here she was alone in the company of a notorious gladiator, in an establishment favored by the lower classes in an effort to escape her own father. Tiberia was correct. Her intentions may be innocent, but she managed to create turmoil wherever she went.

"What do you recommend?" she asked, despising herself more with each passing moment. "Shall I try to leave without being seen?"

"Too late. He's coming this way. Keep your head down and your face hidden. He has no reason to suspect it's you in servant's garb."

"Alexius!" She recognized the newcomer's raspy voice. "How fortuitous to meet you here. It's been too long since I last saw you, my friend."

"Much too long," Alexius replied amicably as he stood from his chair.

"I've been meaning to contact you. I'm certain to win my rightful place as consul in a few weeks. I want to hire at least twenty of your men to use in my celebratory entertainments."

"Twenty men is child's play. A new consul should sponsor at least a fortnight's worth of games to thank the mob for his rise in power."

"Oh, I plan to thank the plebs—have no fear. The twenty men will serve for the amusement of my family and closest friends."

"It will cost more if you plan to fight them to the death."

"Of course," Basilius rasped. "I expected no less."

Strong fingers banded around Tibi's upper arm. Alexius tugged her to her feet and smoothly moved to stand in front of her. "As long as we understand each another. Send your man to meet with my steward. Velus will make the arrangements."

Tibi bristled at Basilius's arrogance. He hadn't won yet. A celebration was premature in her opinion. Alexius's willingness to profit from her brother-in-law's supposed defeat rankled. Did he agree that Antonius was a lost cause? She worried at her lower lip. In Rome, security depended on power and position. Social status often hung by a thread. If Antonius's favor dwindled, so did her entire family's.

Alexius followed her inside the main dining room where every seat was taken and the swell of conversation flowed freely. His hand dropped away from her taut spine. He paid for their food, sent his regards to Dora and made arrangements with Marcellus for the cub's care.

A slave awaited them outside, Calisto's reins in his hand. Long shadows marked the passage of time and the arrival of early evening. The cooler temperature brought people into the street to visit with their neighbors or conclude their business affairs for the day.

Tibi's thoughts refused to settle. The threads of her life were thorny vines being woven into a pattern of unavoidable despair. The arrival of Basilius had been a tipping point, proving that no matter how far she traveled or how obscure a place she went, Nemesis would find her. The threat of her father's wrath and the terrifying changes she had to face in the next few days formed an endless circle of anxiety within her head.

They started back through the labyrinth of streets and alleyways, the smell of smoke thick in the air. An occasional call of a mother to her children or other raised voices punctuated the golden haze of sunset.

"What's wrong, Tibi? You haven't spoken a word since we left the *thermopolium*. If you're worried that Basilius recognized you, you don't need to be."

"How do you know that?" she asked in a waspish voice meant to sting. "You were too busy betraying my family to notice if the old goat even looked in my direction."

Alexius stopped dead. Calisto whined and nearly

bumped into him as Alexius turned slowly to look at her with a mix of angry curiosity and rampant disbelief. "It's true then."

"What?" she snapped, unable to rein in her conflicting emotions.

"You *do* turn into a gorgon at sundown. If I push back your hood and look into your eyes, will I change into stone? How long before your hair forms into vipers?"

"You're impossible." She stalked onward, aware that she was being unreasonable, but unable to help herself.

Alexius latched on to her upper arm and whipped her around to face him. She shrank back from his wrathful height, but he held her with an iron grasp. His narrowed eyes glittered in the half light. "A word of caution, *my lady*. Don't turn your back on a gladiator you've just insulted and never, *ever* dismiss me again as though I'm dirt beneath your feet."

"I'm sor-sorry," she choked, her throat tight with shame and rising fear. She began to tremble. He may have promised not to hurt her earlier, but she'd been lied to before. His wit and charm made her relax around him, but he was a man steeped in violence. She had no way to know if he was trustworthy.

"Now, you'd best explain. What's this betrayal you've accused me of?"

"What else would you call supplying your men to celebrate with Basilius—"

"Good business."

"—if not a sign that you agree Antonius is bound to be passed over by the emperor?"

"I have no interest in politics or the games of government, but this I know. Your brother-in-law is a decent enough politician, but his arrogance has cut him off from the people. Why do think Basilius was in that *thermopolium* this afternoon? Because he's common?"

She shook her head. "No, his family is ancient and as important or more so than that of Antonius."

"Exactly. But Basilius knows the road to power is built on a foundation of the mob's goodwill. Every move the emperor makes is to consolidate his power and pacify the masses. He'll choose his candidates for consul from the senators most favored by the plebs to show respect for the common citizens. Something your beloved brother-in-law either no longer cares about or has forgotten."

"That may be," she said, suddenly understanding why he'd told Basilius two weeks' worth of games was necessary to thank the mob for his rise in power. "But you are one of Caros's best friends. Don't you think you owe his family your loyalty?"

"His *family?*" he scoffed. "Don't pretend a single one of your self-important clan has embraced him—a wretched gladiator—as a true relative."

"I have! I love him dearly."

"You are not your family, Tibi. It's because you *did* accept Caros that I bothered to help you at all." He dropped his hands from her arms as though she'd caught leprosy. "If you bore the slightest resemblance to that pack of rats you call kin, I would have sent you back to them the moment you barged into my home this morning."

Mortified to hear his true thoughts on her appearance in his life, Tibi grappled for a reply, but no adequate apology or explanation came to her. "You must think I'm insane."

"A little," he said gruffly. "Who wouldn't be after what you've faced since yesterday?"

His compassion was the last thing she'd expected. How pathetic she must seem to a man as strong and self-possessed as Alexius.

"But then so am I."

"You?"

"Hmm…" His calloused palm cupped her cheek. The pad of his thumb brushed the curve of her lower lip. "Most of all I think you're lost. You're a ship without sail or direction."

She hung her head, horrified by how easily Alexius—of all people—saw into her soul when everyone else seemed blind. *Lost* described her entire existence. She'd spent her life wandering, searching for a place to belong and always being rejected.

She moved to pass him, raw to her core and afraid that since he'd seen how adrift she was, he might also see how desperately she yearned for him to be her safe harbor.

Hot tears of frustration and heartbreak burned her eyes. She cursed herself as an *idiota*. Last night, she'd viewed being banished to a temple as the ultimate punishment. Now she knew differently. Worse was discovering that the one man she'd ever truly cared for was forever off-limits to her. Why must her heart always long for what she could never have?

"Tibi, wait." Alexius's hand fell on her shoulder, keeping her from running until her legs gave out from under her. He turned her to face him. Darkness had fallen, casting his chiseled features into shadow. "I had no right to say you're lost. Not when I'm in that same rudderless boat."

"How so?" she asked, genuinely perplexed. "You are Alexius of Iolcos, Rome's darling of the Coliseum. Women flock to you. Men idolize you. Even the emperor opens his doors to you in welcome. You couldn't possibly understand what it is to have no place, nowhere to fit in. To despise every day because you're an outsider even among your own family."

"I understand more than you realize, Tibi. I'm a foreigner who longs for home. A gladiator whose entire world depends on the good graces of a fickle mob."

"The mob loves you! *Everyone* loves you." *I love you,* her heart screamed, but fear of his rejection kept her mouth welded shut.

A notch formed between his silky eyebrows. "You think I care about the goodwill of a bunch of strangers? They may love me today, but if I falter so much as a hairsbreadth, they'll be chanting for my death the first time they get the chance."

"Then retire! No one is stopping you," she said, willing him to abandon the dangers of the arena forever. "Leave the field as the champion you are and never return."

The tortured expression that crossed his face cut like a dagger through her heart. When had his pain become her own?

"You don't understand, Tibi."

"Then explain," she said. "Help me understand."

Long, tension-filled moments passed between them. In his eyes, she saw the struggle he couldn't hide as he warred with specters that haunted him from the past.

"You can tell me," she urged softly. "I'll keep your secrets."

His jaw hardened and his beautiful eyes turned grim in silent rejection of her plea. "Let's make haste. Caros and Pelonia may be waiting for you at the *ludus*."

He turned on his heel, drawing Calisto down the moonlit alley. Tibi watched him go. His broad shoulders seemed bowed beneath the weight of the world. In that moment, her deepest wish was to understand his complicated mind and soul, to be the one he turned to for comfort.

Before they left the *thermopolium*, he'd called her *agape mou*—my love. She wasn't capricious enough to believe he'd meant the endearment in a literal sense— he probably called all of his admirers the same thing or something similar—but her traitorous heart refused to relinquish the hope that, given enough time, he might come to trust her. To regard her as a friend, since the circumstances of their lives prevented her from being anything more to him.

Alexius rounded a corner. She hiked the hem of her cloak to midshin and sprinted along the deserted street to catch up. It was difficult for her to understand, but he seemed to feel as alone as she did. With that common ground between them, perhaps, just perhaps, they could somehow find a place in the world to belong together.

Alexius spent the long walk back to the training school listening for Tibi's footsteps to ensure that she never trailed too far behind him. He cursed the Fates who were toying with him as easily as a child launching a parchment boat into white-capped waves. How was it possible that in the space of a few hours one small, exquisite young woman had managed to turn him on his head?

The flaming torches posted on either side of the *ludus*'s iron gates were a welcome sight. Inside the courtyard, Alexius handed Calisto's reins to a stable hand. Velus met him with an anxious expression and two small scrolls, their wax seals already broken.

"What news have you, Velus?" he asked as the three of them traversed the path leading through the peach orchard and into Alexius's private quarters.

The dwarf's nervous gaze darted to Tibi, who'd taken a seat on one of the office's plush blue chairs. He looked back to Alexius and passed him the thinner of the two scrolls. "This is from Caros Viriathos. It was sent from Umbria four days ago. He and his traveling companions were delayed due to some business of Quintus Ambustus. They don't expect to arrive in Rome for at least another week."

Seeing Tibi stiffen and her dark eyes fill with dread, Alexius uttered an oath under his breath. "What else?"

"*This* one," the steward handed over the second scroll, "is from Tiberius Flavus—"

Tibi paled. "Father must know I'm here."

"I doubt it." Alexius reached for the rolled parchment and scanned the document.

"He requests that you give him his daugh—"

"Quiet. I'm reading." Alexius cut off his steward before Velus revealed the worst. More than a request, Tiberius *demanded* that Tibi be returned or Alexius would find himself summoned to the law court. Ensuring that his wayward daughter was properly punished was his right and a matter of honor, or so Tiberius claimed. With the senator's influence and Tiberius's shrewd lawyers, Alexius could spend a fortune on his own counsel and his chance of winning Tibi away from the old goat would remain less than nil.

The realization that he might be forced to send his beautiful Tibi back to a house of hate and maltreatment was more than he could stomach. There had to be some other way to keep her safe. He just had to find it.

He looked up to see Tibi pacing in front of the open

window. She'd lowered the hood, revealing her untidy braid of golden hair. A chilly breeze ruffled the long wool cloak. Her delicate profile was pinched with worry. She looked hunted. He loathed seeing her unhappy.

"Your father is bluffing, Tibi. He doesn't know you're here. Nor will he."

"You can't know that for certain." She faced him, her gaze latched onto the unrolled scroll in his hands. "What are his orders, Alexius? What threats has he issued if you don't deliver me back to him?"

He sent Velus a silencing glance and shrugged. "Nothing of substance."

She wrung her hands. "Things must be more severe than I imagine if you refuse to tell me the truth."

"He says he'll never hire my men again," he lied. Rewinding the scroll, he placed it on the desk and moved across the tiled floor to take her hands in his. "Believe me, I'm not concerned."

Velus snorted.

"Your steward doesn't seem to agree with you."

Alexius frowned at Velus. He tipped his head toward the door in a silent command for the servant to wait in the hall. "I rescued Velus years ago from a beast master who planned to use him for lion feed, yet he likes to believe I'm the one always in need of aid. Apparently, I can't even comb my hair without him."

A wan smile crossed her lips. "I don't want you to suffer in any way because of me. You've already risked much today—"

"I risked nothing." How like Tibi to have some misplaced fear for his safety without any regard for herself. "What can be done to harm me? Do you think your father will storm my gates and pit his paltry slaves against three hundred gladiators?"

"My brother-in-law—"

"Is entrenched in a battle to further his political position." He traced a fingertip along her high cheekbone. "He'll be only too glad his troublesome sister-in-law is out of his way to worry about her whereabouts."

"Thank you very much," she said primly.

He laughed. "Listen to me. I want you to stay here."

"I can't—"

"*Yes,* you can. Until Caros and Pelonia arrive, just as we agreed."

"I believed they'd be here this afternoon." She eased her hands out of his grasp. "Don't you understand? I don't want to be a burden—"

"You *aren't* a burden. You're my guest." The urge to shake her was strong, but not nearly as powerful as the need to throttle her father and sister for stripping her of all sense of self-worth. He found Tibi as close to perfect as humanly possible. How could anyone find her lacking, especially her own family?

How different his own youth had been, basking in the acceptance of relatives who'd adored him and whom he loved just as much in return. His parents had showered him and his sisters with praise and endless affection. How different would Tibi see herself if she'd been nurtured, cared for as she ought to have been?

Fond, long-buried memories surfaced of his life in Greece—so, too, the pain of losing all he'd cared for. For years he'd denied himself the joy of remembering those happier days the same as he'd stopped believing he deserved a worthwhile future.

He realized that Tibi's presence in his life was

changing him. For years he'd felt dead inside, but she made him want to live again. Just as his parents had known within hours of their first meeting that they were meant to be together forever, he knew Tibi was his heart's desire.

"I want you here," he said. "I'm *asking* you to stay."

"But…why?" she whispered, clearly confounded.

Mentally testing and rejecting several approaches to a reasonable explanation, he dragged his fingers through his hair in frustration. He wanted to proclaim his love for her, but a confession of that sort was bound to send her running in fright. No girl with her breeding and background would consider winning a gladiator's affections a compliment.

He cleared his throat. "The truth is…I like you, Tibi. I enjoy your company. I feel responsible both for you and to my friends for your safekeeping. Today, I told you you need a champion. If you truly wish to try to avoid life as a temple priestess, let me help you. Let *me* be your champion. Who better to defend you than a man whose sole talent is winning a fight?"

Tibi went still. She stared at him as though he'd begun speaking Greek midsentence. Although he'd expected no less, her lack of enthusiasm regarding his confession hurt like a kick in the teeth. He was grateful that he'd told her the most tepid version of his feelings because he'd never felt more foolish in his life. For all his experience with women, he'd never been in love with one until Tibi, and her unpredictability was punching a hole in his confidence.

Like most Greeks, he knew he was passionate by nature to the point of being reckless on occasion. If he wasn't careful, he'd wind up on his knees, begging her to stay, to love him in return. A mental image of that pride-crushing scenario sobered him as though he'd jumped into an Alpine lake. "So what will it be then? Will you stay or shall I send you back to that weasel you call Father?"

Chapter Seven

"I have to go back." Tibi's bottom lip quivered. She drew in a deep breath and released it slowly. "Today was my one chance at freedom. Had Caros and Pelonia returned this afternoon, as I'd hoped, the outcome might have been different. As it is, I took a gamble and lost. The longer I defy my father, the more enraged he'll become with me *and* all those who help me. I've seen him beyond reason before. I've no wish to revisit that frightening place. Nor do I want to incite harsher consequences than those I already have to pay."

The urge to toss her over his shoulder and lock her in one of the sleeping rooms upstairs was almost more than he was able to resist. Her rejection of his offer of shelter and safekeeping sent a shaft of pain through his chest the same as a *gladius* slicing through sinew and bone. The sensation of helplessness stoked his fury like nothing else he'd ever encountered.

Aware that she was sensitive to displays of anger, he forced back the dark tide rising inside him and placed his hands on her shoulders with great care. She swayed into him, but caught herself before she leaned on him completely. "I know you are terrified of Tiberius, but he is no threat to me. I'm not his property to punish or command. He doesn't own me—"

"No, he owns *me*. By right and by law. If he learns that you've helped me, he can use his powerful allies to ruin your reputation in business, call you to court, have you fined. He might have his men assault you in the street. You could be hurt or worse because of me…"

The thought of Alexius coming to any kind of harm made her physically ill. The narrow space between them disappeared as she listened to the cry of her every nerve and gave in to the temptation to lean fully against him.

His strong arms banded around her, holding her tight against his solid chest. He pressed his cheek to the top of her head and gently stroked her hair. His warmth and spicy scent cocooned her. For the first time in her life, she felt as though she'd found a haven to call her own.

Heartsick, she chafed at the laws that made her father her master and compelled her home. The time spent with Alexius had been short, but enlightening. He'd given her a taste of the acceptance she'd always longed for, but feared never existed. He said he liked her. Whether or not he was just being kind, she didn't know for certain, but his face, his voice, his touch—everything about him—called to the deepest recesses of her soul.

And yet, how could she heed that call? A legal marriage required her father's consent. Even if her father cared about her and her happiness, he would never accept a Greek gladiator as her husband—not that Alexius had offered for her.

"You give Tiberius too much credit." His warm breath ruffled her hair. "I can defend myself. Stay with me, *agape mou*. Let me help you."

Unable to see an honest way to be with him, she squeezed her eyes shut and soaked in the last precious moment of being held in his arms.

"You refuse to believe he can harm you if you help me, but you're wrong, Alexius." He resisted her attempt to leave his embrace, but she persisted until he let go of her. She stepped out of his reach, the separation causing her heart to ache as though it had been ripped in two. "Violence isn't the only way to maim a person."

"No," he agreed darkly, his eyes hooded by lush, black lashes. "Violence *isn't* the only way."

Tense silence stretched between them. The fire crackled in the hearth. "Will you take me back tonight, then? Or will you have one of your men accompany me?"

"Neither."

"Neither? The night is so dark. I know I came here alone, but I had to take the risk—"

"I'll return you myself," he said, all traces of tenderness gone from his face and body. "But not until morning."

"But—"

"Velus," he called, overriding her objection. "See our guest to a room and send one of the women to serve as her maid for the night."

Alexius dropped into the chair behind his desk and stared out the open window. Distant music and the laughter of his men and their admirers floated on the night wind from elsewhere in the house. His thoughts locked on Tibi upstairs, he barely noticed the star-filled sky or the cold air sweeping through his office.

In times like this, when he was alone with his thoughts and the whole world seemed faraway, he wished he believed as his friends did. He envied Caros, Quintus and their wives, their ability to go to their God with their concerns. They fully believed He cared for them and, as Caros had told him many times, sought to make all things work together for their good.

As soon as they arrived, he planned to seek his friends' counsel and prayers. For as far as he could see, without a miracle his situation with Tibi wasn't likely to end well.

A grim smile curved his lips. His mother, a very outspoken woman with a strong mind of her own, would have complained that his methods of keeping Tibi within his reach were high-handed, but he was grateful his refusal to take her home had so far earned him a night's reprieve from losing her altogether. Aware that Tibi had been courageous and foolish enough to venture out in the middle of the night to escape her father, he knew she might do the same to him if she thought it best. Short of tying her to the sleeping couch, he had no way or right to prevent her from leaving. However, the maid sent to serve Tibi would alert him if she did decide to go without telling him first. If she left, he'd follow and protect her until she reached her father's home.

A knock sounded on the door frame. "Master?"

"What is it, Velus."

"A visitor is here to see you."

"Who is it?" Alexius asked, more than a little annoyed by the intrusion.

"Senator Antonius Tacitus."

Alexius tensed. His hands formed into fists. If Tibi's brother-in-law thought he could steal her away from him, he was crazed! He surged from his chair just as

Velus stepped back to reveal the senator standing in the doorway.

Draped in a dark gray cloak and tunic, Tacitus had obviously dressed with a clandestine mission in mind. His hawklike features too weathered for a man in his mid-thirties, the senator possessed the sort of inbred arrogance that always set Alexius's teeth on edge.

"Lanista."

"Senator." Alexius waved the newcomer into the room.

A man who'd enjoyed wealth, position and the care of an army of slaves since birth, Tacitus dropped his cloak in Velus's general direction, expecting the steward to catch the wool garment before it hit the floor tiles. Velus glared at the senator's back and let it fall, kicking the heavy pile of cloth for good measure before he deigned to pick it up and leave.

Once Tacitus chose a chair across the desk from him, Alexius offered a refreshment, which the senator declined.

"I seem to be popular with your family today." Alexius returned to his seat, careful not to betray his vexation with the senator's overconfident manner or his keen interest in the man's unexpected arrival. "Your wife was here earlier looking for her cousin. Unfortunately, Caros and Pelonia aren't able to return to Rome until next week."

"I'll inform Tiberia of their change of plans. However, you and I both know that's not why I'm here."

A gust of wind rattled the shutters tied back on either side of the open window. Alexius shook his head and adopted a perplexed expression. "I have no idea why you're here, Senator. Please. Enlighten me."

"We all know Tibi came to see you last night.

There's no use denying it. She thought Pelonia might be here. She had nowhere else to go."

"I don't deny it." He leaned back and propped his elbows on the arms of his chair. "I can't confirm her visit, either."

"Can't or won't?"

"Does it matter?"

The senator glared at him. "Where is this misplaced loyalty coming from, *lanista?* Has Tibi offered her body in exchange for your protection? If so, let me warn you. She's a…unique and beautiful girl to be sure, but I defy you to find a more troublesome wench within a radius of a thousand miles."

"If I see her, I'll keep that in mind," Alexius growled, imagining how easy it would be to break the man's arm as payment for his insult to Tibi's honor.

"Good. *If* you see her, will you also convey another message for my wife and me?"

Alexius nodded, losing more of his patience with each word Tacitus uttered.

"Tell her not to go home. Her sister and I are concerned for her safety. Rumors are running rampant about her. In defense of his reasons for breaking the marriage contract, Catulus Lepidus has made claims that are—how shall I put it?—*less* than complimentary concerning Tibi's purity. Gossip is already raking up the old rumors that she's wild and that Tiberius is too weak to control his willful daughter."

Alexius swore under his breath. "I know Catulus Lepidus. He and his father are both rodents. The rat shouldn't have been allowed within a mile of Tibi."

"That may be," Tacitus said, sheepishly rearranging the edges of his cloak. "But Tiberius was fed up with his daughter long before last night's fiasco. For all the years I've known them, she and he have mixed as well as oil and water. The renewed gossip and her defiant disappearance have sent him over the edge, I fear. I believe the possibility that he'll kill her the next time he sees her is very real."

The fury Alexius had been struggling to suppress boiled up like a geyser. The chair scraped back along the floor. He jumped to his feet and rounded the desk. "You tell that swine, *I'll* kill *him* if he so much as *blinks* unkindly in her direction."

Tacitus stood and put half the room between them. "It needn't come to that, *lanista*. If she comes here, do us all a favor and lock her away somewhere."

"*You* are suggesting that an innocent girl like your sister-in-law stay in a gladiator school? Something foul is in the air for certain. I'm surprised you're not more concerned about public opinion. What of her reputation?"

"She has none to protect," the senator answered bluntly. "If it were otherwise, I might view the whole matter in a different light. Given the situation as it is, I see no better place for her than here. Tiberius isn't foolish enough to think he can storm a gladiator school and win."

"You are her family. What of your home? You have the power to ensure her safety, or are you unwilling to?"

"Frankly, I don't think I do." Antonius moved to stand behind a chair. "My father-in-law visits often. It's unlikely that he wouldn't find her there. Tibi is his to command and he is beyond reason and rage at the moment. I believe his antipathy toward his daughters is unnatural. He views them as a curse from the gods since he has no sons of his own and his adopted heir died years ago. He has no love for either girl, but he at least tolerates my wife because her marriage to me strengthened his social standing. Tibi, on the other hand, is a misfit with a long history of ruining his plans. He gives her no quarter and chooses to see her as rebellious rather than strong. Usually, my wife or I can soothe his feathers when she ruffles them. This time is different. He's vowed to see her punished once and for all. I believe him."

Alexius moved to the window, needing the night air to cool his own hot temper. How *dare* Tiberius threaten Tibi when, as her father, he should *cherish* her. What pleasure he'd feel if he broke the old bull's neck. "I think I *will* kill him."

"I can think of no one who'd miss him, but he's not worth the price you'll pay when they toss you in prison."

Alexius turned and leaned against the windowsill. He crossed his arms over his chest and eyed the senator with suspicion. "What do you gain by coming here?"

"I hope to ensure Tibi's safety, of course."

The senator maintained eye contact, but Alexius noted the clench of his hands and tightening around his thin mouth. He'd gambled too often not to notice when a man was hiding something. "Admirable, but there's more. I want to know the truth. *Why* are you here? Tell me or get out and we'll let the Fates decide the best course of action."

Antonius frowned, but eventually admitted, "I can't afford another scandal. My candidacy for consul is precarious at best. I care deeply for my wife, but her sister's questionable behavior and volatile father are…a liability to a man in my position. Most would never question Tiberius's right to chastise his daughter, even to the point of death, but there are moralists who might seek to overplay the situation and sway public favor to one of my opponents' camps."

"A true politician with the heart of a weevil, are you not, Tacitus? A sweet girl's life is in danger, but you are more concerned with the loss of respect her death may cost you than with saving her from harm in the first place."

The senator gripped the back of a chair until his knuckles glowed white in the lantern light. "Scoff all you like, *lanista*, but I bear no ill will toward the girl. I'm here because I *do* want Tibi protected. If she's out of sight, the gossip will die. She'll be safe from Tiberius and my wife will be spared from suffering the loss of her sister—"

"As if that shrew would miss her."

Tacitus stiffened. "My wife is no shrew. She cares much for Tibi, but years of acting as a buffer between her relatives have gained her more than her fair share of bruises."

Satisfied with the senator's explanation and fairly certain there were no surprises waiting to pop up and bite him, Alexius returned to his desk. "*If* Tibi comes here, how long should I plan to shelter her?"

"The election is in a few weeks' time. If you can bear to keep her that long, I'd be grateful."

"And then?"

"We'll see if the winds have changed."

"Fine," Alexius said, thinking he'd gladly keep Tibi forever. "But you owe me."

"Agreed." The senator moved just close enough to shake Alexius's hand on the pact. "Keep Tibi out of sight and you can ask whatever you wish. If your request is within my power to grant, you have my word of honor that I'll see it done."

"I'll hold you to your promise, Senator." Alexius smiled, but did nothing to hide the sharp-edged warning in his tone. "Cross me and you won't like the consequences."

Tacitus froze. His gaze turned wary. He yanked up the hood of his cloak in a gesture that failed to make him seem less intimidated. "Don't threaten me, *gladiator. I* am a senator of Rome. *You* are no more than a foreign dog."

Used to insults of that nature, Alexius grinned as he watched Tacitus head for the door. "I make no threats, *Senator.* I'm merely giving you *my* word of honor. But unlike most politicians, you can count on me to do as I say."

Chapter Eight

The next morning, Tibi woke late. Dread of returning to her father filled her the instant she opened her eyes. She'd spent most of the night tossing and turning, unable to sleep. She didn't remember when she finally settled into the arms of Morpheus.

Usually one to greet the day with ease, she stalled and closed her heavy eyelids to ward off the bright sunbeams filtering through the slats in the shutters. She wished the chirping birds in the tree outside would find someone else to pester.

Hearing the maid, Leta, in the corridor, she left the sleeping couch and stumbled to the table holding a large bowl of water Leta had left the previous night. She washed her face and cleaned her teeth before hurrying to exchange the borrowed tunic she'd slept in for the gray wool she'd worn the day before.

Downstairs, the main floor was empty. Open windows along the walls allowed the clear spring weather to take up residence throughout the house. A gentle breeze rustled the long linen curtains that separated the large rectangular spaces into various rooms. High, painted ceilings, colorful frescoed walls and shiny mosaic-tiled floors proclaimed the home as one of wealth and taste.

Hoping Alexius was near enough to hear, she called out a greeting. No one replied. Uncertain as to where she could or shouldn't go in the unfamiliar house, she followed the sound of the fountains to the central courtyard.

"My lady?" A tray in her hands, Leta found her in the inner peristyle admiring a large Greek urn filled with fragrant white roses. "I was headed upstairs to bring you food and drink. Are you hungry?"

"Famished. May I eat out here in the garden?"

Leta, a pretty girl with long, black braids, smiled, exposing a row of crooked teeth. "You're the master's special guest. You can go wherever you wish."

Cheered by the maid's kindness, Tibi chose a sunny spot near the largest of the three fountains with a clear view of all but one entrance into the courtyard.

"Do you know where your master is?" Tibi asked, eager to see Alexius.

"He's on the training field." Leta set the tray on a low table within Tibi's reach. "I'm to fetch him now that you've left your room."

Once she was alone, Tibi nibbled on a sweet fig while she added honey to the bowl of steaming porridge on the tray. Now fully awake, she enjoyed the birdsong and the sun's warmth on her face while she ate the hearty porridge. How ironic that she found more peace in a gladiator's garden than she did in her own home.

She felt Alexius's arrival before she saw him. A mix of joy and nervousness made her hand shake as she set the empty bowl back on the table.

Her pulse racing, she stood just as he appeared in the

nearest doorway. Struck dumb and helpless to move for the first time in her life, she drank in the sight of him like a woman suffering from an unquenchable thirst. How was it possible he'd become even more handsome overnight?

Broad shouldered and slim-hipped, he stood as tall as a titan—all lean muscle and power wrapped in a dark tunic and smooth, sun-bronzed skin. He must have come straight from a bath. Short, damp, black hair curled around his ears and his lean face was freshly shaven. Light silver eyes glowed like diamonds fringed with thick dark lashes.

He smiled at her and her heart melted. She sank on the low-cushioned bench behind her before her legs gave out from under her.

"I didn't think it was possible, *agape mou,* but you're even prettier today than you were yesterday. I can't imagine how beautiful you'll be in twenty years."

Her face heated. She frantically reminded herself that he was known for charming and discarding much more sophisticated women than she would ever be. "I imagine I'll be quite old and wrinkled."

He moved toward her, conjuring up in her mind an image of a panther on the prowl. "Why don't you stay here and let me find out?"

If only he knew how tempted she was to take him up on his offer, he surely wouldn't tease her. "I told you I have to go back."

"Yes, but there's been a development."

Her brows pleated. "What do you mean?"

He sat on the bench beside her. Leaning back on his arms, he stretched his muscular legs out in front him.

Leather sandal laces crisscrossed his strong calves. "I had a visitor last night."

"Who?" she asked, growing drunk on the clean, intoxicating scent of his skin.

"Your esteemed brother-in-law."

That bit of news sobered her in a blink. "What did Antonius want? Did he demand I go home?"

"On the contrary. I'm to give you a message. He and your sister advise you to stay away."

She took a moment to absorb the warning and its hurtful meaning. "I knew Father was furious," she whispered.

"They fear for your safety." He lifted her chin with his index finger. His intense gaze bored into hers. "As do I."

She slipped away from his touch and stood. Her fingers trailed through the cold water of the fountain. Anger toward her father burned inside her until she feared she'd spit fire. The disappointment of allowing him to wound her again flayed her alive.

He stood and joined her at the fountain. "They advise you to stay here."

Her throat tightened. "How shameful I am to have to hide like a fugitive from my own father."

He grabbed her by the shoulders and forced her to face him. "The shame isn't yours, Tibi."

"No?" she asked, bitterness thick in her throat.

"No. The shame belongs to Tiberius. In my estimation, he's a fool who deserves to be flogged. My father had six daughters, Tibi. He adored them all."

"Maybe they weren't oddities as I am."

"You're *not* an oddity. You're a beautiful and courageous woman. You think for yourself. My sisters were free to do the same, to be themselves." His fond smile was edged with some deeper emotion she couldn't quite name. "They were confident, happy and full of life. Just as our parents raised them to be."

"I thought Greeks prized their women's docility."

He snorted. "In public that's true. In private? I've never met a Greek woman who didn't feel it necessary to give her opinion on any subject."

"Do you men listen?"

"We have to. If we miss what they say the first time, they just get louder until we acknowledge them." His long fingers combed through his damp hair. "What I'm trying to say is that you see yourself through the distorted view of your father and the hypocrites he calls friends. When I look at you, I see…"

"What? What do you see?" She held her breath, waiting.

"I see a woman with every reason to be proud of who she is."

She didn't know how to answer. A thick ball of emotion formed in her throat. She found his words difficult to believe after a lifetime of being convinced that she was worth less than dirt. But maybe he was right. She'd done everything in her power to be a good daughter. Maybe her parent was in the wrong. Perhaps her father *was* impossible to please. "If I'm to stay here, what shall I do? I don't want to be in the way."

Victory sparked in his eyes. "I'll have the cook work you in the kitchen, as a proper woman should."

Her spine stiffened. "I'll serve in the kitchen to earn my keep, but not because—" She broke off when he burst out laughing. "What is so funny?"

He reached for her and pulled her against his chest without warning. "You should have seen your face, *agape mou*. Such instant fire in your eyes and color in your cheeks… You look like a wrathful Aphrodite." His laughter subsided to a tender smile. "We really do have to work on your sense of humor."

She swatted his chest, but found it impossible not to forgive him for teasing when he held her so close. "So if I'm not to work in the kitchen, what *am* I do?"

He hooked a strand of her hair behind her ear. "If you're as good with a bow as you claim, you can be of great help to me if you're willing."

"How so?"

"My archery instructor is in need of an assistant."

Her mouth fell open. "You want *me* to teach *gladiators?*"

"I meant no offense—"

"I'm not offended," she hurried to assure him. "I… I'm… Thank you! No one has *ever* appreciated my skill."

He relaxed. "When I was a boy, I was taught to make use of anything available."

"Aha, now I understand," she said gravely.

He frowned. "What do you understand?"

"Why you feel the need to use every available woman in sight."

To Tibi's complete amazement, color scored his high cheekbones. He started to sputter.

It was her turn to dissolve into laughter. She held up her hand to stop him from offering a round of excuses. "You needn't bother trying to justify yourself. I was only teasing you. But it does my heart good to learn you won't boast of your behavior." Strangely happy and emboldened, despite her many problems, she stood on her tiptoes and looped her arms around his neck, grinning up at him. "Clearly we've hit upon an area where we need to work on *your* sense of humor."

"So you think you're clever." He squeezed her until she giggled. "I'll work on anything you say as long as we work on it together."

After the noon meal, Alexius escorted Tibi to the *sagittarii* field where his lead instructor, Silo, waited to meet with her. The sun was warm, but the day was cool and clear, ideal for archery practice. If all went well and Tibi passed the proper tests, Alexius would allow her to begin work with Silo and two of his minor instructors, training half a dozen new volunteers the next afternoon.

Not far beyond the row of hay-stuffed targets, several pairs of gladiators perfected their stances in the golden sand of the training arena. The clap of wooden practice swords and the instructions issued by his trainers carried on the light breeze. Not for the first time, he questioned the wisdom of allowing his woman anywhere near the men. Walking the delicate balance between making her happy and keeping her safe was a more difficult proposition than he'd first anticipated. He wished he'd kept his mouth shut and never offered her a teaching position. In hindsight, he realized that he'd overplayed his hand. He'd been just uneasy enough to convince her to stay that he'd overstepped the bounds of good judgment.

Only the pure joy on her face when he'd asked her to share her knowledge kept him from changing his mind, as he'd been tempted to do at least a dozen times in the past hour.

He rubbed the knotted muscles at the back of his neck. He'd promised himself he'd never let her out of his sight and Silo swore to protect her with his life. Any trainee who harmed so much as a hair on her precious head would find his days ended that same moment.

Still, if anything happened to Tibi…

"I've reconsidered," he said.

"What?" She stopped midstride and stared up at him with dark, disappointed eyes. "Why? Have I done something wrong?"

The afternoon breezes whipped tendrils of silken hair around her oval face. Her full mouth beckoned him like a treasure trove. She was dressed in wool from head to toe, but he found her more alluring than a siren. "I didn't fully consider the effect you're bound to have on my men."

Her face fell. "There are other women within the *ludus*. Are they not safe?"

He shrugged. "They're not half as beautiful as you are."

Color bloomed in her cheeks. She looked down her front as if inspecting the ugly garment she wore. "Speak sense. I'm not beautiful. Besides, you said your trainers would be by my side to protect me."

"You *are* beautiful… Don't roll your eyes." He sighed and shook his head. "Maybe I'm not being fair to my trainers to expect them to perform their duties and protect you at the same time."

Her gaze dropped to the sand at their feet. She kicked a small rock with the toe of her sandal. "I see your point. I didn't consider I'd cause them extra work. I don't want—"

"Don't say it. You're no trouble or a burden. This has nothing to do with you. My men are trained killers. They can be barbarians."

"Your troupe treated me with respect when I went with them to the Coliseum."

"Hmm…for some reason I remember that episode a mite differently. I believe Gerlach threatened you, didn't he?"

Her nose wrinkled with distaste. "Will the *Germanian* be one of my students?"

His mouth tightened. "Not in a thousand years."

"Then, please, let's see how the next few days go. You have my sincerest promise that I'll be careful. At the first sign of trouble, I'll have Silo take me back to the house. Your trainers won't have to worry about me."

Alexius frowned as a similar promise echoed through his mind from over a decade before. Without warning, the beloved and much-missed face of his sister, Kyra, emerged in his mind's eye. The agony of grief and endless regrets pierced his chest.

"Are you well, Alexius?" Tibi's voice overflowed with concern.

He forced the memory aside and glanced down to see Tibi's slim fingers clenched around his upper arm.

"You looked as though you were in pain. Are you ill?"

"I'm fine," he assured her, more shaken by the memory of Kyra than he cared to admit.

She studied him with a dubious frown. "More secrets? I can see you're troubled by something. It's my fondest hope that you'll trust me enough someday to share your sorrows with me."

"It's not a matter of trust." He looked out over the archery field to the training arena and game pens in the distance. Three hundred of Rome's best gladiators, the multistory barracks, bathhouses, storehouses and kitchens all belonged to him. He was no longer the poor farm boy whose defense of his sister had destroyed all those he'd loved.

"Then what is it?" she asked gently.

"It's a matter of letting the past stay buried, where it belongs."

"Forgive me, but nothing seems buried. You seem haunted by whatever is troubling you."

"Haunted?" He forced a laugh, while at the same time acknowledging that she saw him too clearly. "How like a female to be so dramatic."

She winced as though he'd slapped her. "I may be a *dramatic* female, but I never expected you to be a man who resorts to insults and cowardice."

He stiffened. Not even armed gladiators dared to speak to him in such a manner. "Cease—"

"No, you cease, Alexius. I've told you before that I want to be your friend. I apologize if I crossed a line I shouldn't have. If you have no wish for my friendship, then say so, but don't belittle me. I've stomached enough acid of that kind to last a lifetime. Either treat me with the consideration you've shown me thus far or take me back to my father. I have no love for his treatment, but at least with him I know what to expect, and he can no longer disappoint me."

She'd cut his legs out from under him. He felt smaller in stature than Velus, yet strangely glad she wasn't afraid of him. His ire faded and he tamped down his pride. "I was wrong, Tibi. I'm sorry I offended you."

She swallowed hard and nodded in what he hoped was a sign of forgiveness. "I'm sorry if I was too harsh with you."

He fought a smile, loving her kind heart. For the first time, he realized how much courage she'd had to call upon to censure him. "I'm pleased you spoke your mind. I told you before—you have no need to fear me."

"Thank you. I confess I didn't know if I could believe you."

"And now?" he asked.

She tilted her head and contemplated him with dark eyes large enough to drown in. "I'm starting to think I can."

Pleased, he looked across the distance toward Silo, who waited near a copse of olive trees on the edge of the archery field. His instincts prodded him to march Tibi back to the house, lock her away from his men and keep her safe from the world, but if he gave in to his impulses, he'd lose whatever goodwill she felt toward him. She desired respect. He recognized the signs because he'd spent most of his life fighting to gain the same thing for himself. He held the power to deny her the chance to prove her ability in the area she felt most confident, but if he crushed her spirit, he'd be no better than her father.

Disgusted by the thought of being anything like Tiberius, he set his fears for her aside and put her wants above his own. "Come, Tibi," he urged, as he set out across the sand. "The day is waning and Silo appears to be ready for us."

Tibi refused to question her good fortune when Alexius resumed their trek toward the archery field. He'd truly worried her when he said he'd reconsidered allowing her to train his men. Many times throughout her life her father had given her permission to do something she enjoyed, then changed his mind at the last moment for no apparent reason.

She was encouraged to learn that Alexius was not the same kind of man. His indecision stemmed from a concern for her safety, not a delight in humiliating or punishing her as Tiberius had always sought to do.

As they approached the archery instructor waiting under an olive tree, Tibi grew nervous. She was eager to be a help to Alexius, just as he'd helped her, but what if she was'nt good enough? What if she proved useless? Worse, what if she made a fool of Alexius for recommending her?

Silo, a swarthy, bearded man, met them a few paces away from a wood crate filled with several bows of different types and lengths. Alexius made introductions before allowing the instructor to take over the assessment.

His condescension ill-concealed, Silo waved her toward the crate and invited Tibi to choose the pieces that best suited her.

She glanced at Alexius. He was leaning against one of the olive trees, his muscular arms folded over his chest. His handsome face was a study in boredom. She found his lack of interest less than heartening. He seemed convinced that the entire exercise was a complete waste of time in which she was bound to fail. Was his lack of faith in her abilities the real reason he'd reconsidered giving her the chance to prove herself?

Her shoulders back, she moved to the crate, determined to show Alexius and his patronizing instructor that she was fully capable of performing as well as she claimed.

Harsh voices and the clack of striking weapons carried from the gladiator field as she considered each of the half a dozen bows on offer. Of the three types available, she chose one of each to test in order for the men to see her expertise with each kind.

The first was a basic straight bow made of wood

and shorter than she. One was a longbow, also made of wood, but its length was greater than her height. The last, a composite bow, was Tibi's preferred choice of weapon. It was made of horn and sinew attached to a wooden core with animal hide glue. Smaller and easier to handle than the longbow, it offered the same amount of power. The multiple layers stored added power in the bow, allowing shots to gain an equal or greater distance from the lighter, shorter weapon.

Before strapping on a quiver, she inspected several arrows from their carved bone tips to their soft feathered tails. Convinced that she'd chosen her equipment well, she moved to the gash in the dirt Silo had created as a shooting line, about fifty paces from the first target. Because of the short distance, she kept the standard bow and handed the other two to Silo for safekeeping.

Silo smirked. "Are you sure that's the best choice?"

Tibi smiled sweetly and nodded. She was no stranger to intimidation. She refused to be confused by him, and in this one area, to second-guess herself.

Taking the force and direction of the rising wind into account, she assumed a stance with one foot positioned in front and one behind the shooting line for greater stability. With the arrow in place, she took aim, pulled back the string and let the arrow fly.

Just as she expected, the arrow hit the center of the target. Elated that she wasn't as out of practice as she'd feared, she looked to Silo to judge his reaction. His impassive expression irritated her. "Well?"

"Adequate," he said without emotion. "At least I can be assured you won't shoot yourself in the foot. Shall we try the next one? Or is the wind too much for you?"

Tibi glanced at the next target. At twice the distance

of the first one, the hay-stuffed tunic sported a melon on top to serve as a head.

Without a word, she traded the standard bow for the longbow and moved to the next shooting line. Silo was correct. The wind had kicked up, blowing leaves across the ground and rustling the trees along the field's perimeter. The size of the longbow also presented more of challenge. The greater size of the piece provided more thrust for a longer shot, but pulling back the string strained the muscles of her arm. She released the arrow, hitting the mark she aimed for in the center of the melon.

Again the instructor offered no reaction. Annoyed, Tibi set another arrow then let it fly. Just as she intended the arrow pierced the target's "heart."

"Bloodthirsty," she heard Alexius murmur behind her.

She turned and scowled at him, but as usual he just laughed.

She followed Silo to the third and farthest target. Fashioned in the shape of a circle, the target had been tied to the end of a rope and dangled from a tree limb. The wind had set it swinging like a pendulum.

"Now we'll see if you can really shoot," Silo said, handing her the composite bow. "Or if the other shots were flukes, as I suspect."

Tibi's lips tightened. She took a deep breath and let it out slowly. If Silo meant to fluster her as part of the test, he'd have to try harder. She waited as he used the heel of his sandal to mark the last shooting line. She moved into place, positioned her feet, raised the bow and took aim. The arrow hit the target to the left of center.

"Just as I thought," Silo said. "You aren't quite the expert you claim to be."

"Silo…" Alexius warned.

"Wait," Tibi interrupted. She faced the instructor. "Give me the standard bow."

He did as she commanded. She took up position and sent another arrow sailing toward the swinging target. Although the arrow was shot from the weakest of the bows, it hit right of center. "Give me the longbow," she said.

Silo obeyed. She planted her feet and shot another arrow. This time, the arrow hit center.

She turned to the instructor. "If you still believe I'm no more than adequate, you're blind."

A wide smile cracked the instructor's swarthy face. "*I* believed you after you skewered the melon. That shot was most impressive—especially for a woman."

She heard Alexius utter an oath behind her, but she was too pleased with the outcome of the test to take offense. "Does that mean you won't mind if I help instruct the trainees?"

Silo looked beyond her shoulder. Aware that the trainer wouldn't agree without Alexius's permission, she held her breath for what seemed like an eternity.

"I'll be glad to have your help," Silo said finally. "But whether or not the rest of the men will take instruction from a female remains to be seen."

Chapter Nine

Confident and happy with the trial's successful outcome, Tibi started back to the main house with Alexius by her side. "Tell me the truth," she said as they skirted the gladiator field. "What did you think of my shooting?"

"I was most impressed," he said over the mock battles taking place in the training yard. "I almost felt sorry for the second target. Such violent tendencies you displayed. If I didn't know better, I'd think you were part barbarian."

"It's a family secret, but I *am* part barbarian." She grinned as his eyebrow arched with curious interest. "My grandmother was a native Briton. My grandfather served Plautius during his first governorship of Britannia. The story I was told is that my grandmother was taken as a slave a short time before my grandfather received his military diploma and returned to Rome. She tried to kill him the same day he bought her, but he was so taken with her fiery spirit, light hair and blue eyes that he was overcome with emotion for her. Rather than punishing her, they married within months of meeting.

Pelonia's mother was the third of their nine children. My mother was their fifth."

"If your grandmother's hair was half as lovely as yours, I'm not surprised he was smitten with her."

"Other people have light-colored hair," she said, warmed by the compliment.

"Yes, but yours is unique. Like morning sunlight shining on pure gold. I've never seen its like."

Uncertain how to respond to such praise, she directed the conversation back to the archery test. "Silo seems to think your men won't like having me as an instructor."

"Don't be concerned. You'll win them over."

"Do you truly think I'll have anything to teach them?"

"I'm certain of it. I've no doubt Silo and I can learn a trick or two as well."

"You?" The strong breeze pulled at her braid. "I thought you were an expert with all weapons."

"Give me a lance, a trident or a *gladius* and I'm unbeatable," he said with a confidence born from experience. "As for bows and arrows, I know the basics, but I never claimed to be more than adequate."

"You heard Silo." She smiled up at him as she pushed loose tendrils of hair out of her eyes. "Instruction begins tomorrow at sunrise."

He chuckled. "I hate to disappoint you, but I'm having guests tonight. If I make it to the field before midday tomorrow, I'll consider it a miracle."

They left the training area through an iron gate that opened into a peach orchard. The strong wind whistled through the trees, setting the leaves and limbs to dancing.

They started down a brick path that led to the main

house. The smell of smoke wafted from the nearby cookhouse. The sky was darkening with the setting sun and a servant was lighting torches along the path.

"Do you think any of your guests will recognize me?" she asked

He shrugged. "I can't say. A few of them might. I know one or two of them are acquainted with your sister."

Well aware that gladiators were the favored conquest of wealthy women on the hunt, she was beset with images of Alexius surrounded by beautiful admirers. Her spirits sank. "It might be best if I stay in my room for the night."

"Yes," he agreed without hesitation. He pulled open the side door of the house and waited for Tibi to precede him. "I was about to suggest that myself."

"When do expect your wom...guests to arrive?"

"Within the hour. I'll have Velus send a bath and a meal to your room. You'll want to get your rest. Silo may seem easy in temperament, but don't let him fool you. He can be a brutal taskmaster."

Upstairs, Tibi entered her room and closed the door. One of the servants had lit a set of ceramic oil lamps on the desk. The plain plaster walls crowded in on her. She was an *idiota*. She had to be to fall in love with an untamed man who spent his evenings entertaining swarms of equally wild women. Hating the jealousy coursing through her veins, she leaned against the door's smooth surface and lightly banged the back of her head on the wood before moving deeper into the room.

To her surprise, she saw a small pile of folded, light-colored tunics on the sleeping couch. A comb and a bottle of cleansing oils sat next to the neat stack. She'd have to thank Leta for her thoughtfulness the next time she saw her.

A short time later, servants arrived with a tub they filled with several large buckets of hot water. One of the men closed the shutters on the window overlooking the house's inner garden.

Once the servants departed, Tibi added a dose of the jasmine cleansing oil to the steaming tub. She breathed in the fresh, floral scent as she slipped into the water. Her muscles relaxed as the soothing heat surrounded her up to her neck.

She fashioned a pillow out of one of the drying cloths and leaned her head back against the rim of the tub. Her eyes closed, she marveled at the events of the day. She found it almost impossible to believe that *she* was now a gladiator instructor. Despite the danger of scandal if anyone spread the word about her new undertaking, she basked in a sense of accomplishment and worth previously unknown to her experience.

As she planned her archery lesson for the next day, Alexius's handsome face swam into view in her mind's eye. A smile curved her lips. Desperate, irrational love squeezed her heart. He'd called her beautiful and his compliments did wonders for what little feminine pride she possessed, but they were no match for the extraordinary fact that he'd not only believed in her abilities, he'd given her a chance to prove her skill when no one else had ever bothered.

The water cooled, causing her to shiver. She washed her hair and rinsed it with the last bucket of clean, tepid water before leaving the tub. Dressed in one of the fresh tunics, she combed her hair, giving the cool air a chance to dry the long tresses.

The faint melody of a panpipe drifted through the

shutters, alerting her to the start of the night's festivities. She did her best to disregard the ugly emotions baiting her but found it almost impossible not to give in to the curiosity begging her to spy through the window.

A female's husky laughter floated up from the courtyard. The sound proved too much for Tibi to endure. She reached for the handle on the shutters.

A knock sounded on the door. She jumped in guilty surprise and released the handle as though the scrap of metal had caught on fire. She rushed to let her visitor in, telling herself she was thankful to be diverted from the fete downstairs.

Leta waited in the corridor. The young maid held a tray heavy with various dishes of vegetables, meats and fish. A small loaf of bread smelled fresh from the oven. "Master Alexius thought you might be hungry," the maid said with a smile. "He didn't know your preferences, so there's a sample of some of the delicacies he's offering to his other guests tonight."

Her stomach already in a knot of complicated emotions, Tibi wasn't interested in the food. She waved Leta into the room, determined to hide her inner turmoil from Alexius's kind but chatty servant.

The maid set the tray on the desk, sliding the lamps out of the way as she did so.

"Thank you for the tunics and oils," Tibi said. "They're much appreciated."

"Don't thank me. Master Alexius sent them. I overheard him tell Velus he wants you to be comfortable here."

Alexius's thoughtfulness released a spring of joy inside Tibi. As soon as she saw him she'd let him know how much his kindness meant to her.

Leta moved to the window on the opposite wall. Her

fingers fiddled with the shutter slats as she did her best to snatch a view of the group below without appearing too obvious.

"The usual buzzards have already descended," the maid said nonchalantly. "Livia Marciana, Cosma Tertia and Antonia Corvina are the worst. They're here every night the master allows visitors. All three are rich widows who vie for his attention and hang on his every word. I doubt any of them truly cares for him. They're in a competition with each other to see who can seduce him first. My guess is it will be Livia. She's the sneakiest and the loveliest to look upon. Plus she has the least annoying laugh of all three of them."

Tibi scowled. She knew of Antonia Corvina. The woman was a notorious gossip who traveled unhindered in Tiberia's social circle. The name Livia Marciana seemed vaguely familiar to her, but she'd never heard of the third widow. And after learning of the woman's plans for Alexius tonight, she had no wish to.

"Maybe your master is wise to their scheming and won't dabble with any of them."

Leta giggled. "The master *adores* women. I'm certain he'll choose at *least* one of the trio when their offer is plain for all to see. Why wouldn't he, when they're all so very beautiful and rich beyond imagination?"

Refusing to be impressed with hypocritical women who chased gladiators by night when they'd most likely be scandalized to speak to those same men by day, Tibi stayed silent, leaving the maid to gush alone.

The rich aroma of roasted pork provided Tibi with a much-needed distraction. She made her way to the tray of delicacies on the desk, hoping to find something to tempt her uneasy stomach. She hadn't eaten since morning. Aware that she needed to keep up her strength for the next day's training session, she skipped over the dormice and sea urchins in favor of a perfectly cooked selection of pork that melted in her mouth. The delicious morsel did wonders to revive her appetite. She closed her eyes and savored another bite before sampling a boiled cardoon stem.

"Sergius says their skin is like perfect cream. And their clothes are made of silk so fine it must have been woven for the gods."

"Who is Sergius?"

"My man." Leta beamed with pride. "He's one of the school's champions. Two more fights and he'll have enough coin to pay off his debt to the master. Four fights and we'll have enough money to marry."

Tibi offered congratulations. "Is Sergius downstairs?"

"Oh yes. You can see him there playing dice in the corner of... Oh no. Not again," Leta hissed.

Tibi looked up to see the maid drop the shutter's slat back into place. "What is it?"

The usually sanguine maid turned grim. "Senator Basilius is here for the second time in one day."

Tibi tensed. She headed for the window to see her brother-in-law's rival.

"Do you know the swine?" Leta asked.

"Not personally," she said, wondering at the younger girl's vehemence. "I take it you do?"

"I was his slave until two years ago." There was a wealth of meaning in the short explanation.

"I'm sorry," Tibi said, understanding far better than the maid probably gave her credit for.

Leta shrugged. "Master Alexius rescued me. He's allowing me to work off my slave price. If the gods will it, I'll be free by June."

Pleased for Leta, Tibi couldn't help feeling a pang of envy for the other girl when gaining her own freedom was an impossibility.

The jaunty notes of a kithara had replaced the more refined melody of a flute by the time she folded back one of the shutters to peer down into the courtyard. Lanterns had been lit along the garden's paths, giving the rectangular area a warm, golden glow. The splash of the fountains and the sweet smell of incense lent the night a sultry air. Low-cushioned couches covered in a dark shade of crimson surrounded circular tables laden with large platters of food. Laughing diners reclined and fed one another from the rich fare.

"There's the senator. Over there by that large potted palm," Leta whispered, pointing with her index finger.

"Yes, I recognize him," Tibi said, although her eyes were scanning the scene for Alexius with an immediacy she feared must be improper. "Your master and I saw him at an eating establishment after we left the Coliseum yesterday."

"I wonder why he's here."

Tibi found Alexius, and a dozen men she recognized as gladiators she'd met at the arena the day before, mingling with twenty or so guests on the far side of the courtyard. Dressed in a light gray tunic with a wide, black belt, the silver wristbands he favored and black leather sandals that laced up to his knees, her Greek personified raw power and masculine strength. She found it easy to understand why the female populace favored him. Her own heart raced a little faster each time she saw him until sometimes she feared it might burst from her chest.

"Don't you?"

"Don't I what?" Tibi murmured distractedly.

"Wonder why the senator has come tonight."

From the corner of her eye, she saw Basilius heading straight for Alexius. Velus appeared in the doorway left of the garden. Tibi watched the steward take in the scene and march straight for Basilius. The older man tried to bypass the dwarf, but obviously indifferent to the arrogance of powerful men, Velus prevailed in his subtle but tenacious bid to redirect the senator in the opposite direction.

Tibi sighed in relief. Her loyalty remained with her brother-in-law. "Most likely the senator's here to convince Alexius to promote him to the mob. From what Alexius explained to me, the emperor chooses consul candidates in large part due to their popularity with the masses."

She glanced at the maid, wondering why Leta had gone uncharacteristically silent. "But then, I could be wrong."

"I doubt you are. I hope the master isn't taken in and casts him out on his head."

Tibi hoped so, too, but the senator's prompt ejection from the party wasn't likely. After their disagreement yesterday, Alexius was too savvy to court Basilius's disfavor. He believed the old man was likely to win the consulship and he wouldn't fare well if he'd openly rejected the cunning senator.

Troubled by the political intrigues unfolding in front of her, Tibi considered contacting her brother-in-law with the information, but she couldn't do that without confirming her location. She would just have to try to help her family by convincing Alexius not to support Basilius.

The music and dull roar of conversation filled the garden. Her gaze slid back to Alexius. He and two other men were surrounded by a pack of painted women dressed in low-cut tunics and dripping with jewels. His dark head was tipped back as he laughed. An admirer in a fashionable blond wig and bloodred *stola* moved to his side. She wrapped her arm around his back with a familiarity that made Tibi grind her teeth. She willed him to push the flirt away, but he pulled the woman close with casual ease.

"Who is the bold one?" Tibi asked without thinking.

"Cassandra Lupa. She's a she wolf who used to be *very* close to the master. She scorned him for a wealthy wine merchant last year. Now that she's newly divorced, she wants him back in her clutches."

Jealousy pinched Tibi hard. All her life she'd regretted being female and sought to be more like the son her father always pined for. But in that moment she yearned to be more feminine, a siren who stunned Alexius and ruined him for *all* other women.

His arm draped over the she wolf's slim shoulders, Alexius toyed with the gold bauble dangling from her ear as he continued his animated conversation. Cassandra rubbed Alexius's back, filling Tibi's stomach with queasy distress. Hating the way her heart ached, she dragged her gaze from the byplay and moved from the window. She grabbed her *palla* off a hook on the back of the door and left the room.

"Shall I come with you?" Leta called from the doorway.

Tibi waved her back. "No, I won't be gone long."

Without considering where she was headed, she hastened along the corridor, down the back stairs and, careful to avoid the gathering in the central courtyard, out into the herb garden on the northern side of the house.

The glow of a single lantern made a small arch of

light surrounding the door. The distant melody of the music inside and the fragrant bouquet of rosemary, dill and coriander soothed her rattled emotions. She wrapped the *palla* around her shoulders to ward off the chill in the night air.

Disconcerted by the ferocity of her unrequited feelings for Alexius, she meandered deeper into the garden, the faint moonlight illuminating her way.

She sank onto a bench beneath a lemon tree. Her palms on the cool, smooth marble seat, she leaned back and breathed in the light citrus sweetness of the rustling leaves above her. Stars twinkled in the night sky for as far as she could see. She wondered if the gods really existed or if the God Pelonia served was real. If so, did any of them care about her plight in the least?

The door to the house opened. An elegant couple invaded Tibi's tranquil refuge. The dim light prevented her from seeing their faces and the distance kept her from hearing their conversation. Not wanting to be seen for fear of being recognized, she moved over on the bench and deeper into the shadows as she waited for the right moment to leave.

Finally free of the nest of women who clung to him like boa constrictors, Alexius moved to a solitary spot near a painted column. Less than three hours into the party and he was bored for the first time since Tibi had taken over his life two days before. A quick glance around the courtyard told him none of his company was of the same frame of mind. Even so, he wished he'd canceled the whole gathering in favor of spending a quiet night with the woman he loved.

The beat of the music quickened. A few of his more

inebriated gladiators began to call for their favorite admirers to dance.

"Shall *I* dance for *you?*" Cassandra moved up behind him and entwined her arm with his.

He looked down into his former favorite's seductively painted eyes, wondering why he'd never noticed the avarice in her gaze. Velus had much to answer for. He'd allowed Cassandra entrance tonight without asking him first. She and the *triumvirate* of widows chasing on his heels had been driving him mad. He shrugged out of her grasp. "Not tonight."

She gave him a pout he'd seen her practice more than once in a mirror. "You used to love it when I danced for you."

"Times change." She seemed to think nothing had altered between them in the year since she'd left him to marry a man three times her age whom she'd deemed more suitable. She acted as though he should be grateful for her return when, in truth, he'd failed to notice her absence within hours of her departure.

"Times change?" Her smile faded as the hard truth of his rejection pierced her vanity. She planted her fists on her generous hips. "Times *change?* You mangy dog. Who do you think you are?" she spat. "Have you forgotten that I am a patrician's daughter, gladiator? How dare you dismiss me when you should be thanking the gods that I bother to remember your name."

Alexius struggled not to laugh at Cassandra's theatrics or her need to throw her social superiority in his face. How different Tibi was. She never treated him as less than an equal. "Clearly I'm not a man worthy of you, my lady. It's probably best if you seek more appreciative company elsewhere. Now, I have other guests to entertain."

He offered her his back and sought out his friend Sergius, standing near one of the banquet tables.

"I've never thought of you as a coward," said Sergius. "But your bravery just now is unprecedented."

"How so?"

"When you left Cassandra she looked as though she meant to flay the skin off your back with her fingernails." Sergius popped a handful of berries into his mouth. "What happened?"

As he skimmed over the details, Alexius swiped a chalice of *mulsum* off the tray of a passing servant.

"Congratulations." Sergius's blue eyes were filled with mirth. "You finally put that hag in her place."

"I should have been clearer sooner and saved myself the aggravation of enduring her presence tonight," he said, cringing at the high-pitched squeals of a woman who'd decided to wade into the cold water of the largest fountain.

"Why didn't you?"

"In truth, I forgot all about the greedy wench." Alexius lifted the chalice to his lips and took a deep draught of the honey-laced wine. As he surveyed the fete, he found it impossible to shake his bone-deep boredom with the dancing, games of chance and drunken foolishness overtaking his garden like weeds. The food was delicious, but he'd had his fill. The same boredom prevailed with the women who were all high-born, willing and beautiful, but lacked even half as much charm as Tibi.

He looked to the shuttered window of Tibi's room just beneath the eaves of the portico. She couldn't possibly sleep with the incessant racket. The revelry needed to end. He signaled for the music to stop, but soon realized that the musicians didn't see him through the incense and torch smoke. If he called out, they weren't likely to hear him over the din. Pricked by yet another annoyance, he started toward the group in the corner. Before he reached them, Velus burst into the garden, drawing his full attention.

"What is it?" he asked, alarmed by his steward's noticeable anxiety.

"There's trouble in the herb garden."

Alexius aimed for the door. Velus trailed him. "What happened?"

"I don't know," the steward said, huffing to keep up. "I heard yelling and went to investigate. Livia Marciana was on her way to fetch you. She said a fight had started in the herb garden."

Alexius broke into a sprint. The champions he invited into his home were those he most trusted, but they were all volatile men trained to kill with little or no provocation. Too conscious of the potential damage to his men and property to wonder at the quiet, he pushed open the door and met with silence.

His gaze swept over the garden for as far as the circle of torchlight allowed him to see.

Nothing but the breeze rustling the lemon trees.

Velus caught up with him, his chest pumping like bellows. He scanned the quiet scene. His round face crimped with confusion. "I don't understand. Moments ago, I heard a full-blown war out here."

"Where's Livia?" he asked, his instincts warning him to be suspicious of the whole scene.

"I'm here."

He spun around to see Livia framed in the doorway. Her flowing white *stola* was torn at the neck, revealing a transparent tunic beneath. The expression of fear she wore called for concern.

Alexius moved toward her, careful not to push her into a round of hysterics. "Tell me what happened."

Tears welled in her large green eyes. "I came out here for some air. One of your men attacked me."

"Who?" asked Alexius.

"The darkness... I didn't see the beast's face. Gavius heard me scream and came to my rescue. A fight broke out..."

Livia began to cry in earnest. She fled the door and threw herself against Alexius's chest. He looked to Velus, but the steward shrugged, offering no assistance.

"Quiz Gavius. Find out what happened and if he knows the assailant," he barked, patting Livia's back. Her arms were locked around his waist. He doubted that a summer storm possessed the strength to break her grip.

"Thank you," she offered in a husky whisper once Velus left. Her green eyes were huge, damp pools of distress. Rivulets of black kohl marred her pale, painted cheeks. "I was so frightened, Alexius! But *you* make me feel safe. Please don't push me away. Just this once. Not tonight."

"I'll have Velus make arrangements to see you home."

"No, I need *you*. I need you *so* much." She reached up and kissed him.

Stunned by the cold ambivalence that spread through him like a glacial stream, Alexius ripped his lips from hers and glared down at her with loathing. The game she played was suddenly clear. He wondered if she'd paid Gavius to help carry out her scheme.

Aware of his own strength, he grasped her vise-like arms and dislodged her with gentle but unyielding force. "That was a mistake, mistress. Don't repeat it or

I'll forget my mother's instructions not to ever hurt a woman."

Taking her by the wrist, he led her from the garden. The music and mayhem of the party grew louder in the corridor. Fed up to the back teeth with the last several hours, Alexius shouted for Velus, but his steward was nowhere to be found.

"Fetch your slave and call for your litter," he growled at Livia. "Consider your welcome here at an end."

He left her at the edge of the garden and made quick work of killing the music. Amid the gripes and protests of the fete's premature conclusion, he ordered his men back to their barracks and sent his other guests on their way.

As the garden emptied, Velus finally reappeared. "Where have you been?" Alexius snapped.

"I was looking for Gavius as you ordered."

"Did you find him?"

Velus nodded. "He didn't recognize the brute as one of our men. I suspect Livia ensnared her own slave to help with her dirty tricks."

Anger boiled inside Alexius. Sword practice couldn't come early enough. "I'm going to my quarters. Don't interrupt me unless the house catches fire."

He turned on his heel, grateful for the end of the most vexing night he'd endured in ages. Livia's mischief making galled him and Cassandra's attempted seduction was no compliment. He was no slab of meat to be fought over by a pack of bored, rich hyenas. Nor was he a puppet who danced when someone else pulled his strings.

In his chamber, he blew out the oil lamp on the table and crawled into his bed. As he stared into the darkness, he willed back the angry monster thrashing inside him. The night had given him a new perspective on his life and he didn't like the view. For the first time, he realized he'd been slowly killing himself in ways more dangerous than the risks he took in the Coliseum.

A decade before, he'd been a young man with a hopeful future. His wants had been simple but nourishing to his soul. He'd worked his own land and begun building his own home. Dreams of finding the kind of deep, unconditional love he'd witnessed between his parents and basked in as a child spurred him forward.

But Fate had snapped her boney fingers and robbed him of all he held dear. Flung into the vile pit of the gladiator arena, he no longer thrived when nothing was certain—least of all survival.

Anger had taken root in his heart, growing more each day until there was little room for good in him. When Caros acquired him from his former master, he'd been wild, unpredictable, less than human.

Caros had shown him how to channel his fury into an unbeaten champion's record. Only Caros had ever bested him and that was at the school and unofficial. As long as he had a place to fight when the anger became too much to manage, he was able to fool everyone with his jovial nature.

Now he saw just how much his life of violence had cost him. The constant threat of kill or be killed had taken its toll. Somewhere along the way, he'd stopped believing he deserved any peace at all. In self-inflicted punishment, he'd traded the satisfaction he gleaned from working the soil for meaningless entertainments that left him a little emptier after each game of chance or wild party. Just as bad, he'd settled for condescending women when his parents' example had taught him to search for true companionship and love.

He rolled onto his back and folded his arms beneath his head. Somehow he'd accepted the notion that he was as low as his profession. Without realizing that he'd done so, he'd forfeited the self-respect his upbringing had taught him. He'd believed the lie that he needed other people's approval. No wonder men like Senator Basilius believed his integrity was for sale to the highest bidder and stone-hearted women like Cassandra believed he ought to be grateful for their favor.

His eyes closed. He conjured up an image of Tibi's lovely face. For just a moment he indulged in the impossibility of having her as his wife, of sharing idyllic days with her on his farm in Umbria. How she'd managed to worm her way through the defenses that kept other women from accessing his heart he didn't know, but she made him want to change, to leave Rome behind and embrace the simpler life he truly wanted.

Tibi's willingness to trust him had revived him and his self-worth. For that, he owed her much. More than he could hope to repay. If not for Tibi's influence, he might have taken Cassandra back or allowed the widows or their like to use him to bolster their own vanity. To do so would have been to fall back into bad habits, something expected given his degraded station in life. But Tibi wanted nothing from him but friendship. Her regard gave him the confidence he needed to think more highly of himself.

He cast off the bedcovers and began to pace in the dark. Weighed down by regrets, he longed to be the younger man he'd been, but the past was gone. How could he fix the damage an ill-lived life had wrought? He wanted better for the time he had yet to live. Without knowing where the desperation had come from, he was suddenly starving for the reassurance and joy his friends Caros and Quintus possessed. They assured him that their God would give him what he needed if he believed in Him, but what about the rage twisting in his gut?

Even now, when he was clearer of mind and more optimistic than he had been in ages, anger simmered in his belly, refusing to subside. Surely, his friends' God of peace and love would spurn a man who only thrived because of violence.

He moved to the window and thrust open the shutters. Cold air spilled into the room, across his skin. Moonlight bathed the training area and outbuildings in an eerie white glow.

The field called to him. Out of habit, his right hand clenched, yearning for the familiar comfort of a *gladius* and the relief a fight supplied him. Was he too far gone? Or would leaving Rome and the trappings of the ring be the answer to his problems? Could he be truly satisfied with a simpler life on his land in Umbria? Or would casting aside the hard-won success he'd already earned be nothing more than reckless folly?

Honest enough to admit that whatever life he chose would be colorless without Tibi to come home to, he acknowledged that she could not be his. Half defeated by that simple truth, he accepted that any alterations would be for him alone and because she made him want to be a better person.

He sank back down on the bed. His elbows on his knees, he hung his head, wondering if he was worth the effort or even up to the challenge. What if he threw caution to the four winds and changed his life, only to find the goals he sought were no more than unattainable illusions?

Unable to answer the questions tormenting him, he

settled his thoughts on Tibi. The morning offered her a quiver full of challenges. He would be there, silent, in the background, but doing everything in his power to ensure the success she needed to strengthen her own image of herself. His men would treat her with honor or suffer the consequences, but only she could prove to them she deserved the respect she so desperately wanted.

Chapter Ten

Tibi rose long before the sun the next morning. Troubled by unpleasant dreams during the short time she'd finally slept, she tried not dwell on the shadowed scene she'd witnessed in the herb garden. Livia Marciana had arranged her own assault. Her web of lies shocked and disgusted Tibi, but not half as much as the ease with which Alexius seemed to play into the spider's trap.

Desperately hoping she'd misread what had happened, she splashed her face with cold water from the basin and combed her hair. She wanted to think well of Alexius and considered it only fair to give him the benefit of a doubt. He'd been kind to her. No matter what he did, her offer of friendship stood because of that kindness, but if he'd chosen Livia, she could not love him. Nor, she feared, could she respect him after such a blatant display of poor judgment.

Dressed in one of the dark tunics she'd brought when she left her father's house, she waited for the sound of servants in the corridor before she made her way downstairs.

By chance, she saw Velus in the central garden. With scrolls tucked under his arms and his chubby hands laden with a stack of wax tablets he balanced with his chin, he looked harassed and overburdened—all before sunup.

"Let me help you." She reached for the tablets on top of the stack.

He shied away, almost fumbling the many items as he glanced behind him in a nervous gesture that surprised her. "Thank you, I have them, mistress. Aren't you supposed to be on the archery field?"

"I'm headed there now. I thought I might be too early."

Another quick glance around the garden. "No," he said. "You should be on your way. I expect you're already late. Silo will be on the lookout for you."

Concerned by her tardiness on her first day as an instructor, she hurried toward the corridor that led to the training area at the back of the house. Busy berating herself for not finding out exactly when Silo expected her, she heard a loud clatter in the garden and an irate female voice. "Watch where you're going, you stupid dwarf!"

Outraged on Velus's behalf, Tibi quickly retraced her steps. On the threshold of the courtyard, she froze. Beneath the covered portico on the other side of the fountains and lush greenery, Livia Marciana was standing over Velus berating him for bumping into her. The steward was on his knees desperately collecting the scrolls and tablets scattered across the colorful floor tiles.

Tibi pressed back against the wall, careful to keep out of sight. After the kiss they shared, Livia had left the garden with Alexius. Had she won the wager to ensnare him as Leta predicted? She must have. What other reason would the devious woman have for staying overnight?

Bile rose in Tibi's throat as her suspicions and fears were confirmed. Unprepared for the sense of betrayal that struck her as hard as a merciless fist, she gasped for breath, winded by an intense shock of pain.

Jealousy laughed at her. She couldn't determine which one of them was the bigger fool. Alexius for living up to his reputation and falling for a conniver like Livia, or herself for forgetting his womanizing ways because she preferred to think better of him.

Either way, she was still a fool for having allowed him into her heart. Why hadn't she been wiser and protected herself?

As it was, the situation was unacceptable. Her love was hers alone to give or, in this instance, take back as she wished. When she loved, she desperately longed for that love to be returned wholeheartedly. For years she'd heard of Alexius's exploits. Last night's sample of scandalous behavior confirmed to her that he wasn't up to the challenge of the commitment she desperately needed.

Striving to be sensible instead of ruled by her emotions, she made up her mind that the only road open to them was the friendship she'd offered. If she didn't love him, Alexius was free to cavort with whomever he dared without having the power to devastate her.

She headed to the back of the house. Her chest ached as though her heart had shattered into a thousand shards of broken glass. Irrepressible tears blinded her. She was grateful that no one was there to witness her misery. She swiped the moisture from her cheeks, hurt, sad and increasingly angry with her own stupidity. The situation was for the best. Even if Alexius had returned her love, they had no future. She'd been unwise to forget that simple fact.

Outside, a bracing wind chilled her. Gooseflesh spread across her bare arms, but she was too upset to care. She vaguely wished she'd brought a cloak. Instead of returning to the house and running the risk of seeing Livia again, she continued along the path through the peach orchard.

The smell of smoke from the morning's fires hung in the crisp, clear air. Welcoming the cold as a distraction from her boiling emotions, she did her best to concentrate on the archery lesson she planned to impart. Slowly, she began to regroup and calm down.

She passed through the gate that separated the *lanista*'s private grounds from the rest of the gladiator school. The roar of lions echoed across the sand of the practice field. A rainbow of pink and golden hues spread across the eastern horizon. Lights shone in the barracks windows as did a few torches not blown out by the night winds.

To Tibi's surprise, the main training areas—the gladiator arena, the caged *bestiarri* grounds where trainees fought exotic animals, the equestrian and archery fields—were empty. Uncertain where else to go, and with the house off-limits due to Livia's presence, she waited for Silo beneath the olive trees within sight of the row of targets she'd shot yesterday.

As the rising sun dispelled the gray gloom of dawn, slaves arrived to rake the sand and feed the animals caged along the far side of the elliptical arena.

Wondering how the panther cub fared with its new feline mother, she did her best to ignore the swell of nervous anticipation for the coming day.

Alexius striding across the open expanse was the last

sight she'd expected to see. In the golden light of morning he looked like a flesh-and-blood Apollo, the hem of his cloak whipping out behind him in the wind. She leaned back against the olive tree for support, aiming to appear nonchalant instead of overtaken.

He smiled as he approached, sending her traitorous heart into a frenzy of longing. She hated her reaction, given the vows she'd made not to love him less than an hour earlier. Deciding that she may not have sway over her wayward emotions, but that she definitely controlled her own mind, she forced herself to stand straight, determined to stop being such a weakling.

"Good morning."

The richness of his accented voice poured over her like warm honey. A slight rasp that hinted of his recent sleep made her shiver. She closed her eyes to break his hold on her. For her own protection, she had to remember he'd just spent the past several hours indulging in the charms of another woman.

"Good day," she said, her manner as stiff as her spine.

"Why are you out here this early?" he asked, slipping off his cloak in a single fluid shrug.

"Velus told me Silo was waiting."

"Silo's inside the barracks, still eating." He settled his cloak around her shoulders. Although knee-length on him, the wool garment reached to her ankles. Warmth from his body and the spicy scent of his skin enveloped her. A sigh escaped her lips before she realized it.

"Where's your cloak? You're freezing," he said.

"I forgot it in my room."

"I'll send a slave to fetch it."

She began to take off his.

"No." He reached for her hands. "Wear mine until yours comes. I want you to stay warm."

"Thank you, but you shouldn't have to be cold just because I'm forgetful."

He smiled. "I'm fine. Keep it."

"But—"

"Don't argue with your *lanista*."

She glanced down at their entwined fingers. His dark hands were big, scarred and warm. Before the episode with Livia, she would have reveled in his touch and accepted his care as proof that a special bond existed between them.

Now, confusion toyed with her. Hope whispered that she'd been wrong. The Alexius she knew personified sincerity, making her unable to see him as a liar and a cheat.

"I confess I didn't expect to see you until much later. I thought you mentioned your guests would keep you off the field this morning."

"I sent them home early last night. I realized the noise must be interfering with your rest."

"Really? All of them?" If she hadn't seen Livia she would have been touched by his consideration.

"Yes, all of them."

Offended by the lie, she pulled her hands from his. She wondered what other falsehoods he'd told her over the last few days. She'd known the compliments on her beauty and wit were exaggerations, but what of the poignant stories about his past? His family? He'd said he felt something unique between the two of them. Jealousy and distrust made her wonder just how "unique" he felt toward Livia.

"I'm sorry I ruined your party." Her voice was as

cool as the morning. "You needn't have gone to any trouble on my account."

"You didn't ruin anything. The truth is, I was glad to see everyone go."

"Everyone?" she asked, giving him another chance to tell the truth.

The faint lines in his forehead deepened as he studied her. "Is something amiss with you, Tibi? If you're worried about today, you needn't be. If I weren't confident you'd do well, I wouldn't allow you out here."

Yesterday, his assurance would have gone a long way toward soothing her anxieties. Today, she didn't believe him. The loss of trust was a violation. She'd been robbed of something precious.

"Tell me the truth," he said. "What's happened? You don't seem like yourself, *agape mou*."

"Don't call me that," she said, agitated. The endearment mocked her after his romp with Livia. "I'm not your love. I'll never be."

He stepped back as though she'd struck him. "You sound so certain. Is that because *you* can never love *me?*"

She glanced away, her throat working to dislodge the sharp ball of emotion choking her. Relieved, she saw Silo and a trio of other men walking across the field, their arms loaded with bows and several quivers full of arrows. "Of course." She swallowed thickly, the remaining shards of her heart splinted into ever smaller pieces. "What good can come of either of us loving the other?"

In a short time, the trainees began to arrive in force. The raw recruits quickly swelled from two, to four, to six. Judging by their accents, most of the men were

Italians, but one hailed from Gaul, and another from across the Adriatic on the coast of Dalmatia. Near the back stood a ferocious-looking *Thracian*.

All the men were more than average height, with three or four almost as tall as Alexius. Each of them was huge and swollen with muscle. They were battered and scarred, with the majority bearing bruises, black eyes and at least one bandage.

Alexius leaned on the trunk of an olive tree behind her, his arms crossed over his chest. Her senses heightened by his close proximity, she tried not to be overly sensitive to the silent, but intimidating force of his presence.

Silo called for attention. The chatter quieted. Men who waited beneath the trees, stood, dusted themselves off and moved forward. They formed a tight half circle around her before Silo made introductions.

She smiled and offered a greeting to the wall of indifferent faces. Six pairs of unimpressed dark eyes stared back at her in reply.

Denying her instinct to run and hide in her chamber, she offered a brief history of her archery experience. Still no response. She looked to Silo, "Perhaps we should just begin."

Silo nodded in agreement. He moved to the stack of bows and called the trainees forward. Based on his height and upper-body strength, each man chose the weapon that best suited him. Tibi explained how to restring the bows and, amid their complaints, made them practice until each man mastered the process.

To her relief, Alexius disappeared after the midday meal. Everyone seemed more at ease. While the men waited, they made friendly wagers and created challenges to test each other's strength.

The sun was high overhead, transforming what had been a cold, gray morning into a warm, spring day. She removed Alexius's cloak and hung the garment with care from a branch of one of the olive trees.

Her bare arms drew a round of whistles and hoots from the trainees. Thankful for the dark, shapeless tunic that covered her from throat to ankles, she colored, but ignored their teasing.

Secretly pleased that the group seemed more inclined to accept her, she called the men to order. She held up an arrow and proceeded with the second half of the day's lesson. "Using a well-made projectile is essential to hitting your target."

"Are we going to make one of those as well?" the *Thracian* interrupted from his place in the back.

"Of course. How will we proceed to shooting without arrows?" she replied over the round of sarcastic comments that followed his jest. "First, you'll have to gather the sticks. However, you may want to consider using limbs from the surrounding olive trees. Once you peel away the bark, the fresh wood is easier to manipulate into a straighter missile during the drying stage."

Disbelieving grumbles skittered through the troupe.

"Of course, that is the easiest part," she continued, without skipping a beat. "Catching the birds for use of their feathers can be the most daunting task."

Shouted instructions and the clap of wooden swords from the nearby training areas punctured the silence. Tibi chuckled, unable to keep pretending that she was serious in light of their disenchanted faces.

Slowly, the troupe began to realize they'd been duped. Uncertain smiles turned to appreciative laughter and their once-apathetic gazes lit with a grudging spark of approval.

* * *

Alexius chose his favorite weapon. He pointed the tip of the straight, Greek-styled sword toward Sergius, his friend and one of his most honored champions. "Join me on the sand. I need a good fight."

At the center of the elliptical field, Alexius rolled his shoulders in a futile bid to release the tension in his muscles. Desperate to be free from his inner turmoil, he'd been looking forward to this moment since the party last night.

Sergius settled into a defensive posture, all signs of his usual humor gone from his dark eyes. "Are we battling to the death?"

"Do you wish to die?" Alexius asked.

"No, but you look as if you mean to kill me."

Alexius tensed. He was usually better at disguising his inner feelings, but his encounter with Tibi earlier in the morning had shaken him more than he cared to admit. He'd watched her train his men, his pride in her courage outmatched only by his love for her.

But she did not want him.

The pain of her rejection hurt as though he'd been sliced open. If he'd been higher-born, a citizen or even a simple Roman, instead of a foreign farmer's-son-turned-gladiator, would she have considered him fit enough to care for then?

Every nerve in his body sensed her presence close by. Determined to starve his hunger to see her, he kept his back to the archery field and focused on the battle before him.

Sergius raised his shield and clapped it with his *gladius*. Alexius swung his sword and lunged forward, nicking the other man's forearm.

Gaping at the stream of blood on his arm, Sergius

kicked sand in Alexius's face then attacked like a barbarian.

Alexius blinked the sand from his eyes and laughed,
finally getting the fight he needed. He plowed forward,
whirling his weapon with the swiftness and force of a
storm.

Sergius fell back.

Alexius followed. His opponent recovered quickly
and jabbed with his sword, almost catching Alexius in
the ribs.

The atmosphere erupted with excitement. The surrounding trainees stopped their practice and cast lots
on the winner. Voices cheered from the sidelines.

His sword flashed in the sunlight and caught Sergius on the leg. He swung again, striking his friend's
shield. Sergius retaliated in a forward rush. His face
contorted, his muscles straining against the force of
Alexius's attack. "I have plans with Leta tonight. If
you're going to kill me, do me a favor and wait until
after I see her."

Swords clashed. With every swing of his weapon,
Alexius released a little more anger. He grinned,
amused by his friend now that he'd worked off some
of his tension. "How is your lovely woman?"

Sergius struck again. "She's perfection as always,
but she's a bit worried about your new houseguest."

Alexius faltered midswing, but made a swift recov-
ery. "How so?"

"She says Tibi is in love with you. She thinks you'll
break the poor girl's heart."

Stunned by the announcement, Alexius dropped his
guard. Time stopped. His gaze darted across the sand to
Tibi on the archery field. The sight of her with her arm
wrapped around one of the trainees made him freeze.

White heat sliced across his ribs, followed by a cracking sound and a pain so sharp it left him winded.

His sword slipped from his fingers. He fell to his knees, clutching his side. Everything and everyone around him whirled into a sudden flurry of activity.

Warm blood oozed from the throbbing wound and between his fingers. Its metallic odor filled his nostrils. Sweat broke out on his brow.

Sergius dropped his sword and sank to the ground in front of him. Light clumps of sand splashed onto Alexius's dark brown tunic. Between frantic apologies, he yelled for help.

Remus, one of the physicians always on hand at the *ludus*, pushed his way through the circle of gawkers surrounding Alexius.

"It's not bad," Alexius said, catching his breath as the older man's fingers probed the deep gash.

"It's not good, either. You may have a cracked rib or two. This cut needs tending right away or it will start to putrefy and poison the blood."

The prognosis didn't bother him. After the number of injuries he'd endured over the past ten years, he was too well acquainted with wounds to care about one more.

Only Tibi concerned him. Where and how had Leta gotten the notion that Tibi cared for him? Was it possible that her uncertainty matched his own? Had she lied to protect her pride when she said they had no future?

Hope soared before he could clip its wings. He moved to stand. An arrow of pain shot through his side, forcing him to move more slowly than he liked.

"It's bed rest for you, Alexius," the physician said. "At least a week if not longer."

Mentally debating Remus's advice, Alexius allowed

Sergius to help him to his feet. He ordered his men and instructors back to work.

With as much dignity as his injury allowed, he limped back to the house, refusing to look weak in front of his men. Despite the outcome of the battle, his anger was oddly dormant. If Leta was right and Tibi cared for him in even the smallest way, he had a new, worthwhile reason to live for the first time in a decade.

Although he and Tibi had had different home lives and come from different backgrounds, he understood her better than she realized. The circumstances of their pasts had taught them both to be wary. Because he had plans to make, he could spare a day or two to recuperate out of necessity, but no more. He refused to let Tibi see him as helpless, not when it would take all his strength to win her confidence and a chance to prove how much he loved her.

Chapter Eleven

"Look, a fight!" Silo shouted with more excitement than Tibi thought the event warranted. They were in a gladiator school, after all. Surely more than one brawl erupted every day.

She lifted her hand to shield her eyes from the glare of the sun and looked toward the gladiator field. A crowd had gathered. They moved as one, up and down the sand, along with the fighters. Their cheers were audible from across the open distance.

Unable to see the challengers, she went back to her work. Now that the trainees were finally shooting, a few of them actually seemed interested in learning the proper techniques to succeed at archery.

"Move your right foot forward," she instructed the *Thracian,* whose name she'd learned was Gaidrēs. "And raise your left arm a bit." She reached around his brawny back and pushed his elbow up with her fingertips.

"Impossible!" Silo hissed. A wave of disbelief passed over the other archers intent on the fight. "The master's wounded!"

Master? Alexius! Tibi spun around. The crowd parted,

giving her a glimpse of Alexius on his knees, before swallowing him up again. She hitched her tunic and broke into a flat-out run in his direction. A change in terrain from soil to sand nearly tripped her. By the time she reached the spot where he'd fallen, he'd left the field.

She saw him and another man cross through the iron gate that led to the peach orchard and his home beyond. The gladiator trainees had gone back to their practice and a few were beginning to notice her presence on the field.

Ducking her head, she sprinted after Alexius. As she passed through the orchard, the shade of the peach trees offered a cooler temperature to her overheated skin.

Inside the house, she saw Velus in the corridor giving orders to a trio of servants.

"Where is Alexius?" she interrupted, without slowing her pace.

"In his chamber, my lady, but don't—"

She turned a corner, no longer within hearing distance. She chose a diagonal path across the garden. The sweetness of blooming spring flowers was even more pronounced than on the previous day.

Her heart racing with concern, she took the steps two at a time. On the second floor, she turned in the opposite direction of her own chamber and went straight to Alexius's room. Male voices spilled into the hall— laughter punctuated by wheezing moans of pain.

Praying the laughter meant Alexius wasn't bent on the afterlife, she leaned against the frescoed wall and drew in a deep breath. She was shaking. What if she'd lost him?

Adopting an air of serenity she was far from feeling, she moved into the doorway. Alexius was stretched out on top of the wolf pelts tossed across his sleeping couch. The dark tunic he wore covered him to just above the knees. His sandals had yet to be removed and the laces crisscrossed the long length of his muscled calves. The sight of him smiling and apparently far from death filled her with an ocean of relief.

Alexius's room fit him perfectly. Sky-blue walls and wide, arched windows reflected his open manner. Thick bearskin rugs softened the gold-and-brown mosaic-tiled floor, while heavy furniture carved by a master's hand mirrored the dark, mysterious hues of his complex and exotic nature.

The conversation between the men faded as they realized she was there. The man who'd accompanied Alexius from the field sat in a chair beneath the windows. He saw her first. Eyes as black as pitch latched onto her face. His sharp cheekbones were smudged with dirt and spatters of blood.

Alexius's dark head swiveled on his pillow. A smile curved his lips and lit his silver eyes with such tenderness that her hearted melted. Struggling to remember her vow to take back her heart, she wondered how she'd ever believed she could withhold her love from him.

He held out his hand, his fingers curved to beckon her. "Come in."

She moved deeper into the room as he continued with introductions. "Tibi, this is Sergius, my friend and one of my finest champions. Sergius, *this* is Tibi."

The warmth in his voice when he said her name brought heat to her cheeks. "She's the cousin of Caros's wife, Pelonia. She's my guest here until they come to Rome sometime next week."

Sergius acknowledged her with a nod of his head. "Leta has told me much about you."

"She's told me about you as well."

"Good things, I trust."

She nodded. "If she's to be believed, you are the finest man to ever walk the earth."

He grinned. "My darling girl never lies."

Alexius snorted. "Except on your account, obviously."

Sergius punched Alexius on the shoulder and both of them laughed.

Tibi moved closer, but kept half the room between her and the two men. Her gaze pinned to Alexius's face. Other than a slight paleness beneath the natural bronze of his skin, he looked relatively hearty. "I'm glad to see you're alive, *lanista*. What happened?"

"I let this mongrel best me."

"*Let* me?" Sergius scoffed.

"Of course, I let you. I have to throw you a bone every once in a while or you'll lose interest in learning new tricks."

"You're wounded, so think what you like if it makes you feel better," Sergius said, his tone as dry as dust. "But I could have sworn you folded because of something I said."

Sudden tension replaced the good-natured ribbing between the two friends. Sergius raked his hand through his hair as though he knew he'd crossed some invisible line he now regretted. Even Alexius was frowning. What had happened?

"Perhaps I should come back later," Tibi suggested.

"No!" Sergius jumped to his feet, the chair banging the wall behind him in his haste. "I have to return to the field...that is, if you wouldn't mind staying with this bear until the physician gets here."

"Physician?" Her gaze swept over Alexius looking for a wound bad enough to require more complex medicine. "If a physician's coming, why isn't he here already?"

"He went to fetch supplies." Sergius sidled past her.

"For what purpose?" she asked before realizing he'd fled though the open door behind her.

She moved to the sleeping couch when a slave delivered a bucket of steaming water. Another girl placed a basin on a table close by.

Able to see Alexius more clearly, she realized that there was a thick cloth pressed against his side farthest from her. His arm lay at an odd angle. "Is something wrong with your shoulder?"

"No."

"Your side?" she asked. His hesitation told her she'd found the wounded area. "How badly are you hurt?"

"It's nothing." He frowned. "Just a scratch. I've endured much worse."

The thought of him suffering made her want to smother him with sympathy. "If it's just a scratch, then why won't you let me see it?"

"Because when you faint at the sight of all the blood, I won't be able to catch you."

Her eyes widened in alarm, then narrowed. "What are you implying? That I'm weak and—"

"I knew you were bloodthirsty." A deep sigh escaped him. "Come here. Look all you like, but don't say I didn't warn you first."

Tibi skirted around the edge of the sleeping couch, closer to his injured side. She moved past the chair propped against the wall. Sun streamed through the open windows at her back.

Alexius moved his arm. She leaned over him and reached for the folded linen.

"Wait!"

She froze, her hands hung in midair. *"What?"*

"Sit beside me." He patted the space by his hip. "There's less of a chance you'll hit the floor when you fall."

"I'm not going to faint. A little blood doesn't bother me."

"Define *little*."

Her worry spiked. In the short time she'd been here, he'd grown paler. *Where* was the physician? "A great deal of blood doesn't bother me, either."

He leaned his head back against the pillow and closed his eyes. "Then sit here beside me because I want you to."

Alexius kept his eyes closed. Fearing that Tibi would leave if he moved, he resisted his longing to reach for her. Her soft fingertips brushed a lock of hair from his forehead and trailed down his temple, relieving the pain in his skull he hadn't been aware of. His wound burned and every shallow breath sent a sharp burst of fire through his rib cage, but all the torment was worth it to have her touch him.

"Alexius, you have to stay awake. Keep talking to me."

The urgency in her voice spoke of her concern. He cracked one eye open as she leaned over him. Her soft hair tickled his nose. He didn't want to worry her, but the loss of blood and her delicious scent were starting to make him light-headed.

He forced his eyes open. Their gazes locked. Her full lips were a whisper from his. He only had to lift his head to taste them.

She jerked back. Color high in her cheeks, she looked flustered and that fact pleased him.

"I'll sit with you if you like, but over here." Without

taking her eyes off him, she reached behind her to pull the chair closer to the couch. She sat down. "Now tell me what happened. How did your friend beat you?"

His eyebrow arched. He didn't like the sound of that question. Sergius hadn't beaten him. Finding out that Tibi might care for him had been the culprit. "His sword caught me in the ribs."

"If you'd been in the Coliseum, you might have been killed."

"Most likely." Seeing her blanch, he decided he could grow used to her concern on his account. "Good thing I was on the practice field instead."

Remus knocked on the door frame, a leather satchel filled with medicines in his hand. "How is my patient?"

Alexius grunted. Tibi took hold of his hand and ran her thumb over the back of his scarred knuckles in a soothing motion.

"He's growing surlier by the moment," she told the physician. "I trust you can fix him."

She stood and traded places with Remus at the end of the couch. The old man scooted the chair out of his way and removed the compress. He clucked his tongue in disapproval as he cut away the ruined tunic.

Tibi moved to Alexius's side. He watched her lean over him and grimace as she studied the hacked flesh. Her dark eyes flared and the creamy skin of her cheeks drained of color. Her nose wrinkled with distaste. She bit her full lower lip and nervously pushed a long, wayward tendril of blond hair behind her ear. She *didn't* fall over in a faint, as he'd predicted.

Good to know.

Without warning, Remus pushed on his sore ribs. Alexius bit back a moan, refusing to let Tibi think less of him.

"Worse than I expected," Remus said. "I'd say you have a least three cracked ribs instead of two, as I originally thought."

Disgusted by the diagnosis, Alexius shook his head until he noticed Tibi's compassionate gaze. When she gently cupped his cheek, he wasn't above wallowing in her sympathy.

"Hand me that bottle of vinegar," the physician ordered, enlisting Tibi as his aide. "We have to clean the flesh before I stitch it up. If not, the possibility of infection and festering will worsen."

Tibi did as she was asked and handed Remus a clean piece of linen along with the bottle she opened. Put off by the strong acidic stench of the fermented juice, Alexius tensed. He'd lived this particular scene too many times in his life not to dread the oncoming torture.

Remus tipped the bottle. A liquid inferno hit the laceration. Air hissed through Alexius's teeth. Sweat drenched his face and chest. He swore under his breath.

Tibi dashed to the basin, dipped a clean cloth in the water and hurried to place it on his clammy brow. The pain eased just as another dose of fire hit his flayed skin.

Alexius gritted his teeth. Other times he'd been as badly hurt, he'd simply counted through the pain until he passed out. Not today. As Tibi squeezed his hand, mopped his brow and whispered encouragement, he prayed he'd stay wide awake.

"Will he be all right, Remus?" she asked, a catch in her voice that made Alexius squirm. "Is he going to live?"

"One never knows in these situations, but he's survived worse." The physician sent him a pointed glance. "Of course, he needs to rest, which he fights against."

"He'll rest. Won't you, Alexius?"

He didn't answer. They all understood that she wasn't really asking him. He didn't want to commit himself when he knew how fed up with inactivity he'd be in a few short days. But if his resting made her happy…

"*Won't* you, Alexius?"

"I'll rest," he grumbled.

"Until Remus says you're well?"

"I can't make that promise."

"You can't? Why not?"

"He gets bored," said Remus, his arms crossed over his chest. "He'd rather be on the field issuing orders."

"What if I keep you entertained?" Tibi asked. "Will you consent to rest then?"

"Are the entertainments open to negotiation?"

"Of course," she agreed. "Whatever you wish."

He grinned when she didn't seem to understand his jest.

"I'll read to you, we can play *latrunculi*—"

"*Board* games?" he interrupted. "I'm not a child."

"All right," she said patiently. "We can just talk."

"About what?"

"The choice is yours—politics, philosophy…Greek tragedies."

"I understand now," he grouched. "By *rest*, you mean to ensure that I fall asleep."

Her lips twitched with laughter. He was glad to see he'd reeled her back from the verge of tears.

"Please say you'll do as Remus suggests. You have to heal. I don't want any harm to come to you."

"Because you care?"

She glanced away. "If I say yes, will you do as you're told?"

Uneasy with his increasing inability to resist her, he knew then that he was beaten. "All right. But only because *you* asked."

Chapter Twelve

Four days later, Alexius prowled his chamber, waiting for Tibi. His ribs ached. The sutures holding his side together pulled and itched until he thought he'd go insane.

An hour earlier, Velus had delivered his midday meal, but the fried clams and mix of boiled vegetables appealed to him as much as a plate of worms.

Since his injury, he'd rested as he promised, but he longed to get back to the field. The endless inactivity wore him down more than any wound ever could. The empty hours left him with too much time to ponder his past and the underlying blackness of his present.

Tibi was his one ray of light. As she'd promised, she did her best to keep his mind off his confinement. She'd read to him from Homer's texts. Her Greek was atrocious, but he found her attempts to give each character a different voice amusing. And after realizing that the legendary Jason hailed from Alexius's hometown, she acted out the tale of the prince's quest for the Golden Fleece. He chuckled remembering her disgust for Jason's fickleness when he left the fair Medea for the Corinthian princess, Glauce.

Last night, they'd discussed politics over dinner. Not

his favorite subject, but the play of candlelight on Tibi's lovely face and her passionate defense of the recent uprising in *Dacia* had kept him entranced. Too interested in using the opportunity to discover the subtleties of Tibi's personality, he didn't remember much of what he'd said. He hoped he sounded intelligent as they debated the options open to Emperor Domitian to rectify the state of affairs. If not, Alexius reasoned, he could always blame the pain medicine he was supposed to be taking.

Of even more interest to Tibi, he'd found, was the fact that the Empress Domitia had recently returned to the palace after a year of exile. "It's because the emperor loves her," Tibi had said. "He must have been terribly lonely without her."

Alexius had choked on the lemon water he'd been drinking. He'd heard gossip of a far different reason for Domitia's return, but he found Tibi's optimistic belief in love too sweet to disillusion her.

When he finally heard the even gait of Tibi's sandals in the corridor, he rushed to his couch as fast as his damaged ribs would let him. He pulled the furs up to his chest and did his best to look pathetic.

She knocked on the door frame.

"Come in," he called, sounding sleepy.

"Did I wake you?" She crossed the threshold. A cheerful smile curved her lips as she walked toward him. She'd pulled her hair back from her face and braided the soft strands into a long blond ribbon down her back. The unadorned tunic she wore matched the dark brown of her eyes and set off the creamy smoothness her skin.

By the gods, he wanted to leap up, pull her into his

arms and kiss her. Instead, he shook his head. "I've been waiting for you. Where have you been?"

"On the archery field, just as I was supposed to be."

"You should have been here with me," he said in a moody tone he didn't have to pretend. He stretched, not enough to hurt himself, but enough to make him wince—a trick he'd learned to snare her into touching him.

Sure enough, she placed her palm on his brow. He relaxed, instantly less agitated.

"Your fever is all gone," she said with unfeigned relief.

As expected, he'd suffered a fever the day after his injury. No worse than other times he'd been wounded, the boiling heat had consumed his whole body within hours of receiving his stitches. He'd been delighted that she stayed with him through the night, cooling his brow with moist cloths and holding his hand.

He realized that he was enjoying her care much too much. He couldn't seem to help himself. In the past, his admirers had clung to and clucked over him because they wanted compensation in one form or another. He'd been eager for them to leave him be. Tibi wanted nothing, or so it seemed. The more time she spent with him, the more he craved her presence.

"You were worried about me, weren't you?" He knew she had been, but he wanted to hear her admit it.

"Not a bit. Don't be ridiculous."

"Liar." He closed his eyes as she brushed back his hair with gentle fingertips.

She laughed and sat beside him. "Naturally, I've been very concerned about you. I'm your friend, after all. Besides, where else am I supposed to go if you get yourself killed?"

"That's the *only* reason?" he asked, growing sleepy from the comb of her fingers through his hair.

"I guess not. I have my reputation to consider as well."

He opened one eye and peered at her. "Your reputation?"

"Mmm…I'm considered enough of a menace as it is. Think how the gossips will crucify me if my host ends up dead while I'm here."

He settled deeper under his furs and scratched his stitches. "You're a wicked girl, Tiberia."

"Tiberia?" She grimaced. "That's my sister. No one ever calls me by my full name unless I'm in serious trouble."

"Then I'm surprised you're ever called Tibi at all."

She swatted his shoulder and he moaned as though she'd stabbed him. A smile in her eyes, she shook her head at him and started to rise from the sleeping couch. He caught her hand to keep her close.

"I missed you," he said, all humor gone. "Don't be late again."

"I told you I was on the field. The men are taking quite well to their lessons. The time got away from me."

He leaned his head back against his pillows and tamped down his annoyance. His day didn't start until she arrived. He spent the hours she was gone wishing for her return, while she obviously preferred to be somewhere else. He needed to get back on his feet before he made a habit of waiting around for her like some pathetic, forlorn puppy.

"Perhaps I should make all my instructors women. To keep the men interested in their training."

"That's not a bad idea. The tactic seems to work," she remarked, refusing to let him bait her. She trailed her fingers from his grasp and inspected his untouched meal. "Why haven't you eaten?"

"I'm not hungry."

"You have to eat."

"No, I don't."

"Let me rephrase. You *need* to eat to regain your strength."

"I'm strong enough."

"Don't be petulant." She smiled to take the sting from her words. "What if I fetch you some fresh food? If you eat it all, I'll reward you with another game of *latrunculi.* I'll even let you win this time."

He glared at her profile. Was she serious? Or had she somehow discovered that he was desperate enough to be with her to be reduced to playing board games. "Are you mocking me, Tibi?"

"Not mocking." She covered his untouched plate with a warming dome. "Teasing, perhaps, but I'd never mock an injured man."

He uttered a disbelieving snort.

She faced him. "Especially a man in such dire straits that he squanders the time he's supposed to be sleeping by prowling in his chamber like a prisoner."

"Velus!" he hissed. "What did that old goat tell you?"

"Don't blame your steward. He makes excuses for you. Do you think I'm so deaf I can't hear you shuffling about in here when I'm walking in the corridor right outside?" She pinned disappointed eyes on him. "You have stitches, Alexius. If you're not careful, you'll rupture them. Not to mention cause more damage to your ribs."

"This isn't my first bout with cracked ribs or sutures, Tibi. I usually have one or the other most of the time. I know how to live with them. Besides…I was out of bed because *you* were late," he defended. "You're supposed to keep me entertained."

She burst out laughing. "Underneath all that handsome brawn, you're still a little boy who wants to be coddled by his loving mama and six long-suffering sisters, aren't you?"

"No," he muttered, soothed somewhat by the fact that she admitted to finding him handsome. "I don't like my agreements broken."

She sat down on the chair beside the sleeping couch. "Does it really mean that much to you to have me here?"

With other women, he might be leery of a trap, but not with Tibi. He decided to see if honesty got him anywhere with her. "From the instant you leave, I start counting the moments until you return to me again."

Her expression softened, but there was an underlying wariness, too. "You have to know any woman would be touched to hear those lovely words, but please don't toy with me, Alexius. What of Livia? If she were here, would you tell her the same thing?"

He pulled back, fast enough to jolt his ribs. "Livia? Livia who?"

Her tenderness fled, replaced by anger. She stood. "Livia *who?* Livia Marciana, that's who. I know you have a reputation as a user of women, but exactly what kind of man are you? I saw you kiss Livia in the herb garden during the party last week and I know she stayed here that same night. Don't tell me you've forgotten her so soon."

Never one to fight lying down, Alexius pushed off his furs and rose slowly to his feet. He'd seen Tibi annoyed, irritated and miffed, but never truly angry. Quick to realize something nefarious had happened behind his back, he ignored the insult in her accusation and focused on the reality that she cared enough about him to be upset.

Even better, she chose not to harbor what troubled her and sought out the truth.

"Tell me what happened from the beginning, Tibi. What exactly did you see?"

Her lips pressed into a tight line. "I saw you at the party with all those…those harpies. I went for some air in the herb garden. I saw a woman order a slave to molest her, then try to paint one of your men as the culprit. The light was dim. I didn't see the schemer's face and I didn't know she was Livia until her performance with you a short time later."

"When you saw her kiss me."

She nodded.

"The kiss made you angry? Jealous?"

Her whole body went stiff. "I was very…disappointed in you for believing her and for surrounding yourself with such devious company."

"I didn't believe her," he said, angry enough at Livia to want to strangle the conniving wench. "I ordered her home and barred her from coming into my house again."

She chewed on her bottom lip. Her eyes fumed with hostility. "I'm sorry, but I can't believe you. I saw her in the central garden before sunrise the next morning."

Too furious to defend himself, he made his way to the door and into the hallway. "Velus!" The bellow sent a sharp jab through his ribs. "Get up here. We have some lies to unravel."

Too angry to look at him any longer, Tibi turned her back on Alexius and stared out the wide bank of windows. Whether or not it was her imagination, the air seemed heavy and unseasonably warm.

She wished she'd never touched on the subject of Livia. No matter that learning the truth was always best, one way or the other. Her show of temper embarrassed her and the display of jealousy did little to support her claim that she was solely interested in Alexius for his friendship.

Although able to see the archery field from her current vantage point, the grassy stretch was empty except for the row of targets. To keep from having to converse with Alexius, she focused on the trainees learning how to wield a trident and net in the center of the gladiators' sandy arena.

"Master?" Velus said.

She turned around to see the steward's sheepish entrance into the room.

Alexius rubbed his ribs. She knew he must be in a great deal of pain. He reached for the injured spot more and more often. She was angry with him, but his refusal to take his need for rest seriously still concerned her. He claimed he was used to the pain of stitches and battered bones, but the damage had to have time to heal properly—no matter how stubbornly the wounded believed to the contrary.

"I think there's been a misunderstanding," Alexius told his steward. "Since you know everything that goes on in this house, I'm thinking you might be able to help us figure out the problem."

"If I can." The dwarf wrung his small thick hands.

"My guest believes Livia Marciana stayed with me the night of the party last week."

The steward studied his feet.

"However," Alexius continued, "I distinctly recall ordering you to send that witch back to her cave."

"I can explain."

"I thought you might." Alexius sent a speaking glance to Tibi before refocusing on his steward. "What happened? Did you disobey my orders?"

"Yes," Velus admitted. He wiped a stream of sweat from his temple. "But for a good reason. Please take pity on me."

Uneasy with the steward's obvious distress, Tibi stepped forward. Although her interest in the story was keen, she didn't need Velus put on trial when he seemed eager to admit the full truth.

"Velus," she said before Alexius continued with his interrogation. "I'm sorry. This mess is my fault. I think I must have made a mistake."

"No, my lady, the fault is mine. I disobeyed and didn't confess because I thought I wouldn't get caught."

"Let that be a lesson to you." Alexius scowled. "How often do you go behind my back?"

Tibi intervened. "He claims to have a good reason. Will you give him a chance to explain?"

Alexius invited him to proceed with a wave of his hand.

"I went to do as the master ordered." Velus avoided Alexius and spoke to Tibi. "I found Livia working her wiles on Senator Basilius. I told her she'd been ordered to leave, but she refused to go. While I stood there, she offered the senator a thousand *denarii* toward his campaign for consul and the support of all her patrons if he'd take her part to make me let her stay. He agreed and threatened to cause the master problems if I forced the widow to go."

"What sort of problems?" Alexius interjected in a tone sharp enough to cut.

"I don't know for certain," Velus admitted. "He implied that he'd make sure other gladiator schools received the best contracts."

"Nonsense," Alexius scoffed. "He was trying to intimidate you."

"Most likely. It was late, master. Since you'd retired to your room, I didn't see the harm in letting her stay and avoiding all potential problems. I found her a chamber downstairs, delivered the wine she ordered and sent her on her way early the next morning."

"When I saw her in the garden," Tibi whispered.

"That makes no sense," Alexius said. "What was her point in those arrangements?"

"I heard mention of a wager," Tibi said, hesitantly.

To her surprise, Alexius flushed. His gaze flicked to Velus. "I warned those she-cats. They assured me the bet was hearsay. Did you know any different?"

Velus fidgeted. "I suspected."

"How much did each of them risk?"

"Last I heard, three thousand *denarii*—a thousand each. I let Cassandra into the fete that evening to give you an advantage and a distraction. You always seemed to prefer her over any of the other women who come here."

Alexius rubbed his side. "Why didn't you just tell me of their schemes or, better yet, send them home before you let them enter the house?"

"They were your guests, master, not mine. I thought you were aware of their tricks and were amused by them or didn't care."

Not surprised by the needless schemes when all of Rome thrived on intrigue, Tibi had heard enough.

She left the room without another word, needing an escape—time to think. Alexius called her name, but she ignored him and kept walking.

Downstairs, she went to the central garden. The perfume of roses and jasmine surrounded her. She welcomed the breeze on her face. Dark clouds soared overhead and she realized the heavier air she'd sensed earlier was due to the possibility of rain.

She sat on one of the marble benches near a fountain. Disgusted by Livia Marciana, she saw the whole situation clearly now. As Leta suggested, Livia and her cohorts had made a wager that one of them would seduce Alexius. Livia being the most determined of the trio, contrived her own attack in the herb garden, knowing Alexius would be called to investigate.

When he rejected her and sent her home, Livia made a new pact with Senator Basilius. In turn, Basilius intimidated Velus on Livia's behalf. Having stayed overnight, the scheming woman would have looked to be the victor, allowing her to collect the money from her friends and pay off the senator, all while keeping a healthy profit in her own purse.

"Tibi?" Alexius said, close behind her.

Steeling herself, she stood and faced him. Velus was nowhere to be seen. She assumed he'd returned to his own quarters.

"Please don't punish Velus," she said, her heart beating in a wild tattoo as she watched him walk up the palm-lined path. "I'm convinced he was trying to act in your best interests."

He held up a hand to stay her. "Don't be concerned. I know he's loyal even when he's misguided. I told you before that he thinks I can't even comb my hair without him."

"Can you?"

"Before you came into my life? Always." His mouth tightened. "I'm sorry you had to hear all that ugliness."

Her fingers trailed through the cool water of the fountain. "You're not responsible for the plot Livia hatched, nor are you to blame for my jumping to conclusions."

"So I'm absolved of all blame in your estimation?"

She nodded. "As far as I can tell. I made a mistake and assumed the worst. For that I'm deeply sorry. I hope you can forgive me."

His sculpted mouth turned downward at the edges. He looked exhausted, disgusted and unexpectedly disappointed, considering that she'd apologized. He took hold of both of her hands and she trembled as he kissed the back of each one. "There's nothing to forgive. You have no way to know this, but for months my life has been congested with boredom and regrets. Foolishly, I refused to change. If I had listened to my conscience and corrected my ways, Velus wouldn't have been placed in a compromising situation. You wouldn't have witnessed me with Livia and there would have been no reason for you to think ill of me."

"Alexius—"

"No, let me finish." He cleared his throat and looked away, apparently ashamed by what he insisted on telling her. "I wasn't always the way I am now. My parents taught me to work hard and be honest. I used my hands to nurture the soil instead of for killing. I made plans for my future. I hoped to marry and have a respectable family the same as other men. Then my life changed."

Fascinated by his willingness to share his past with her, she waited, willing him to continue.

"Of all the things a gladiator loses—his freedom, his

self-respect, all claims to his own life—the loss of his future is the most terrible, in my estimation. Gladiators learn not to think about tomorrow. They may say they have a plan for their lives, but they don't—not really. Life is reduced to the days, sometimes the hours, between each battle. Time doesn't exist beyond the next fight."

He reached over and brushed the pad of his calloused thumb across her cheek. "We... *I* looked for whatever I could find to fill the gaps and stifle the anger that haunts me. Over time, I accepted shallow, silly behavior like Livia's as natural. I regret my stupidity. Even more, I'm sorry my failings created a chance for you to believe the worst of me and I earned your low opinion."

Her mixed feelings on his character untangled. She saw that the gossip she'd heard about him over the years had sullied her view of him. She understood that he wasn't perfect—no one was—but only a man of innate integrity recognized his mistakes and learned to be a better person from them.

The lines in his face appeared deeper than usual and the pain in his eyes showed her the loss of pride his confession cost him.

"You don't have to tell me anymore," she said. "I understand."

The first few drops of rain started to fall. Tibi looked up at the dark sky just as cold water splashed on the tip of her nose. Alexius drew her over several steps beneath the covered walkway. The storm began in earnest. A loud waterfall of rain poured off the eaves between them and the lush greenery of the garden.

Sensing that Alexius needed a deeper peace than she was capable of granting him, Tibi sought to offer him as much comfort as possible. Careful of his ribs, she wrapped her arms around his narrow waist.

Alexius pulled her close. He pressed his lips to the top of her head. "Tibi, I walked through life asleep until you woke me up. If you'll give me the chance, I'll prove to you I'm a better man than you've had cause to believe until now."

Overcome with joy and uncertain that she could think more highly of him, Tibi held him as tight as she dared without hurting his wounded side. She racked her brain in an effort to understand why he cared for her opinion, but she found the reasons elusive. Encircled in his arms, she leaned back and searched his handsome face for answers. In his eyes, she saw the depth of his regrets. Hope mingled in the background as he waited for her reply.

"Alexius, in all my life I've never met a man more honorable or worthy of my highest regard. I don't understand why you need forgiveness from me, but I give it without reservation. I told you before that you can always count on me to be your friend."

"Friend?" Confusion—or was it disappointment—rippled across his face, but quickly fled. An ironic smile touched his lips. He let go of her and raked his hand through his thick black hair as he backed up a few steps. "Yes, we're friends. That's more than I have a right to expect."

The rain continued to splash against the garden stones. Tibi wondered what Alexius would say if she told him the whole truth—that she'd given him the right to expect every part of her days ago. She opened her mouth, ready to put her pride on the line and ask him when she saw him covertly rub his side.

Realizing he'd been on his feet for far too long, she

forgot her question and looped her arm with his. "Let's take you back to your room. You need to lie down before you pull out your stitches."

Alexius studied her. He sighed. The tension of the last hour vanished as though the wind blowing through the garden had carried it away. He winked and grinned. "Will you tuck me in, my lady?"

"Most certainly." She smiled up at him, happy to see that something she'd said or done had brought her playful Greek back to her. "After all, what are friends for?"

Chapter Thirteen

"Excellent, Gaidr̄es. Remember to account for the wind and keep your right foot planted a bit farther above the shooting line next time. You'll be sure to hit the center," Tibi instructed from the side of the archery field. "You'll find the greater stability makes all the difference."

The huge *Thracian* corrected his stance, adjusted his aim to accommodate the strong northerly breeze and shot another arrow. Just as Tibi predicted, his arrow hit the middle of the target. The students on either side of Gaidr̄es hooted and slapped him on the back to congratulate him, but Gaidr̄es looked to her for approval. Tibi nodded in acknowledgment of the excellent shot. The *Thracian* had quickly become her favorite student. His natural ability with a bow and willingness to practice long after the other students finished each day made him a joy to teach.

The bell rang, announcing the midday meal. Tibi praised her men for another day of work and complimented them on their improvements before wishing them a pleasant day, since Silo took up their training after the noon hour.

She and the men stored their bows. She waited for Silo to lock up the arrows. Each day the instructor walked her back to the gate that led to Alexius's private gardens.

"The men are improving," she said as they crossed the sandy field. "Another few days and several of them can start learning to shoot a moving target."

"Yes, they're doing better than I anticipated," Silo agreed. "You are a superb teacher. The men want to please you."

Delighted by the compliment, she bid Silo farewell and entered the peach orchard alone. The metal gate banged behind her. The chain rattled as Silo adjusted and locked the padlock.

Hurrying down the shaded path, Tibi could barely contain her excitement over the special plans she'd made for the rest of the day. Velus assured her that Alexius was on the edge of climbing his chamber's walls. Both steward and master needed space from the other before one of them ended up in pieces.

In the two days since they'd cleared the air about Livia, Alexius had reordered the household accounts and devised a new record system for Velus to follow, regardless of the fact that the previous one worked without fail. Clearly, Alexius needed a distraction and she'd devised the perfect solution.

Velus met her at the back door of the house. "Finally," he said, making no attempt to hide his impatience. "If the master calls me upstairs one more time today, I won't be responsible for my actions."

Tibi bit back a smile at the fed-up dwarf and tried to appear sympathetic. "What happened?"

"First, his porridge was too hot, then it was too cold," Velus began the litany of Alexius's complaints.

"His pillows needed fluffing, then he needed to be shaved. Last month's accounts didn't meet his satisfaction. Apparently, I ordered too much pork, but not enough olives. This month I'm to order more fish sauce and, although he's never mentioned it once in the three years I've served him, pickled cabbage is one of his favorite vegetables and Cook never provides enough of it."

"You poor man."

Velus frowned. "Believe me, I never thought of myself as a proponent of violence, but if you don't remove him from here soon, as you promised, I may just poison him…although, taking a heavy mallet to his head gains more appeal by the moment."

"Is the basket ready?" she asked. "As soon as I change my tunic, we'll be off and you can enjoy some peace and quiet."

"You are a goddess, my lady." Velus pointed to a large woven basket on the table beside the door. "I packed the food—cabbage included—and the furs you asked for over an hour ago. I also arranged for a litter and hired the strongest men I could find to carry the both of you."

She bent down and kissed Velus on the cheek. "Thank you for caring about his comfort even when he's driving you insane."

The steward reddened. Clearly pleased by her gratitude, he hid his pleasure behind a loud snort. "I didn't act for his comfort, but mine. If he reinjures himself being bounced in a litter, who knows how long he'll need to recuperate before I can be rid of him."

"Good point." Hiding her laughter, Tibi headed upstairs to her room. She washed off the grime from the practice field and changed into a clean tunic. With unusual care, she rebraided her hair and added a touch of jasmine oil behind each of her ears.

Gathering her cloak, she ventured to Alexius's room down the corridor. She hadn't seen him since the night before and her heartbeat quickened in anticipation.

She stopped in the doorway of his chamber. A swift glance showed the furs and pillows piled in a haphazard manner across his sleeping couch. A rickety tower of wax tables sat beside a mountain of scrolls on a desk in the corner. Alexius stood in front of the open bank of windows, his back to her. From behind, he looked vibrantly alive and not hurt in the slightest. The strong breeze ruffled his black hair. The black tunic and sandals he wore showed off his bronze skin. Engrossed in the action on the gladiator field below, he gave her time to simply drink in the beloved sight of him.

"I take it you're feeling better," she said at the same time she knocked on the door frame. "Velus seems to think so, in any case."

Alexius faced her. "There you are, *agape mou.*"

The endearment warmed her heart. She knew she should stop him from using it, but in truth she didn't want him to.

"I was watching you, but I lost track of your whereabouts when you left the field."

Encouraged by his welcoming smile, she crossed the threshold. "I came back to the house about half an hour ago."

He left the window and met her in the center of the room. "You were worth the wait. You look pretty enough to ravish."

She felt her face catch fire. "You shouldn't say things like that."

"I'm sorry. I forgot for a moment we're just friends."

At a loss for a snappy reply, she asked, "Did I pass the test?"

"What test?"

"You said you were watching me on the field. Were you evaluating my training techniques."

"Yes, of course that's what I was doing." He shrugged. "Why not? I own the school. It's my right to check on my teachers, no?"

She'd asked a reasonable question. Why did he sound so defensive? "You need to do whatever you think is best as long as you spend plenty of time off your feet."

"I've been on my back long enough. Another hour and I was bound to grow roots."

"You and I both know you left your couch days ago." She glanced at the tablets on the desk. "Did you finish going over your accounts?"

"For the school *and* the household," he grouched. "Velus might as well be an old woman the way he carries tales about me."

She fought a smile. "If it helps, he didn't volunteer the information. I pried the ugly details out of him."

Unconvinced, he grunted. "I stayed in my room as long as I did because you insisted."

Tibi's ears perked up at that. Since when did she have the power to influence his actions? "I care about your health."

His eyebrow arched. "You should. It's your fault I'm in this condition."

"How so?" she demanded. "*I* didn't stab you."

His lips tightened. She realized he'd given more information than he meant to and refused to say more. She changed the subject. "The physician—"

"Left an hour ago."

"You can't be healed after a mere six days."

"No, but I'm well enough. Tomorrow I'll be back on the field. I need to show my face to the men or I'll start to lose their respect."

She nodded in understanding. After being surrounded by gladiators for the past week, she'd learned quickly that they resembled wolves in need of a strong pack leader. "Very well. Tomorrow you return to training your men, but what of the rest of today? What shall we do?"

"Anything but another round of *latrunculi*."

She hid a smile. "Why not? You might eventually win once if we play enough."

He ignored her.

"I have a surprise for you, in fact."

That piqued his interest. "What kind of surprise?"

"I'm not telling you. You'll have to trust me."

"I already trust you. You are the one who doesn't trust me."

"Not true, Alexius. I trust you more than anyone." The confession startled her.

"Since when?" he dared to ask, taking hold of her hands.

"I don't know," she admitted. "I think my instincts have always been on your side."

"That's good to know." His thumbs swept over her knuckles. "Now, about my surprise—"

"Have you eaten today?"

"No. I ordered a tray, but Velus has been grumpy of late and lax in his duties."

"Velus, grumpy? I can't imagine why."

"I'm at a loss as well. He must be getting old."

She coughed to hide her laughter. "Maybe he'll feel better tomorrow. As for today, I'm taking you somewhere special to me. The exact location is the surprise.

We have to go by litter for most of the way, then there is a very short walk."

"I'm intrigued. When do we leave?"

"We can go now if you're ready. I asked Velus to pack a basket of food for us. You won't have to go hungry."

"Ah, I see. You and my steward are in league together. Little wonder he didn't care if I starved to death."

She mimicked one of his shrugs. "Poor baby. Shall we go?"

"Of course," he said, copying a tone she often used. He offered a slight bow and waved his open hand toward the door. "After you, my lady. Lead and I will follow."

Alexius watched the trees along the road through the gossamer drapes surrounding the litter. He shifted on the bench that comprised the transport's seating arrangement and stretched his legs out on the planks in front of him. He resisted the need to rub his ribs as though his life depended on it. If Tibi suspected any discomfort on his part, she'd insist on returning to the *ludus*. In need of a change of scenery and intensely interested to see a place Tibi considered one of her favorites, he gritted his teeth against the constant shift and bounce of the litter that shot arrows of pain through his side.

"It's not much farther," she assured him. "Would you like another pillow? Another blanket?"

"I'm not an invalid."

"I never hinted that you were," she said tolerantly. "I didn't want you to be uncomfortable and I know you must be the way they've thrown us about in this litter.

We might as well have ridden in a wagon with square wheels. Truth to tell, I'm starting to feel a bit nauseated."

He took hold of her hand, his impatience instantly soothed. "Lean on me and close your eyes. I'll steady you."

"Your wound—"

"Is on the other side. I promise you're more concerned about it than I am."

A long moment passed before she gave in to his suggestion. The furs covering her lap shifted as she moved closer. She disengaged their hands and entwined her arm with his before resting her cheek against his shoulder.

The contentment that settled around him filled him with unease. He hadn't known this much peace in years. Facing the future without Tibi was bleak, no less than a torment. Casting the truth of their predicament from his mind was a constant temptation. He longed to give himself over to the unrestrained happiness she brought him, but only a fool would dare to forget Tibi wasn't his or that, at most, she'd be with him just a few more days.

Her weight shifted. From his window he'd seen her on the field at sunrise. She must be tired and falling asleep. Silo kept him apprised of her excellent teaching methods. Pride in her skill came easy to him.

Enjoying the warmth of her pressed against his side, he moved his arm to cradle her closer. He leaned his head against the cushioned back of the litter and closed his eyes. For days, he'd been in a quagmire, desperately searching to find a way to make her his own. At every turn, an insurmountable barrier blocked his path.

Even if he managed to convince her to marry below

her station, making her his wife was an impossibility. The law required her father's consent for her to legally wed. Obtaining Tiberius's blessing for a marriage between his daughter and a gladiator was as probable as the sun refusing to rise.

The litter swayed and bounced. He shifted in his seat. For her own sake and because he respected her too much, he wouldn't ask her to be his mistress, no matter how much he wanted her.

"What's troubling you?" She lifted her head. "Is it your side? Perhaps we shouldn't have left home."

Wishing she did consider the *ludus* her home, he looked down into her beautiful face. Her dark eyes were clouded with slumber. "It's not my side. I have other concerns on my mind."

"Then tell me." She stifled a yawn. "I'll try my best to help you if I can."

He brushed a kiss across her forehead. "I want something of great value to me, but I don't know how to get it."

"The item is not for sale?"

"The owner won't sell it to me."

"What is it? A plot of land? A stallion?"

"More like a mare." He winced, remembering that she'd denied being a horse the morning she came to him.

"Ah. Does the owner refuse to sell her to you specifically, or to anyone in general?"

"To me specifically."

"How mean of him." She settled back against his chest and mused out loud. "Too bad you're not a thief, you could steal the animal."

"I've thought about it, believe me." He pressed his

nose against her soft hair and breathed in the sweet perfume of jasmine.

She swatted his chest. "I was jesting."

"I know." He pressed his lips to her temple. "Don't worry. Taking what I want wouldn't work in this instance. Neither will fighting for her."

The litter swayed sharply as they turned a corner. "If the owner won't sell the horse to you, perhaps he'd allow someone else to purchase the mare. In turn, you could buy her from the second party."

"That's a fine idea, but I fear anyone in a position to buy this particular mare would never relinquish her."

"She must be a true prize."

"Greater than I ever imagined."

The litter slowed, then stopped. As the transport was lowered to the ground, Tibi sat up and pushed back the curtain to peer outside. "We're here…almost. I told you there's a short walk. Are you up to it?"

His eyes narrowed. "Are you trying to bait me, woman?"

"Me?" she asked as wide-eyed and innocent as a child. "Never."

He reached for her, but she grabbed her cloak and scrambled outside, laughing. "Be good. I don't want you to pull out your stitches."

Her playful mood was infectious. He climbed out of the litter. A verdant landscape surrounded them. The six men who'd carried the vehicle were all of different heights. Little wonder their ride had been rough.

"The day is perfect," Tibi said, looking upward. "Have you ever seen such a clear blue sky?"

"It's beautiful," he agreed, without taking his gaze off her face. "I've never seen a lovelier sight."

Her mouth twisted and her eyebrow arched. "Are you mocking me, gladiator?"

"Who, *me?* Never."

She picked up a satchel stuffed with furs and settled the strap on her shoulder. "The other basket over there has our meal. Can you carry it? Or do you need my help?"

Hearing the mischievous taunt in her voice, he determined that even if the woven leather basket weighed a thousand talents he'd somehow pick it up and carry it a dozen miles. He reached for the handles and lifted the basket. Fortunately for his jostled ribs, it weighed about as much as a pillow.

"Where are we off to?" he asked.

"This way. Be sure to watch your step."

They left the hired men with the litter and started down an overgrown trail that sloped to the Tiber and followed the water's edge. The brackish smell of the gently flowing river competed with the sweet fragrance of wild honeysuckle and bushes of wild roses.

Lichen-covered bricks, once arranged with aesthetics in mind, lay cracked or at odd, uneven angles. By design, poplar, olive and cypress trees lined the meandering path. Weathered stone benches, placed at equal distances apart, invited visitors to sit and admire the play of sunlight on the crumbling marble statues of gods, goddess, flute-playing satyrs and magnificent horses.

"Where are we?" Alexius asked. "I've been all over Rome and never imagined a place like this existed."

"It's otherworldly, is it not?"

Tibi joined hands with him as if she did so every day. He accepted his good fortune without comment and entwined his fingers with hers.

"This is what's left of one of Emperor Claudius's private imperial gardens," she said.

"Claudius? It must be over thirty years old then."

"At least," she agreed. "The imperial palaces and gardens line both sides of the river, but somehow this small strip of land was forgotten or overlooked. If we continue in this direction, we'll eventually run into the guarded wall that marks Emperor Domitian's land. The opposite way leads to the palace of his niece, Julia."

"You must come here often."

She nodded. "This garden has been my haven for much of my life. Our family home has access to the river. On sunny days, my mother used to bring my sister and me here by boat when we were children. We played for hours. We'd make flower chains, climb trees or play games of hide-and-seek. Sometimes we pretended the statues came to life. My sister was always the princess in danger—"

"What were you?"

She gave him a wry smile. "I was whatever evil creature she was most afraid of at the time. A handsome demigod never failed to come to her rescue and kill me. I became quite deft at dying," she added with proud lift of her chin.

He laughed. "Weren't you ever the princess?"

"No, Tiberia is much better suited to the role."

"And she's still playing that particular part, isn't she?" he added in appreciation of her sarcasm.

Her wide brown eyes blinked up at him. He grimaced inwardly, realizing she'd been serious and not sarcastic in the least.

"You don't like my sister very much, do you?" she asked. "I noticed that the first day when we spoke about her."

His hand tightened on the basket's handles. "Truthfully, no. I realize you may see the best in her, but to me she's spoiled, vain and doesn't appreciate you nearly as much as she should."

The easy flow of the river and distant bird calls filled the pause in conversation. "It's not her fault she's the way she is. She's been beautiful and elegant since birth," Tibi defended. "She is blessed with the talent of knowing what to say and how to behave. No one was surprised when she gained the attentions and affection of a senator. Father picks her to pieces like a hawk picks a mouse, but you're the first person I've ever met who genuinely disapproves of her."

Thinking of Caros's rants against the elder sister, he knew better, but kept that information to himself. "My apologies for being the odd man out," he said in a way that made it clear he was sorry for nothing. "But enough of your sister. She's of no interest to me. You were telling me about your exploits here in this garden."

"Oh, yes, where was I?" She led him off the path and into a thicket of tall grass. A half circle of lemon trees shaded the spot that was surrounded by more rosebushes and wild pink cyclamen. An old, broken fountain lay in pieces near a rusted sundial. "Sometimes I come here to read or shoot when I need a private place to practice away from Father."

She opened the satchel she carried and pulled out a large woven rug that she unfolded and spread on the ground to tamp down the grass. Next came a thick black blanket of sewn-together beaver pelts to cover the rug and create a soft island to sit on.

Alexius sank to his knees on the luxurious fur and placed the basket he'd carried in front of him. Tibi knelt down on the other side of the woven container, undid the latch and rummaged through the various packs of food stored inside.

"Why don't you rest while I assemble all this? If you fall asleep, I'll wake you."

He did as she suggested, choosing to lie on his un-injured side in a patch of sunshine that filtered through the lemon trees. He bent his elbow and propped his head on his palm. Enjoying the warmth of the sun on his skin, he watched her unwrap a bundle of freshly baked rolls that were seeded with rye.

"For a woman as bloodthirsty as you are, you can be surprisingly domestic."

She grinned but otherwise ignored him as she opened packet after packet of oiled parchment con-taining fat pork sausages, several kinds of cheese, and foul-smelling pickled cabbage. She wrinkled her nose at the rotten aroma.

"Here," she said, her face wreathed with disgust. "I've heard this is your favorite."

"You keep it." He pushed the packet away. "I hate cabbage. Always have."

She frowned. "Why did you tell Velus otherwise?"

"He was too smug in thinking he knows everything about me. I'll tell him I've changed my mind in a few days."

She sat back on her heels. "That means today you've sentenced us to have a vegetable neither one of us likes."

"So we'll eat the sausages and cheese."

"It's not good to waste food. There are hungry people all over the city."

"Do they like cabbage? We have plenty to share."

A roll hit him square in the face. He chuckled and ripped off a piece of the bread to taste. "I didn't realize you're concerned for the poor. Have you visited one of Adiona's orphanages?"

"I used to visit often until Father learned of my interest and forbid me to go any longer. I ignored him at first, but he found me out. He threatened to report Adiona and Quintus's religious leanings to the authorities if I didn't heed his command to stay away."

Alexius swore under his breath. Exactly what kind of evil beast *was* her father? "Tiberius is against charity?"

"No, not all, but he doesn't believe it's appropriate for his daughter to associate with beggars and thieves. Even if they are children."

"Do you truly believe he'd be wicked enough to report Quintus and Adiona?"

"I don't know if he'd do as he threatened, but I never cared to put him to the test." She offered a sly grin. "But all is not lost. My father provides me with a monthly allowance to afford the silks and furs he insists are necessary for me to be adequately dressed as his daughter. If you haven't noticed, my tastes are less formal. I make certain half of all he gives me goes to the orphans. I'm sure he wouldn't be pleased to know he's feeding so many of those beggars and thieves, but I'm determined to help one way or the other."

He shook his head. His large monthly donation to Adiona's endeavor seemed second rate compared to Tibi's gift. He gave because Adiona browbeat him into doing so. Tibi gave because she truly sought to help. "Very crafty, *agape mou*. I'm proud of you."

"You don't think I'm being deceitful?"

"Perhaps, but for the right reasons. Maybe there will be a day when you can give without all the trickery."

She reached for a blade of grass and split it in two. "I hope so."

"There's no doubt. If nothing else, one day your father will be d—"

"Don't say it. You speak true, but as long as he lives, I can hope he'll change." She bowed her head. He watched her for a moment, giving her time to think. The lemon trees behind her swayed in the breeze. A long tendril of soft blond hair had worked free of her braid and she hooked the silken strand behind her ear. Her inner turmoil was palpable as she reached for a cyclamen bloom and tore the bright pink flower apart.

He wished there was some way for him to ease her melancholy. If she belonged to *him*, he'd never keep her from the path she chose to follow. He wanted to rail against her father, to make her see that she didn't need the old man or his elusive blessings. But how did he convince her when he didn't understand the need to make a hateful father proud? His own parents had been kind and compassionate, their love and approval freely given. The thought of one of them being a miser like Tiberius was as foreign to him as some far-off Nubian desert.

She tossed the decimated petals aside and looked up with a cheerful, slightly forced smile. "Enough of my woes. Let's eat. I know you must be near the grave from hunger."

She handed him a rye roll stuffed with cheese and sausage before preparing the same for herself. To his disgust and amazement, she pinched some of the cabbage between her finger and thumb, then placed the smelly vegetable on her sausage.

"Don't," he said. "I'm sure even the hungry wouldn't expect you to eat that."

She sank her teeth into the sausage, cabbage and all. Her tentative chewing turned avid. She reached for more cabbage. "How delicious. Try some."

"No, thank you. Another few days without food and I might be hungry enough to try that poison, but I doubt it."

"Come, don't be afraid. I tried your Greek meal—"

"Because it was delicious. This has nothing to do with fear and all to do with smell."

"Just a taste." She pushed the sausage toward him. "If you don't like it you can spit it out."

"The stench is blinding." He leaned forward and took a bite. The acid and crunch of the cabbage mixed surprisingly well with the smoked meat and soft brown bread. "It's not terrible," he conceded.

She grinned. "Would you like more?"

"I'll pass."

Later, Tibi leaned against one of the lemon trees. No longer hungry and flirting with the idea of sleep, Alexius relaxed on the soft fur with his head on a pillow in her lap. Her fingertips brushed lazily through his hair or drew light patterns over his forehead and closed eyelids.

The leaves rustled above them. The discomfort in his side was a dull throb he managed to ignore for the most part. "When men dream of an idyllic future, this is the kind of day they have in mind."

"Mmm…even with the pickled cabbage to mar it?"

"Even then." He grinned and opened one eye to look up at her. She'd tipped her head back against the gnarled tree trunk. An expanse of soft, fair skin tempted him to kiss her slender throat and the soft underside of her chin.

The grasses rustled to the right of him. He rolled

to his feet and reached for the knife on his belt, all his senses on immediate alert. Seeing nothing of concern, he glanced to Tibi. Her eyes flared imperceptibly at something behind him.

"Be at ease, it's only a rabbit," she said with distinct dislike. "There's no one here to disturb us."

Alexius craned his neck, locating the little gray culprit just as it turned and hopped in the opposite direction. He sheathed his knife. "You don't like rabbits, Tibi?"

"No, not particularly."

He sat back down. "They're delicious in a brown sauce with sautéed onions and pork fat."

She swiped his shoulder and leaned back against the tree trunk.

"Why don't you care for them?" he asked, sensing a good story. "Small defenseless creatures seem like something you'd rally to defend."

"The reason is no fault of theirs and I bear them no ill will, but they bring back bad memories." She stretched her legs out in front of her and arranged her tunic to deny him even the smallest glimpse at her long, supple limbs. "When my father learned I'd taken up shooting, he took me on a hunt with a group of his friends. I thought I'd finally discovered something to make him spend time with me. When we arrived in the woods, I had second thoughts on killing, but he and his friends taunted me and said they expected no less from a girl. To prove them wrong, I shot the first creature I saw the next morning. It was a small brown rabbit… but it wasn't a clean wound."

She didn't elaborate. She didn't need to. He could imagine the slow death of the animal and the pig of a sire too unmerciful to make quick work of the matter for his young daughter.

"I swore I'd never kill again."

"Have you kept your promise?"

"Yes. Although, it hasn't escaped me that now I'm training gladiators to dispatch more than rabbits."

"You might be saving their lives."

She picked another cyclamen bloom. "Yes, but at the possible expense of another."

"You don't have to go back to the field."

"I know, but now I'm fond of the men. Gaidrēs and Ovid are my best students. They truly seem to enjoy the sport. I can't bear to think of any of them being harmed when I might be able to teach something to aid them."

He frowned. He hated the Fates and the way they had of reminding him how much he and Tibi were ill-suited.

"What's wrong, Alexius?"

"Nothing. I'm thinking how different we are, is all. You, so softhearted you can't bear to harm a rodent. I, so hardhearted I'm willing to kill men for a living."

She paled and bowed her head to hide her face from him. Had she somehow forgotten who he was and what he did? Did she despise him now for the reminder?

Without a word, she stood and smoothed out her tunic, leaving him alone on the island created by the beaver fur. "I don't think you're hardhearted, Alexius. In fact, I think your profession gnaws at you more than you admit. You told me before not to broach this subject, but my interest is sincere…as is my concern for you. Please…I'm asking you to tell me why you fight when you don't have to."

They were in the open air, but he felt pushed into a corner. Searching to escape the cage closing around him, he stood and turned his back on her. He wanted her close, but the answer she sought was the one thing certain to send her running. Rage for all he'd lost, all he wanted and could never have, flared inside him and erupted like a fountain of acid. "I *do* have to fight," he growled. "*That* is the crux of my problem."

Chapter Fourteen

"All right," Tibi said in a soothing voice she might use
on a rabid animal. He turned around. There was trepi-
dation in her eyes, but far from running, as he feared
she might, she eased closer in his direction.

Fists at his side, he closed his eyes and grappled with
the enraged beast thrashing for release. Haunted by the
source of his pain, he regretted allowing Tibi to see his
loss of temper. She must think he was a lunatic. What
kind of man exploded over what should be a simple
question?

To his amazement, he felt her arms band around his
waist. She pressed her cheek to the center of his chest in
an act of selfless comfort that sent the beast he'd failed
to conquer running for its cage. Without thought, he
crushed her against him. He kissed the top of her head,
her temple, the gentle curves of her cheek and chin.
Their eyes met in a moment of deep, intense connection. He claimed her lips with a kiss infused with all
the adoration she inspired in him and belonged to her
alone.

"I love you, Tibi," he whispered near her ear. "I
shouldn't tell you so, but I do and I *always* will."

"Why shouldn't you tell me?" she breathed.

"I'm not good enough for you…I never could be after what I've done and the life I've lived."

"Shh…" She quivered against him. She rose up on tiptoes and looped her arms around his neck. Her face was filled with wonderment. "Speak no more of being good enough or not. Be you the emperor or…or a hair plucker at the baths, you're my heart's one desire. I love you, too—with every fiber of my being. I've known since the day you took me to the *thermopolium*. I was too afraid to hope you might someday return my feelings, but my love grows more for you with each breath that fills my lungs."

Afraid that he'd stumbled into a dream, he held her tight, terrified he might wake up. "I know I can't have you forever, Tibi, but you're all that I want. The thought of losing you is worse than…"

"Than what?" she asked, her eyes misting with tears.

He swallowed the rock of pain choking him and buried his face in the fragrant curve of her throat. She deserved to know how acutely important she was to him, but the truth at the center of the matter flayed him on a rack of guilt.

"Never mind," she whispered. "I don't wish to cause you distress. You don't have to share it with me."

"I want to. I *need* to tell you the truth," he said, his voice husky with suppressed grief. "It's just that I've buried the pain so deep for an eternity. I don't know how to explain or even where to begin."

Tibi buried her fingers in the soft curls at the nape of his neck. Euphoric from his declaration of love for her, she wanted to surround him with care and devotion. If it were possible, she'd wipe away every drop of pain he'd ever endured. Hoping to ease some of what troubled him and distract him from his anguish, she brushed a kiss across his temple and whispered, "Let's sit down. All this time on your feet can't be good for your ribs."

He allowed her to lead him back to the beaver-pelt blanket. He collapsed more than sat in her former spot, his back supported by the trunk of the lemon tree. She took the place next to his uninjured side and enjoyed the way he pulled her close, as though he truly desired her near him.

The flow of the river, the buzz of a bee and the song of a kestrel filled the long moments while Alexius wrestled with his past.

"I told you before about my family," he said finally. "What I didn't tell you is that it's my fault they were murdered."

"Murdered?" She arched back, horrified by what he must have suffered. His love for his family had touched her from the first moment he'd spoken of his parents and sisters. To learn they'd all come to tragic ends added to the devastation. "I don't understand how their deaths could be your fault."

He rubbed his eyes and began in a gruff voice, "The day I turned sixteen years old, my father gifted me with a plot of his land to tend. Custom suggested I marry in the next few years and my *abba* wanted me prepared to support a wife if the right girl came along.

"I had grand ideas. My family's only lack was money, and I planned to correct that. In my dreams, I was going to turn my plot into a thriving enterprise big enough to rival that of the wealthiest family in Iolcos." He smiled bitterly. "I suppose I've never known my place in life. That's why I don't take kindly to people like your sister and the senators who think, by rights, they're better than ordinary mortals."

"Whether you're rich or poor, you're far from ordinary, Alexius. You are the best there is," she said with unvarnished sincerity.

He squeezed her and continued. "I worked hard and at season's end, harvested a bountiful crop. My family helped me and rejoiced in my success. My sister, Kyra, pitched in the most because she and I were closest in age and friendship—only eleven months separated our births. On market day, I told Kyra to stay home. I knew she'd be angry, but I had my mind set on selling the harvest and making plans with all the coin I'd take in that day, not keeping her out of trouble."

"What trouble?" Tibi asked. "Are the markets of Iolcos so hazardous women don't venture there?"

"No. Kyra was special in that regard and instance. She was lovely, the most sought-after girl for miles. Ulixes, the eldest son of the wealthy family I mentioned, wanted her for his own."

"And she didn't wish to marry him?"

"He had no plans for marriage. He was already a husband. In his mind, she wasn't good enough to wed anyway because of our family's poverty. He planned to make her his mistress and believed she should be honored by his 'favor.'"

"Swine!"

"Yes." He closed his eyes and swallowed hard. "But Kyra was much like you—too freethinking for a female and always landing in trouble."

She stiffened, but he held her closer and kissed her brow. "She followed me to town without my knowledge. I should have taken her home once she made her presence known, but I would have missed the market and lost much of my crop before I had another chance to sell it. Concerned about the coin as I was then, I let her stay with me."

The sunlight began to soften as the afternoon waned, bringing a new coolness to the day. Tibi reached for her cloak beside the food basket. She wrapped it around her shoulders and snuggled closer to Alexius's warm side. "I think anyone would have done the same."

"I know, but that doesn't change what followed and I'd do *anything* to turn back time." He took a deep breath and released it slowly. "Ulixes and his cohorts arrived while we were packing up the empty baskets for our return home. He sniffed out Kyra and began to pester her immediately. She knew of his snobbery toward her and wanted nothing to do with a married man. Kyra being Kyra, she couldn't simply ignore him. She berated him in front of his friends. I stepped in and sent him on his way. Or so I thought."

Alexius stroked her hair, talking faster and faster as if a dam had burst. "We left in the late afternoon. Our farm was farther out of town than most, but we would have been home before dark. Ulixes and three of his men attacked us on a quiet stretch of road. I fought as well as I could, but at sixteen, I was no match for the four of them. They left me for dead and…and abused Kyra. She died from their violation a few days later."

Tibi's chest ached for his loss and pain. "I'm so sorry."

"My father took them to court," he continued in a flat voice as if he hadn't heard her. "Ulixes's wealthy family bribed the magistrate. My grieving father hadn't sought reparations; he'd simply wanted an apology. Instead, he was forced to pay an unearthly sum when Ulixes claimed that my father's petition amounted to slander. When *abba* went to pay the money he could ill-afford to spend, Ulixes taunted him with the sounds of Kyra's cries as she'd begged for mercy."

A sob caught in Tibi's throat. "You must have wanted Ulixes dead."

"Yes," he said in a low voice so cold she shivered. "While I healed over the next weeks, I planned my revenge. As soon as I was able, I hunted down Ulixes and killed him, along with two of the other men who'd ravaged my sister."

"What of the third?" she asked, feeling both horrified and justified by his actions.

"He escaped and told Ulixes's relatives what I'd done. Naturally, his father went to the authorities. I was arrested and sentenced to death. I felt no remorse for my actions, but accepted the justice meted out to me. What I didn't anticipate was that my enemy's kin would seek revenge of their own. Months after I'd been sold out of prison to the gladiator *lanista,* I learned they hadn't been content to see me die for the revenge I took on their son. They sent assassins by night to kill my blameless family. My eldest sister, Eleni, was away visiting friends at the time. When she returned home she found everyone dead. I heard that the sight drove her mad."

He started to move away, but she refused to let go. It wasn't until he tightened his hold that she realized he'd been giving her a chance to flee if she planned to reject him.

"Where did your sister go?" she asked, struggling to contain her sorrow.

"It's a mystery I can't unravel. Several years passed before I had enough money to search for her. By then, Eleni had disappeared without a trail to follow."

Tibi bent her head and lifted the back of his strong, scarred hand to her lips. There were no words of comfort to offer equal to the level of heartbreak he'd suffered. In her own life, she'd tasted grief and unhappiness at the hands of her father, but nothing she'd borne compared to the tragedy that had cost Alexius his whole beloved family.

The shadows of a flock of birds passed over the thicket as she and Alexius held each other in silence. She tried to push back her sadness, but a single sob worked free from her throat. She buried her face against his shoulder.

"Tibi, *agape mou,* I didn't tell you about my past to hurt you. If I had my way, you'd never experience pain again. I told you to answer your question, to give you the whole truth and make you understand why I have to fight. Before I was sold to the *lanista,* I sat rotting in prison, cursing the gods and those hags, the Fates. A rage formed inside me then that even now I struggle to keep buried. My anger is like a wild creature clawing to be free or a volcano on the brink of eruption. When I fight in the arena, I can unleash the beast and know for a time, no matter how short, I'll gain a measure of relief and a sense of my true self. If I stop fighting, I'm afraid..." He choked on the word. "I'm afraid I'll lose control and hurt, not a trained gladiator armed with weapons, but someone powerless to defend himself against me."

She eased from his embrace and stood. "I understand your dilemma now, but I think there *must* be some other solution."

He smirked. "Caros claims I need his God."

She picked a small white lemon blossom from the tree and pressed the sweet bloom to her nose. "Perhaps

He *can* help. Caros used to be such a dark and forbidding man, but now he's filled with joy. You said yourself the change in him is too great to ignore."

"And why would a God of peace care anything about a violent man like me?"

She bit her bottom lip, searching for a reasonable answer. "Pelonia's told me many times her God loves everyone, no matter who they are or what they've done. Maybe it's true."

Scowling, Alexius leaned his head against the tree. His eyes closed. He crossed his arms over his middle. Slivers of sunlight glinted off his silver wristbands. He looked exhausted and defeated, something she'd never thought she would see. Little wonder: telling her about his tortured past must have exacted a terrible toll on him.

With neither of them able to discover a resolution to their problems, she knelt beside the basket. The fur-covered grasses sank beneath her weight. Careful not to disturb Alexius when she hoped he was falling asleep, she began to quietly stow the parchment wraps and recork their empty bottles of water.

Once Tibi put everything away, she coaxed Alexius to lie down on the fur, his dark head on one of the pillows.

Confident that Alexius was getting some much-needed rest, she decided to take one of her favorite walks along the river before she woke him to return to the *ludus*.

"Tibi?"

Alexius reached for her, but his fingers found soft beaver fur instead of smooth, supple skin. Disappointed, he rolled to his back and blinked the sleep from his eyes. He must have slept at least an hour. It was the darker side of twilight. The trees were an inky smudge against a sky the color of a deep purple bruise.

He rubbed his brow, wincing at his remembered confession to Tibi. Embarrassment pummeled him like hail, although he had to admit that the storm inside him seemed calmer for the first time in years.

"Tibi," he called. The chirp of crickets was all that replied. Worry sparked to life. Had she deserted him? She'd said she loved him *before* he admitted to what he'd done to Ulixes. She was too gentle of heart to reject him outright, but perhaps she'd reconsidered the wisdom of loving a gladiator with such a violent past.

But would she have deserted him without a word?

That didn't seem like her.

"Tibi!" No answer. He surged to his feet, straining against the darkness to find her. He knocked over the basket of uneaten food as he left the thicket. Moonlight filtered through the poplar and pine trees of the abandoned garden. An owl hooted somewhere nearby. Where was she? "Tibi!" he shouted.

Growing more worried with every step, he charged toward the river along the uneven path. So soon after reliving his sister's assault, his mind raced to the worst possibilities. What if she'd fallen into the frigid depths or been bitten by a poisonous serpent? He started running. The river's edge revealed nothing of her location—no footprints or sign of anyone of any kind. Light from the moon and stars reflected on the water's rippled surface. The gentle lap of the current was the only sound to fill the eerie silence.

He searched up and down the river. Calling Tibi's name, he listened for any faint cry for help or other sound she might make in the darkness. The blackness of night impaired his efforts. Torn between terror and anxious frustration, he ran the distance to the litter and the men hired to stay with the transport.

To his relief, he found the litter bearers playing dice by the glow of two torches. "Come, men! Bring the light. My woman is missing. I need your help to find her!"

The leader of the group released three of his band to go with him. Makeshift torches were fashioned from tree limbs.

"One of you return to the *ludus,*" Alexius ordered the remaining trio. He absently rubbed his strained ribs. "Explain to my steward, Velus, what's happened. Tell him I'm in need of men and lanterns for a more extensive search."

"I can't do that, sir," said Napos, a stringy individual Alexius had been introduced to as the group's leader. "Me and my men are bound by oath to stay with this litter—"

Enraged by the fool's lack of concern, Alexius lunged for him. Napos scurried away, stricken by obvious panic, but not fast enough to escape. Alexius grabbed Napos by the front of his stained tunic and lifted the quaking man off his feet. "By the gods, do you think I care about this rattletrap? I'll buy ten litters to repay your master if anything happens to this piece of trash in your absence." He released Napos with a shake and a shove that sent the leader reeling. "Now, run, little man, *run!*"

Napos half ran, half stumbled backwards. "What if your steward doesn't believe me? I have no seal to prove I'm on an errand of your bidding."

Alexius cursed. Napos spoke true and Velus had

always been a suspicious sort—an excellent quality he'd always appreciated in his steward until this moment.

Quickly weighing his options, he looked back toward the river. The three torches were fading points of light in the distance. "Tell him if he doesn't heed you and send supplies within the hour, I'll give him back to the beast master who sold him to me."

The two underlings that remained jumped to fashioning torches while their nervous leader rushed in the direction of the main road.

Sometime later Sergius and four other men from the *ludus* arrived with torches, lanterns, water and horses, Calisto among them. His throat rough from calling Tibi's name, Alexius issued gruff orders. Along with the litter bearers, the men divided into pairs and set out to explore the garden's every nook and bramble.

Ignoring the cold of night, he and Sergius investigated a dilapidated temple, moving fallen stones and statues until they both agreed that Tibi wasn't under them. Several pairs of men combed both sides of the Tiber. To Alexius's relief, Tibi's precious body wasn't found, encouraging him to believe she hadn't fallen into the frigid water and drowned.

Hours passed. The sun began to rise in a burst of red and gold streaks across the deep blue sky. Terrified, Alexius continued to lead by example, refusing to give up when exhaustion begged him to do so. Tibi was more than his love, he realized. She was his heart and his last hope for a future. If he lost her, he might as well dig his own grave and stop breathing.

"Did you search as far as Domitian's wall?" Alexius demanded from a set of men returning from that direction.

"We checked everything," the weary men assured him. "Even the fallen, hollowed-out trees are empty."

Sergius shuffled beside him. "We have to go back to—"

"No!" Alexius barked. "Not until we find her."

"She's not here."

"Don't say that!" he growled, his voice as rough as gravel. His hands clenched into fists.

"Don't unleash your fury on me, my friend." Sergius grabbed him by the shoulders. "We have to go back to the *ludus*. There's nothing else to do, Alexius. We've looked under every stone and blade of grass. The litter bearers have already left and our men are hungry and worn out. You're dead on your feet. What good will it do anyone if you collapse?"

Recognizing that Sergius was right, he spit on the thought of giving up. "Would you leave if Leta had gone missing?"

"I wouldn't want to, but I hope I'd be wise enough to realize when to take good advice." Sergius closed his eyes and sighed in resignation. "Go back to the *ludus*, send fresh men to continue the search if you must. If Tibi hasn't been found by the time you've rested, I won't hesitate to come back out here with you."

Alexius glanced across the gray morning to his men. Haggard and exhausted, they were asleep standing up. "All right, we'll go back, but I will find Tibi." He raked his hands through his hair. "I *have* to."

Chapter Fifteen

"How long did you think you could hide from me, girl?"

Like a wayward slave, Tibi stood before Tiberius in the garden of her family's home. Fear and the smell of fish sauce from her father's uneaten meal churned her stomach.

The sun had set at least an hour before. Slaves had lit multiple torches and hanging oil lamps in each archway. Light flickered across the greenery, the elegant tiled designs decorating the floor and the columns that held up the porch's painted rafters.

Back in the hateful reality of her family home, the precious days spent with Alexius seemed like a dream, like a lifetime ago. Her father's slaves, Lixus and Orosius, had ambushed her on her walk near the water's edge. Still shaken from the experience of being dragged from the riverbank, gagged and thrown into a boat by her father's men, she worried about Alexius and how abandoned he'd feel when he awoke to find her gone.

Quaking in her sandals, she did her best to hide her terror. "I planned to stay away for just a little while, Father. I knew I'd displeased you after that fiasco with

Lepidus. I honestly never intended to embarrass you and I hoped your anger might have a chance to subside if I put some space between us."

"Spare me your lies and excuses," he sneered. He rose from the red, tufted couch he rested on and tightened the black silk belt he wore around his thick waist and green tunic. He poked his index finger toward her face. "You ran away to save your worthless hide from being taken to the temple where you might *finally* do some good for this family. Thanks to the slaves' talk, everyone from the city matrons to the butchers knows of your disobedience. You've shamed me and yourself throughout Rome. The whole city is flapping with gossip that my rebellious daughter has once again proven too much for me to handle. Even pantomimes are mocking me in the streets with their wretched skits."

"The gossips are wrong," she whispered, stricken by the knowledge that he troubled himself more with the opinion of strangers than with the slightest concern for her welfare. "Do you even care where I've been or if I'm all right?"

She met with stony silence and flinty eyes. "I can see you're breathing. That is plenty."

"How did you find me?" she asked, expecting his hostility, but oddly not as hurt by his coldness as she had been in the past.

"How does a cat find a mouse? By visiting her favorite holes." He picked up a blue glass pitcher and poured honeyed wine into a matching chalice. He swirled the potent liquid as he spoke. "You think you're clever, but you have much to learn, my little mouse. I have eyes all over this city. Patrons three deep, each of whom owes me favors and loyalty. All your favorite places have been watched. My men have searched Claudius's old garden at least twice a day since you disappeared from here. But had you shown your face at the bath or gymnasium, the theater, that Forum tunic maker you frequent, the library or even one of those orphanages I forbade you to visit, you would have been found and brought back to me."

Her temper sparked. He'd expended so much effort to find her and all to prove to his neighbors that he was strong enough to bend her to his will. "I'm sorry to cause you such trouble."

He lifted the chalice to his lips. "Not sorry enough, but you will be."

She felt her face pale. Her knees weakened. What did he mean? What new punishment had he devised for her to suffer? She lifted her chin, wishing with all her being that she'd never left the *ludus* or Alexius's loving arms. "Do you plan to kill me?"

"I should, but if I were going to end your life, I'd have exposed you on the day of your birth."

She blanched. Babes born deformed, sickly or deemed unfit—almost always girls—were often left to die in the elements. She wasn't deformed and as far as she knew she'd been a healthy infant, albeit female. She focused on a potted fern to help maintain her composure. If she wanted to get a definitive reason for why her father had always despised her, this was her chance to ask. "Why *didn't* you put me out?"

"Believe me, I planned to."

Her chin quivered. "Because I wasn't the son you wished for?"

"In part, but that's the least of the matter." He placed the chalice on the table beside his couch and sat back down. "Your mother was involved in an affair with a married man she claimed to love. There's a chance you might be his."

Too shocked to speak, Tibi staggered to the nearest chair and sank into the soft red cushions. He'd meant to lay her low with the news and aimed his poisoned arrow well, but she managed to hold her head high, refusing to let him see her bleed.

"I learned of her indiscretion a few weeks before she came to term with you," he said without emotion. "The scandalmongers were laughing behind my back. All of them claimed I was too weak to keep my wife under control."

"Just as they say you can't control me."

He nodded. "Like mother, like daughter. Where do you think the line of gossip came from so soon after you won that archery competition?"

He idly picked at the potted fern beside him. "I told your mother to ingest silphium or wormwood to rid her body of you before you were born, but she refused. I threatened to expose you, but she promised to divorce me if I did. The threat carried weight because in those days most of my coin came from her side of the family. On the other hand, she didn't want her lover named as the reason for our divorce. She and I made a pact instead. I'd let you live in return for an eighth of her dowry, the promise she'd leave the other man and become the docile wife I demanded."

"Tiberia?" Tibi whispered.

"She has my look about the eyes and is mine as far as I know. If nothing else, at least she's proved useful in her marriage."

"Who might my father be?" Tibi wondered aloud, beginning to recover a measure of inner calm.

"He's dead." Fire flared in his dark eyes, belying his

phlegmatic attitude toward the subject at hand. "That's all you need to know."

He reached for his glass and took another drink of wine. "At the time, the agreement between your mother and me suited me greatly. The portion of dowry I received was the same as I'd have gleaned in a divorce." He shrugged. "And there was always the chance you might have been a boy."

"Would you have loved me then?"

"I doubt it. Every time I look at you I remember how your mother went behind my back and deceived me." He waved his hand, splashing the wine from the chalice. "At least keeping you silenced the gossips for a time and repaired your mother's bruised reputation. After all, what shamed husband keeps a child if he believes there's a chance the brat might not be his?"

"You think there *is* a possibility I'm yours? Or are you confident I'm not?" she said, hoping he wasn't her father and frustrated by his refusal to name the man who might be her true sire.

"No one can know with full certainty. I thought we'd see a likeness of one or the other of us in you, but even then you foiled my plans. Your dark eyes could come from any one of a thousand men in Italy and the rest of you takes after your barbarian grandmother."

The evening's breeze rustled the firelight. Suddenly glad her blond hair and pale skin made her an oddity that frustrated Tiberius, she felt liberated to learn the true reasons behind his antipathy toward her. She saw now that she was not the problem he'd labeled her since her earliest memories. All the effort she'd expended to please him was in vain, but not because of any intrinsic flaw on her part. His eyes were clouded by his own failure as a man and a husband, yet he was determined to see *her* as the picture of disappointment.

Eager to leave and return to Alexius, she appreciated her gladiator more by the moment. He'd shown her more respect and honor in a week than she'd experienced in the previous eighteen years. He'd helped her see how she should be treated and what behavior to accept from others. Tiberius failed on all counts. Whether he was her true father or not, the heartless man no longer held sway over her outlook. What kind of callous man sought to grind a girl into dust for the sins of her mother? As far as she was concerned, she'd already wasted too much of her life trying to please the merciless tyrant.

No longer.

From now on she planned to spend the rest of her days glorying in the love of a magnificent man who accepted her freely and without reservation.

That Alexius loved her amazed her still, but she believed him because he'd helped her see her own value. If he would have her, she'd marry him tomorrow, tonight or even within the next hour, if possible. Tiberius had best give his permission and not stand in her way to wed, either. The information he'd imparted concerning her birth had been meant to hurt her. Instead, he'd cut her free and created an arsenal of ammunition to use at her discretion since he, not she, cared so very much for public opinion.

"I'm leaving." She stood and called for a slave to fetch her cloak. "I do regret any embarrassment or difficulties I've caused you in the past. As I've said, that was never my intention. I'm grateful you didn't leave me to the elements as an infant, but as of right now I wish to end our…association."

"I think you're mistaken, Tiberia."

Hearing her full name, she began to tremble. Conditioned to fear the worst, she sought out the nearest way of escape.

Tiberius snapped his fingers. The woman bringing her cloak changed course and scurried in the opposite direction. At the same moment, the burly slaves who'd kidnapped her from the river appeared in each of the two side doorways.

"What are you planning?" she demanded of Tiberius, her heart racing like a rabbit being chased by a wolf.

"You were born under a cloud of embarrassment and shame. This last act on your part must be dealt with, for I'm done being forced to defend my reputation because of your rebellious ways. Once and for all, I mean to prove I am master of this house."

She ran for the one unimpeded door.

"Silvo!" Tiberius shouted for his steward.

The huge Campanian filled the open arch that led to the interior of the house. She struggled to get past him, but Silvo was too strong for her. Merciless hands gripped her shoulders and pulled her back into the courtyard. Orosius's arm of iron banded around her waist and lifted her off her feet.

"Lixus, fetch the cane," Tiberius ordered.

Tibi's cries for mercy fell on deaf ears. Her screams for help rang through the house as Orosius carried her from the garden and into the yard where her father chastised his slaves. Cool, misty air dampened her skin. She kicked and twisted to get loose from the huge slave's hold, but he held her deftly as he chained her wrists to the whipping post above her head.

"I'm sorry, my lady," Orosius whispered near her ear. "I have no choice."

Hot tears flowed down Tibi's cheeks. Splinters poked her wrists and inner forearms. She'd never been caned, but she had been beaten enough to dread the onslaught of agony.

Angry and terrified, she closed her eyes and cried out to the gods for mercy, but it was Pelonia's God that came specifically to her mind. "Please, Jesus," she whispered against the rough wood of the post. "Please, help me."

"Lixus, where are you?" Tiberius shouted behind her.

"I'm here." Tibi heard running. "All is ready."

"Then begin. It's time my troublesome *daughter* learned a lesson she won't soon forget."

Chapter Sixteen

Alexius charged through the gates of the *ludus*. He jumped down from Calisto's saddle before one of the stable boys had time to kneel and offer his back as a step. His fear for Tibi's safety had doubled during the wild ride across the waking city. Panic and reason vied for precedence with one overtaking the other every so often. Hammered by frustration, he cursed the gods, then begged them for mercy. White hot rage bubbled in his belly, promising mayhem if he didn't find her soon.

"Master!" Velus rushed toward him as Alexius climbed the front steps. "Your guest—"

Relief sparked. "Has Tibi…?"

"No," the dwarf corrected with a shake of his head. "I'm sorry. She hasn't come back yet. Master Caros along with his family and friends arrived an hour after sunrise."

Disappointment crashed over him. He ordered more men to return to the abandoned garden. Any other time he'd be ecstatic to see his friends, but Tibi was missing. They presented a distraction from his quest to find her and he resented the intrusion. "Have you told them what's happened?"

"No, I thought you'd prefer to do so."

"Where are they?" he snapped.

"The women and nursemaids are seeing to the children upstairs. Their husbands are waiting for you in your office."

The cooler, darker interior of the house surrounded him. Panic-stricken and exhausted from hours of futile searching, Alexius clawed his dirty hand through his hair and swore under his breath. Small nicks and cuts crusted with dried blood marked his skin, proclaiming his search under every thornbush and dilapidated statue. His injured side raged with fire, though he'd walked through miles of river.

He stalked across the house in the mood for bloodshed, not rounds of merry greetings.

From out in the corridor, he saw the two large men in his office. They were talking as though the bright spring day beyond the open window was a true reflection of the world and not the dark chaos plaguing Alexius.

Both men were tall and well-muscled with black hair. Caros, the brawnier of the two, bore the scars from over a decade in the gladiatorial trade. He remained one of Rome's most famous champions. In the three years since he'd wed Pelonia and become a Christian, Caros had changed in ways Alexius hadn't thought possible. Gone was the lethal coldness that made seasoned killers tremble. Instead, he was a contented husband and father with a peace about him that other men envied.

Quintus, a wealthy merchant once enslaved for his faith, had no visible scars from the many months he'd trained as a gladiator, but his discerning eyes were as sharp as a *gladius* with the ability to slice to the heart of any matter. His marriage to the renowned beauty

Adiona Leonia had sent shock waves through the city
two and a half years earlier. The fact that Quintus had
managed to win Adiona, a sworn man-hater whose out-
rageous wealth rivaled that of a queen, made him somewhat of a legend throughout the city.

"There he is." Caros smiled. The gladness in his expression turned to concern the moment Alexius crossed
into the office. "What's happened, my friend? Are you
ill? Has someone died?"

Alexius's jaw tightened. He refused to consider Tibi's
death or how his heart would perish along with her. To
his eternal embarrassment his throat closed up and his
chest constricted. "It's Tibi..." he managed to choke.

"Tibi?" Caros frowned in puzzlement. "You mean
Pelonia's cousin, Tiberia the Younger?"

Unable to speak further, Alexius nodded. His gaze
swung between Caros and Quintus like a wounded
animal's begging for mercy. Instinctively, he knew he
could count on them to help him. Until that moment, he
hadn't realized just how much he'd missed these men,
who were as much brothers to him as friends.

Both men crossed to him in the middle of the room.
Their faces reflected true anxiety for his unusually
downcast state. Giving him a chance to collect himself, Quintus pulled up a chair and Caros pressed him
down into the padded seat.

"What's happened to her, Alexius?" Caros asked.

"I can't find her." He swallowed convulsively. Over
the rock lodged in his throat, he gave them a quick account of their trip to the garden the previous day. He
left out the personal details and ended with finding Tibi
gone when he awoke at sundown.

"Why were you with her in the first place?" Caros's

sky-blue eyes narrowed on him with suspicion. "You gave me your word—"

"And I've kept it! I haven't touched her no matter how much I've been tempted this past week."

"Past *week?*"

Alexius groaned, regretting his loose tongue. Struggling not to be vexed by all the questions, he acknowledged and appreciated Caros's concern for his cousin by marriage.

Caros scowled. "You'd best explain."

Alexius gave him the skeletal version of events since Tibi's arrival the previous week.

"You mean you've been using an innocent young girl to train *gladiators?*" Caros raked his hand through his hair.

"I didn't force her." Alexius surged to his feet, wincing at the sharp pain in his side. "And I'd do it again, if it pleased her. She thrived on sharing her skill. Silo and I agree—she's one of the best archers either of us has ever seen."

"That's not the point—"

"No, it isn't," Quintus interjected a voice of calm. "You're in love with her, are you not?"

"I don't deny it." Alexius moved to his desk and leaned against the carved edge. "I love her more than I've ever loved anyone in my life! Now I can't find her. The men and I tore that garden apart. We searched both sides of the river for miles. I don't know where else to look. I'm going mad thinking she might be hurt and depending on me to find her."

"When did this all start?" asked Quintus.

"My guess is the first time he saw her," Caros said. "The day I wed Pelonia three years ago."

"Three years?" Quintus whistled through his teeth.

"I thought the months I loved Adiona from afar were torture, but I meant—"

"It was."

All three men looked toward the doorway at once. Adiona stood in the open arch, a vision in flowing light blue silk. Her glossy black hair was arranged with effortless elegance and her amber eyes glowed with love as she gazed at Quintus.

"Utter torture," she reiterated as she glided across the tiled floor to her husband. At his side, she smiled up at him as though he lit the sun each morning.

Again, Alexius was struck by the change in the woman he'd known for the past six years. Once icy enough to give a man frostbite for looking in her general direction, she'd always been outwardly stunning. Marriage and faith had changed her cold persona and given her an inner glow that warmed everyone who came near her.

She turned her amber eyes on Alexius. "How is my favorite Greek? The children are clamoring to see their uncle Alexius."

"Not well."

She frowned. "What has happened?"

Quintus put his arm around her slim waist and pulled her close to his side. "Pelonia's cousin, Tibi, is missing."

"Does Pelonia know?" Adiona asked with instant worry. "Who is looking for the girl?"

"She doesn't know yet," Caros said, his expression closed. "Alexius has just returned from the river where Tibi disappeared. Other men are on their way as we speak."

"Then we must tell Pelonia. She'll want to pray with us for her cousin's safe return."

"We will. We're trying to fish the details out of Alexius first."

She pinned Alexius with a knowing look he didn't fully understand. "Speak up, gladiator. We have prayers to begin."

"I've already explained! She came here last week in distress caused by a row she'd had with father. I agreed to keep her here until Caros and Pelonia arrived because Senator Tacitus suggested she wasn't safe in her own home. Yesterday, we went to a garden she wished to show me on the banks of the Tiber. I fell asleep and when I woke up, she was gone."

Adiona looked up at Quintus. "I told you."

He kissed her brow. "You were right. He's already admitted that he loves her."

"Really? When?"

"A few moments before you arrived," said Quintus.

"Why are you not surprised?" Alexius rubbed his ribs, pain and exhaustion wearing him low.

"Pelonia and I guessed your feelings years ago...." She looked quizzically at his side. "Are you bleeding?"

"It's nothing."

"It *is* something." She left Quintus and crossed to the desk for a closer look. He caught a whiff of her cinnamon perfume once she reached him. "You *are* bleeding. What's happened to you?"

"A small wound from practice last week. I must have strained the stitches looking for Tibi this morning."

She went to the door and called Velus. "Fetch the physician," she told the steward when he entered the corridor. "Your master's wound is bleeding afresh."

"A physician isn't necessary," Alexius complained. "I have to find Tibi."

"Yes, a physician is most necessary. Pelonia and I

have been asking the Lord to bring you and Tibi together for years. How will that happen if you insist on bleeding to death out of stubbornness?"

"You've prayed for us?"

"Of course. You're our dear friends. We all pray for each of you daily."

Alexius shook his head, stunned they'd cared enough to appeal to their God on his behalf. "I'm grateful."

"You're welcome. Hopefully, you'll put yourself out of your misery soon and realize how much you need Him." She gave him a smile filled with compassion. "In the meantime, I'm not going to let you thwart our prayers. If you care for Tibi, accept the help you need. Once Tibi's found, she's going to require more than a corpse to wed. We want you both to have a long life with a happy marriage and at least half a dozen children for you to spoil."

His grip tightened on the edge of the desk. The hope she'd been building in him crumbled. "That is the worst of the situation. She can never be mine. Even if she agreed to marry me, her father—"

Adiona patted his cheek as though he weren't a very bright lad. "Alexius, my friend, look around you. You're in a room full of miracles. Surely you've realized by now from the work He's done in all of us these past few years, our God is capable of making a way where there is none."

He glanced beyond her shoulder. His office glowed with morning light. A confident Caros and Quintus looked on, nodding in agreement.

Not for the first time, he wished he possessed their faith and reassurance. He felt as though he was standing at the top of a broken bridge. He wanted to jump over the missing section in his path and join their God on the other side. But what if he miscalculated the distance and went plunging to his death?

He knew his friends believed he didn't take life too seriously, that he could be counted on for a laugh and that he saved his reserve for the arena. They hadn't considered the anger that dwelled inside him or the real possibility that their peaceful God wouldn't want him because of it. "I'll believe in Him if He brings Tibi back to me safely."

"All right," she said too easily for his liking. "If you want to put off knowing His grace until then, so be it. However, *you* will have to be the one to tell Him your choice. I'm not going to do it for you."

The physician, Remus, knocked on the door frame before Alexius formed an adequate response. Adiona excused herself to go find Pelonia and explain to her that Tibi has disappeared.

At the physician's insistence, the men left the office for Alexius's room. Alexius sat on his sleeping couch, trying not to disgrace himself with groans of pain while Remus pushed on his ribs.

"You've snapped a half dozen stitches at the very least." Remus clucked at him. "Naturally, the reopened wound has caused all this blood. Why were you up? Where's that pretty blonde girl who was supposed to be keeping you entertained in bed?"

Alexius's gazed darted to Caros. His friend's arched eyebrow and folded arms made it clear he'd heard the mouthy physician. "Caros, it's not what you think."

"Then do me a favor and explain."

"I was bedridden. Tibi came up here after her morning instruction each day. We took meals together. She read to me, we talked, things got so bad, I let her convince me to play *latrunculi*—"

"Cease, now I know you lie. If you—"

"It's true! Believe me or not, it's up to you, but I had no intentions of using and discarding Tibi. She's too precious to me."

Caros frowned, but let the matter rest. While Remus prepared his supplies, Alexius left the couch and waited in front of the window, his gaze pinned to the empty archery field.

"How are you feeling?" Quintus asked.

"Like I've lost the last flicker of light in my life."

"I understand."

"I doubt it," he said, beyond the point of hiding his bitterness. "The woman you love is a few doors down, caring for your beautiful daughter."

"If you remember, Adiona was poisoned once. She almost died in my arms."

Alexius leaned forward and grasped the windowsill. He hung his head. His side ached, but not half as much as his heart did. "How did you wade through the agony of waiting?"

"I prayed and the Lord showed me a way to save her."

"Your Jesus doesn't know me or what I've done. You're a good man, Quintus. I can see why He'd help you, but why would He bother with me?"

"He knows you better than you do, Alexius. All your secrets and flaws. You have nothing to hide."

"What a frightening thought. Is that supposed to make me feel better?"

Quintus squeezed his shoulder. "The truth is that *you* don't know *Him*. He's eager to help, not because you're good enough or not, but because He loves you and wants you to trust in Him."

Remus joined them. He handed Alexius a ceramic cup. "Drink this. You look parched."

Alexius downed the honeyed wine in one gulp. "Do you have more? I'm thirstier than I realized."

"Yes." Quintus frowned at the physician. "I'll get it. But only because I'm much kinder than you were to me when I was the one getting stitches."

Alexius grinned, remembering earlier days and Quintus's first fight in the Coliseum. Quintus brought him another full cup. Alexius drank more slowly this time. "It's water."

"Too much wine can't be good for you when you've lost so much blood."

"Can I come in?" Pelonia said from the doorway. A tiny woman, she looked like a fawn entering a cage of lions.

Caros crossed to meet his wife. He bent down to welcome her with a kiss before he followed her into the corridor.

"I need to lie down." Suddenly weak, Alexius dropped the cup in Quintus's direction who barely managed to catch the ceramic mug before it shattered on the floor. Alexius stretched out on his couch, hating the lack of strength invading his limbs.

"Alexius?" Pelonia had returned. She leaned over him and placed a kiss on his cheek. She smelled of cloves and other faint spices. A dark beauty with smooth olive skin and dark hair, she had huge, doe-brown eyes that bore a striking family resemblance to Tibi's. "I haven't much time. Can you hear me?"

He nodded. "Yes, but if I didn't know better I'd think my friends betrayed me and plied me with mandragora."

A brief silence confirmed his suspicion. Anger raked

though him. Glaring at Quintus and Caros, he struggled to sit up.

"Alexius, be at ease," Pelonia said. "Remus gave you the root in the wine. Quintus fetched you water."

Pelonia's gentle hand on his shoulder was too much to fight against. He lay back down, steaming in frustration and drug-induced weakness. "I have to find Tibi!"

"I know. We will. I promise. Adiona told me what you've done for my cousin this past week. I thank you from the bottom of my heart. I'm here because I want you to rest. The hour since you came home isn't enough. You've done all that you can for now. I'm going to visit Tibi's sister, Tiberia. Perhaps she knows Tibi's whereabouts or can help us look."

"That shrew doesn't love Tibi." His head listed on the pillow. "She won't care."

"I know she does, but sometimes these situations are…difficult." She brushed his hair off his brow. "You do believe *I* love Tibi, don't you?"

"Yes."

"Then trust me. I'm going to do everything in my power to find her. That's why you need to be strong for when she's home."

"It's time," Remus interrupted. "If I don't begin now, the mandragora will begin to wear off before I'm finished."

Alexius closed his eyes. "Promise to send word."

"I promise." He felt Pelonia's small hand squeeze his. "From the moment I hear the first murmur."

Alexius awoke groggy from the effects of the mandragora. His skull ached and his side throbbed. He vaguely recalled Remus announcing that he'd ripped several stitches. He felt cleaner—someone had washed off the first few layers of grime from his arms, face and throat.

He opened his eyes and took in the room. It was almost dark, nearly the exact time of day he'd woken yesterday to find...

"Tibi!" He bolted into a sitting position. Pain lanced his entire body.

"She's not here," Velus said. "Lie back down."

"Has there been any word? Has Pelonia returned?"

"None yet." The steward pressed a cup into Alexius's hand. "The physician said to drink as much of this as possible."

Rubbing his head, Alexius refused. "The last drink he gave me was laced with that cursed sleeping root."

"This is water with lemon."

He eyed the cup with distrust. "You're *certain* there's been no word?" he asked over the rim.

"Not one." Velus lit a lamp, casting a small circle of light around the side table and across the pillows on the sleeping couch. "Are you hungry?"

He could eat a boar by himself. "No. I want nothing, except Tibi."

"I doubt that she tastes very good, although with a touch of lemon and olive oil—"

Alexius threw the cup at Velus, hitting him in the shoulder. The ceramic cup broke into pieces on the floor, splashing water across the mosaic tiles.

Unconcerned, Velus swiped flecks of water from his tunic and bent to pick up the shards. He wiped up the water with a towel, then lit two more oil lamps around the room. "You may want nothing, but the rest of us would deeply appreciate it if you took a bath, my most benevolent master."

Usually a response of that nature would have made

him laugh, but with Tibi gone, he found no cause for humor in anything. "Why haven't you already called for the tub, old man?"

Muttering something under his breath about dull wits and shaving, Velus left to have hot water prepared. Alexius lay on his back. He rubbed his smooth cheeks, understanding that Velus had shaved his face while he slept. Beyond caring, he stared at the ceiling and the flicker of lamplight on the plaster.

As far as he was concerned, the day had been a curse straight from Hades himself. The putrid mix of frustration, anger, helplessness and guilt reminded him of a decade earlier when Kyra had been assaulted. The weeks following, he'd stared at the rushes of his father's ceiling while he recovered and plotted murder to avenge his sister. This time there was no brute to hunt down or trail to follow. As surely as Hades had carried Persephone off to the underworld, so, too, had Tibi disappeared without a trace.

A night wind blew through the window, setting the shadows to dancing. A reminder came to him of Adiona's words along with an urgent need to repeat them.

He felt like a hypocrite asking for help, considering the number of times he'd rejected their God in the past. But where else could he go, what else could he do when all his instincts begged him to pray?

He didn't know how to begin except to start as he'd heard his friends pray on previous occasions. He spoke in Greek, half afraid that he'd muddle the translation from his heart if he used Latin. "Father God, my friends recommend You. How can I deny You when I've seen You change their lives for the better in so many ways? I believe in You, but I don't see how You could possibly need or want me. I'm a murderer and a gladiator with hatred buried deep in my heart. Anger breeds in me like a living thing that won't be slain. I've tried everything I know to rid myself of this beast, but it refuses to leave. If You can help me, I ask that You change me. Make me the man You want me to be."

He took a deep breath. The hole in the bridge he feared to cross seemed smaller by the moment. "But if I'm beyond redemption or You don't want me, I understand. Whatever You choose, I ask for Your blessing on the woman I love. Her name is Tiberia the Younger, daughter of Decimus Tiberius Flavius. She is kind and lovely, as close to perfection as I've ever seen. She's lost, but You must know where to find her. Hold her close. *Please* keep her safe in Your hands."

He sat up, careful of his ribs. His feet on the floor, his elbows on his knees, he hung his head in full humility. "I ask You to bring her back to me, but if she has no wish to return, at least, allow me to know that she's well. If You do, I'll know you accept me and I'll serve You the rest of my days."

He didn't know what else to say or ask except that Caros always prayed in Jesus's name. He did the same.

Waiting, he didn't know what to expect when silence was the sole reply.

"Why are you on your feet?" Velus approached, leading a small procession of servants bearing a tub and enough buckets of water to wash him *and* his horse.

Lost in his thoughts, Alexius ignored his steward. He wasn't aware of when he'd walked to the darkened window. Was Tibi out there in the city somewhere hurt or lost?

Impatient to find her, he chased everyone from his chamber and hurried to scrub off the muck from the river. He pulled on a clean tunic and grabbed a bag of coins from the money chest on the far wall.

Downstairs, the sound of voices drew him to the courtyard garden. Lamps and torches lit his way, giving the frescos and tiled floor a golden sheen. The dinner hour approached, bringing with it the aroma of roast lamb and fresh bread. His stomach rumbled. He hadn't eaten since his last meal with Tibi. The thought that she might be hungry and thirsty gutted him. Unable to eat, he expected the evening fare to be served soon, but he planned to be gone before the first platter arrived.

He entered the peristyle to find his friends and a handful of strangers, not preparing to eat, but in prayer for Tibi's safe return. Relief crashed over him at the sight of the small band of Christians. He'd seen their prayers work before. He waited on the steps, thinking he'd have to swear the servants and slaves to silence.

Adiona lifted her head and noticed him standing beside a column. She smiled and stretched out her palm in welcome. In that moment, he could have entered the Coliseum with more confidence than he did his own garden. His feet heavy, he moved forward and took hold of her soft hand. She bowed her head and continued her prayers without saying a word to him.

At a loss to know what to do, he bowed his head, too. His own prayers spent before he came downstairs, he listened to the hum of multiple voices praying at once. What otherwise might have been noise or meaningless babble somehow blended into a song of unison.

The *domus* seemed to breathe in relief as a door opened somewhere behind him. Expecting Pelonia, he released Adiona's hand and went to investigate.

"Where is your master?" Pelonia asked, handing her cloak to one of the servants.

"I'm here." Alexius gave the servant holding Pelonia's cloak orders to have Calisto prepared. One way or the other he was leaving the house to look for Tibi. "Did you find her?" he asked, silently begging God for confirmation of her safety.

Her pretty face wreathed in disappointment, Pelonia shook her head, her pearl earrings swaying with the movement. She crossed the few steps between them and wrapped him in a her embrace. "I'm sorry. I would have sent a message sooner if I'd had news to give you." She released him and stepped back. "Tiberia wasn't home when I arrived this afternoon. I waited two hours before she came back. She believed Tibi was safe here with you. She hasn't heard from her and doesn't know where she is, either. I'm afraid she fears the worst. It seems Uncle Tiberius has had men posted all over the city at Tibi's favorite places and then some. He knew she frequented the garden she visited with you. It's reasonable to think his men found Tibi and took her back to him."

Dread poured though Alexius, knowing Tibi had good reason to fear her father's wrath. "Let's be off, then."

"Tiberia and I have already been. Tiberius barred the door against us."

"Then he has her."

"I tend to agree, but I can't confirm if he does."

Cursing the old man, Alexius slammed his fist into his palm. "Why didn't Tiberia send word of her father's actions? Had I known his tactics, we would *never* have left the *ludus*."

"I don't know," Pelonia said, her brown eyes red from unshed tears and filled with stress.

"*I* do. That shrew wanted Tibi found."

"No, Alexius. If that were true, she could have betrayed Tibi's location to their father all along."

"Not if she wanted to appear like a caring sister. Appearances are everything to that one."

Pelonia sighed. "Be reasonable. I assure you Tiberia is as wretched about all this as we are."

"I doubt it." He rubbed his pained side. Not since Kyra's assault had Alexius been as afraid for another person as he was for Tibi. "Antonius believed her life was in danger. If Tiberius has found her, what will the old goat do?"

"Again, I don't know." She closed her eyes and massaged the bridge of her nose. "Truly I don't. I'm trusting the Lord to keep her from harm."

"I'm going to fetch her."

"You won't get through the front door."

"I hope Tiberius *does* try to stop me."

Her eyes flared at the implied threat. She grabbed his arm to keep him from leaving. "Alexius, think. We don't even know if she's there. The city gates will close within the hour. Even if you managed to reach Tiberius's *domus*, slaves will have it closed tighter than a clam for the night.

"Listen to me, my friend. Tiberia and I spent the last three hours considering our options. One of them is to surprise Uncle in his own house."

He stilled, knowing a good tactical decision depended on being informed of the facts. "And?"

"If you force your way in, there's a healthy chance he'll harm Tibi just to prove that he has the right."

"What are the other options you devised?"

"We can wait for Antonius to go tomorrow and determine if Tibi is there."

"You can't expect me to sit here all night and twiddle

my thumbs," he ground out between clamped teeth. "I can't! I'm not *able* to do nothing."

"I know. I want to do whatever is possible as well, but I know my uncle. It's unwise to surprise a viper in his own nest."

Adiona joined them, the pale color of her flowing *stola* glowed white in the lantern light. "What's happened?" she asked, signaling to lower their voices or risk disturbing the praying group in the garden. "Is Tibi with you?"

"No," answered Pelonia, quick to explain the situation.

Adiona grimaced. She looked to Alexius. "Tibi's going to be your wife. What will you have all of us do?"

He scraped his hand through his hair. "I want to kick his door down and snatch her from her father's hateful clutches."

"Sounds perfectly reasonable to me," Adiona said matter-of-factly.

"Adiona!" Pelonia's gasped whisper carried across the entryway. "What of the harm that scenario will create?"

"I don't see any difficulties arising from his plan." Adiona smiled at Alexius. He groaned inwardly. Her tone suggested there was so much trouble attached to his desired course of action that he'd be an addled fool to attempt it. Growing more agitated by the moment, he glared at her. As a former matron of Rome, she was well-versed in political intrigue, stratagems and maneuvering louts like Tiberius. "What do you suggest I do, my lady? Follow Pelonia's advice and seek out the senator tomorrow?"

"What's going on?" Caros said. He and Quintus joined them.

"Adiona is about to tell me how to fetch Tibi from her father without causing a small war."

Quintus glanced at his wife, his eyes full of pride. "If anyone knows how, she will."

Caros put his arm around Pelonia and held her tight as she informed him of events.

"Which means Alexius must convince Senator Tacitus to find out if she's there one way or the other," Adiona said. "If memory serves, there's no opinion Tiberius considers greater than that of his powerful son-in-law."

Alexius turned for the door. "I'll return soon."

"We'll come with you," Quintus and Caros said at the same time, but he didn't stop to wait.

Outside, he shouted for the gate to be opened. Calisto was waiting as he'd ordered when Pelonia first returned.

With a snap of the reins, he urged the horse to a full gallop, in a race to beat the closing of the city gates. Moonlight and a few randomly placed torches lit the near-empty streets.

Calisto's pounding hooves matched Alexius's frantic heartbeat. "Please, God, just as You showed Quintus a way to save Adiona all those years ago, show me a way to reach Tibi."

The huge iron gates were being closed when he reached the city walls. Armed cohorts turned everyone away. Tents, campfires and people sleeping in open ox carts littered both sides of the road that offered free passage the next morning.

Furious that he was only moments too late, Alexius considered scaling the walls out of pure frustration. Instead, he approached the gatekeeper and shamelessly used his fame and a few well-placed *denarii* to bribe his way past the guards who were impressed to meet a gladiator champion of his status.

Alexius had no trouble finding the senator's palace on the Palatine hill. Large brass bowls of fire illuminated the wide front steps and well-tended front garden. Corinthian columns supported a wide, red-painted portico lined with statuary and potted plants manicured to perfection.

He passed the palace, seeking out Tiberius's smaller *domus* instead. The lights had been extinguished in the main house for the night. He followed the plastered wall along the street until he reached the end of the property. A gate made of iron bars revealed a path leading to the rough two-story building that served as slaves' quarters. A small fire surrounded by a ring of smooth stones provided some light. Three women sat in the shadows on the front steps braiding each other's hair.

Alexius tied Calisto's reins to a low-lying tree branch on the dark side of the street. He waited in the shadows for a cart to go by before he crossed back to the gate and called to the women to get their attention.

Two of the slaves came forward, suspicious enough of him to stay beyond his reach. The third waited on the steps, most likely ready to run for help if he proved dangerous.

"Good evening, my doves." He offered them the smile that he knew from experience worked wonders on women of all types. "I'm looking for some information for a friend of mine. I'm hopeful you'll be willing to help me."

"My, you're a pretty one!" said the first woman, a buxom brunette with pockmarked skin and a toothy smile. "I'll share information with you…and anything else you have in mind."

Alexius grinned. "That's kind of you, sweet. Unfortunately, I only have time for talk tonight. I'm looking for Tiberius Flavius."

Her smile turned into a sneer. "We're his slaves. How do you know him?"

"I'm here for my friend."

"And who's your friend?" The second slave drew closer, tossing her long braid over her shoulder as she did so.

"Just a friend."

The first slave looked him over with unconcealed suspicion. He guessed he earned her trust when she continued, "The master's *domus* is over there if you're looking to find it. What do you want with the old buzzard?

"Hopefully to wring his overfed neck and pluck him for stew." The second, younger girl laughed at her own joke.

He glanced toward the house he'd passed down the street. "Is he gone or does he go to bed with the sun?"

"He's home. Wish the buzzard would fly away, but he's been cooped up for the past week," the brunette said with a twist of her thin lips.

"Why is that?" Alexius tried to read the woman's face, but the dim, red glow of the fire made it difficult to see more than shadows. "Has he been ill?"

"No. He's the kind of sour soul who'll live forever just to torment everyone."

Encouraged by their dislike of Tiberius, Alexius brushed the bag of coins tied to his belt just enough to make the contents clink.

"What of his daughter, the younger Tiberia? My friend is looking for her."

The brunette crossed her arms around her middle

and looked pointedly at the bag of coins. "What does your friend want with her?"

He casually untied the knot and slipped a copper coin from the leather pouch. He held it through the bars. "He's worried about her. She disappeared yesterday."

The second girl came close enough to snatch the bribe from his fingers. "No, they brought her *back* yesterday. I saw her with my own eyes."

"You did?" He forced a smile. "Bless the gods. My friend will be most gratified to know she's safe."

"I wouldn't say that, exactly." The brunette held out her palm. Alexius supplied her with her own copper piece. "The master's been in a squawk ever since the lady defied him last week and ran away."

"Why did she go?" He noticed that the third girl had left the steps and come closer to better hear the conversation.

The brunette shrugged, sending her oversize *stola* dangerously low. She told him the same story Tibi had about the broken betrothal, Tiberius's fury, insults and threats. "Who wouldn't run from a brute like that if they had the chance?"

"I know I'd run like a horse with his tail on fire if I wouldn't be beaten for it and dragged back here," the second girl added. "I guess Lady Tibi's not so different from us in that regard."

Alexius looked toward the star-filled sky while he brooked the urge to rip the gate off its hinges and hunt down Tiberius. "She was beaten?"

The second girl held out her hand. He gave her a coin. "I have a friend who's a friend of one of the house slaves. According to my friend, *her* friend saw Lady Tibi caned. She said the girl is covered in welts and bruises from her shoulders to her ankles."

Bile rose in Alexius's throat. Somehow he managed a look of mild interest while his hands gripped the bars of the gate. He squeezed, wishing the cold iron was Tiberius's black heart.

"I think it's a shame she's treated that way," the younger slave continued. "She's always been nice to me."

"Cardea. Rohesia. Vinius is coming. You'd best not let him see you out here gossiping with a stranger."

His informants wasted no time running back into the house. The third girl followed them at a slower pace, glancing back at him every few steps. Livid with Tiberius and promising to exact retribution for the old man's actions, Alexius returned to Calisto. Sick at heart over Tibi's treatment, he struggled to keep a clear head. He led Calisto from the copse of trees back to the street.

"You there." A woman's voice came from the direction of the gate he'd left moments earlier. "Come here."

"What do you want?" The moon had hidden behind a cloud, limiting the already meager light. His hand on the knife sheathed at his belt, he moved closer to the voice. "I'm in no mood to be trifled with."

"Nor am I, gladiator."

That knocked him back. "Who are you?"

The third slave moved from out of the shadows. He relaxed. "What do you mean by calling me gladiator?"

"There's no need for games. I know you, Alexius of Iolcos," she said.

He scowled, trying to place where he might have seen her before. "How?"

"I used to be a house slave for Senator Tacitus. His interest in the games and you champions is incessant. I saw you at the fete he threw for you and your men last autumn. Lady Tibi was there also."

"I imagine the lady attends quite a few parties at her sister's home."

"Yes, but the way you looked at her that night… Doubtless she went home singed."

He rubbed the back of his neck, remembering the event. He hadn't seen Tibi in months. She'd worn a tunic the color of a ripe peach. "How much will it cost me to keep you from telling anyone I was here?"

She didn't hesitate. "A *denarius*."

Figuring the girl thought she'd asked for a fortune, and not wanting her to demand more, he complained about being robbed as he fished the silver from among his other coins. With exaggerated reluctance, he handed it to her through the bars.

She held the piece up to what remained of the firelight. Deeming it the amount she sought, she gave him a satisfied grin. "And another…if you want me to take you to your lady."

Chapter Seventeen

Finally losing his veneer of calm, Alexius rattled the bars in frustration. "Don't toy with me, wench! Where is she?"

The slave girl jumped back, her face deathly white in the blackness surrounding them. She turned and sprinted toward the slave quarters.

"Wait! Come back. Please!" he called, not above begging when seeing Tibi was at stake.

The girl stopped and contemplated him over her shoulder. "You looked liked a ferocious bear just then. You frightened me."

"I'm sorry. Please, come here. I swear I won't hurt you. I'll give you a fortune if you take me to Tibi."

Leaves crunched beneath her feet as she took a few hesitant steps back toward him. Her face was creased with wariness. "How can I trust you?"

"I'm willing to trust *you*."

"I can't kill you. I fear you can snap my neck like a blade of grass."

"Why would I harm you when I need you?"

She bit her lower lip, considering his argument. "I want five *denarii*."

"You have it. Where is your master's daughter?"

Night insects chirped in the darkness. "You'll have to wait here while I fetch the keys. I'll bring my boy to watch your horse. He'll need a *denarius* also."

She ran up the dirt path and disappeared into the slave quarters. Alexius led Calisto back to the trees across the street and waited in the dark with his horse. Aware that he might be walking into a trap, he didn't care. Taking the chance was worth finding Tibi.

"Are you still there, gladiator?"

He sprinted across the street. "I'm here."

A young boy stood beside the slave. The keys rattled as she worked the lock. Apparently, she was more nervous than she seemed and he realized that by *fetch* she'd meant steal the keys, probably a second set kept by the cook. "What is your name, little thief?"

"Ismene. This is my son, Itulus."

"What of the dogs? Surely, your master keeps them."

"He does. A pack of Molossi. They have yet to be loosed for the night. Several of us slaves have more work before sleep. The steward waits until we're all on our pallets before unleashing the vicious beasts." The key finally turned. She warily opened the gate.

"I'm not going to hurt you," he reassured her. He waited for Itulus to cross the road and listened for the birdcall signaling the boy had found Calisto. To keep from being trapped, he propped the gate shut with a piece of firewood.

"Let's stay close to the wall," he told Ismene. "It's a dark night, but the shadows there are darker still."

Near the house, they used the fruit trees for cover. At the back of the *domus,* large poplars stood on either side of the door. The faint smell of smoke drifted across the yard from the slaves' dying bonfire. Ismene rattled the keys again, increasing Alexius's anxiety as she felt for the right one in the dark.

"By the gods!" she hissed. "I can't find it." She took the ring and stalked several paces away from the trees. She held up the keys to the sliver of moonlight available. "I still can't see it. Her room is there." She pointed to the second floor. "Why don't you climb the tree and enter that way?"

He squinted in her direction, trying to judge if she was joking. "Just how many robberies have you committed to think climbing trees and scaling walls is a task of no account?"

She sighed impatiently. "Do you wish to see the lady or not? We only have so long before the dogs are released."

"Which window is it?" he growled.

"That one." She pointed to an indiscernible spot. "You can't see it from here, but there's always at least one lamp left for the lady. As you climb higher, you'll see the glow."

"What if the shutters are closed?"

"They'll be open," she replied with confidence.

"And where will you be?" he asked, beginning to think she was pulling a prank on him.

"I'm going to continue trying the keys. But you saw how long it took for me to try just one. Once I'm inside, I'll check the house and see where the guards are. You won't have to climb back down."

No, he would not. If there was any way to move Tibi, he'd have her with him. He hadn't come all this way to leave her in the clutches of a madman.

Recognizing the lunacy of his actions, he found the lowest limb and hoisted himself up, his need to see Tibi goading him on like a hot poker. He groaned in pain as his stitches pulled and lightning flared through his cracked ribs. Struggling to catch his breath, he looked back to his companion. "I'm trusting you."

"You can. I want that five *denarii* and to have a secret the master would kill to know. Now go and let me get back to these keys."

Reaching the second story was surprisingly quick once he found his rhythm climbing up the tree. Just as Ismene had told him, he began to see light the closer he came to the open window.

He listened for voices or sounds of any kind. Hearing none, he felt along the house as he eased out on a limb toward the window ledge. The ledge hit him just below the waist. Standing on the limb, he looked inside the window, grateful none of his men were privy to seeing him.

The faint light revealed the door on the far side of the chamber was closed. Beside the portal, a mirror hung over a table filled with colorful glass jars and bottles.

From what he could see, the room was empty. He climbed inside.

He found Tibi lying on her stomach on a sleeping couch to his left. Her face was turned toward the wall, her long blond braid hanging over the side of the couch and trailing to the floor. Her arms were at her sides beneath a thin white cloth that covered all of her except her head and the top of her bare shoulders.

The black bruises that crisscrossed her fair skin made him see red. In an instant, he realized there was no way to move her without a litter and the fear and frustration of having to leave her was almost more than he could stand.

He knelt beside her, his sorrow for the pain she'd suffered driving him to his knees. With a trembling hand, he touched her brow and felt the scorching heat of a fever. "Tibi?" he whispered.

Except for a soft sigh, she didn't respond. With the back of his hand, he touched her cheek, feeling the damp of tears she cried even in her sleep.

Seeing no basin or other container of water to cool a cloth for her brow, he lifted the open bottle on the side table and sniffed the sickly sweet scent of opium. Thanking God someone had been merciful enough to give her medicine for her pain, he moved the cloth on the back of her legs. Just as the slave had said, the bruises covered every part of her skin.

Plans to murder Tiberius began to form in his brain. How easy it would be to find the old goat's room, break his neck and toss him down the stairs. No one would ever know he hadn't fallen by accident, and who was there to care?

Surely even Tibi didn't long for her father's approval after the torture he'd put her through today.

He felt a presence approaching in the corridor. He stood and moved behind the door. The portal opened. "Gladiator," Ismene whispered, "are you in here?"

He pulled Ismene into the room and shut the door. "Look what that evil wretch has done to my beautiful girl."

Ismene moved to the couch and lifted the cover enough to see Tibi's back. She winced. "I expected as much."

"What do you mean?"

"The master was livid this past week while she was gone. He wanted her punished and beating the slaves wouldn't do. If she'd been here, who knows, but as it is, he had too many days with nowhere to release his anger."

Alexius jerked. Was he capable of this much harm if he kept his fury bottled inside him?

"We need to leave," Ismene said. "The lady's maid will return soon and the dogs will be loosed."

"I can't—not yet."

"You have to. If you're caught here, these bruises aren't the worst of what she'll endure."

Unwilling to let Tibi suffer any further, he bent to brush a kiss across her cheek. "I'm coming for you, *agape mou.* Trust in me. In just a few hours I'll be back to take you home."

Alexius didn't bother to go back to the *ludus.* He marched up the steps of the senator's palace and waited outside until sunrise when he was certain the steward would answer the door.

The brass door knocker bearing the Tacitus family seal made a great ruckus under his influence. "Open up!" he demanded.

"Go away!" said a male voice which Alexius assumed belonged to the steward. "Come back at a decent hour, or better yet tomorrow, and we'll consider letting you in."

"I have important news concerning Lady Tiberia's younger sister."

Curious silence prevailed on the other side of the door while he waited. His fingers clenched and unclenched as he contemplated the best way to remove the marble door from its brass hinges. Finally, he heard the muted rattle of keys and the slide of multiple metal locks. The door opened slowly. The sweet smell of incense was rife from the morning rituals.

He pushed past the steward and into a circular entry ringed by armed slaves. Unconcerned by the half dozen swords glinting in the lantern light, he focused on the middle-aged steward. "Where is your master, the senator?"

"I'm here." Antonius stood at the top of a wide staircase, looking down his hawklike nose. Sharp, black eyes raked over Alexius as he descended the steps, his senatorial toga arranged to perfection. "Everyone knows of my love for the games. Normally, I'd be pleased to receive a great champion like you, Alexius, but not when I have meetings scheduled with my patrons within moments. Horace says you have news of my little sister. If so, speak it."

Not intimidated, Alexius stepped forward. "You're to cancel your meetings and come with me. Tibi's been caned on her father's order. Tiberius respects you. You *must* see that she's released into my care."

Tiberius scowled. "I'm not unconcerned, mind you, but what you ask is impossible. I have other matters just as pressing as Tibi's welfare—perhaps more so."

"There is *nothing* in this world more important than Tibi!"

The senator backed toward his armed slaves as far as possible without looking like a coward. "I'm in the midst of an important campaign."

A doomed one, Alexius thought. "Are you expected to win?" he asked, already aware of the answer.

"The dice have yet to be cast."

"Which means you expect to lose."

The senator thrust back his shoulders and lifted his chin to a regal angle. "Perhaps, but I won't give up without a fight. To fail to win the nomination for consul will be a signal to some that I'm weak and no longer enjoy the emperor's favor, as I once did."

Alexius glanced around the circular entry, the ancestral statues and other trappings of senatorial power.

"Your loss is your own fault, senator. Three years ago, the people loved their new man, but you forgot them in your quest to glorify yourself."

Color dusted the senator's sharp cheekbones. "Even if you're correct—and I'm not admitting you are—I know of no way to change that fact. There's only so many babies I can kiss and hands I can shake for a nomination that takes place in a week."

His head aching from lack of food and sleep, Alexius rubbed his forehead. A plan began to form in his mind, a plan he wouldn't have considered on his own, but that now seemed like an answer to his prayers. "Perhaps I can help you."

"How so?" the senator asked, desperate enough to be intrigued.

"It's well-known that I'm favored by the mob. Sponsor a contest the day before the election. I'll represent you and lend you my support. Not everyone will follow me, but—"

"But enough will to draw the emperor's interest. What happens if you're defeated? I'll be out of a great deal of coin."

"I'll be dead. Between the two of us, I consider myself the one with the most to lose."

"You'll do this if I get Tibi for you this morning?"

"And secure Tiberius's signature to let us marry."

"Impossible! He'll never agree."

"That's your burden to carry, not mine. You're an orator, Senator Tacitus. Win Tiberius to my side and I will win the mob to yours."

"You're insane, Antonius," Tiberius ranted. "My daughter married to a *gladiator?* Do you even ken what you're asking?"

Alexius paced outside Tiberius's office. Tibi was suffering in her chamber right above him on the second floor. If not for his promise to Antonius to remain downstairs until the pact with Tiberius was signed, he would have already gone to her with speed.

"Yes, I do understand. Do *you* understand that if you don't oblige me, my chance for the consul nomination is next to nonexistent? If my reputation suffers, your own influence will dwindle, since much of your status is attached to my name."

"But he's a gladiator!"

"There are worse things."

"Name one."

The silence almost made Alexius chuckle.

"An actor," Antonius finally offered.

Tiberius grunted.

"What does it matter? We already have one of their sort in this family."

"Pelonia isn't *my* daughter," Tiberius shouted.

"You want Tibi to marry," Antonius said reasonably. "At least this marriage will have a purpose. Alexius is rich and popular. Consider that the marriages of your two daughters will ensure you recognition wherever you are in Rome. Tiberia's marriage to me provides the security you need to enjoy the higher classes. And Tibi's marriage will give you free passage with the lower orders."

Alexius rolled his eyes. He must truly be in love not to mind joining Tibi's pretentious family. How she'd avoided their nonsense was a triumph, in his opinion.

"Listen to me, old man," Antonius said, the argument intensifying. "Your hateful reputation precedes you and Tibi's is tarnished beyond repair. Between the two of you, there are enough scandals to sink a galley.

Tibi is not going to receive a better offer and sending her to a temple will not alleviate the current problems crushing this family. Either give your permission for her to wed Alexius or consider that I'll publicly disavow you."

Impressed by the hard-nosed tactic, but beyond caring what Antonius said as long it produced the desired result, Alexius stood and began to pace.

"You wouldn't!"

"Sign or consider the matter done."

Alexius wasn't certain if the sudden quiet was capitulation or the calm before a storm. He heard something clatter, like a stylus hitting a desk.

"There, the filthy contract is signed! Take your Greek dog and my worthless daughter from this house and make certain they never set foot here again!"

Alexius raced up the steps to Tibi's chamber. Antonius's own litter waited outside to take her home. Alexius had already sent word to the *ludus* and arranged to have a physician present when they arrived.

The pitiful sight that greeted him ripped his heart apart. Tibi was in the same spot and position he'd left her in the previous night. He touched her brow. The fever lingered. The effects of the opium were wearing off. The muscles of her abused back were starting to jump in protest against their treatment.

He shouted for a basin of water and fresh cloths. Crouching beside her, he brushed the hair out of her eyes. "Tibi? *Agape mou*, can you hear me?"

There was the faintest nod of her head.

"Your father's agreed to let you wed me. I'm taking you home with the hope that I can eventually win your agreement. For now you need to rest and get well. I'm going to take care of you if you don't mind."

Another faint movement.

"I know you're suffering, but we have to leave here. I have no more medicine."

He might have imagined it, but he thought she winced. For her, the two miles to the *ludus* were going to seem like one hundred. He prayed that she'd lose consciousness.

He secured the light cotton cloth covering her. "I have to pick you up." He slowly turned her on her side. Her body convulsed and a shriek of pain burst from her chapped lips. He eased her back to her stomach.

A slave delivered a basin and cloths. Alexius cooled her brow, her throat, her wrists.

"By the gods!" Antonius exclaimed from the doorway. "She didn't deserve this."

"I told you." Alexius glared at the other man. "Tiberius isn't going to get away with this…this barbarity."

"I agree he shouldn't." The senator seemed embarrassed. "I'm sorry I didn't pay more attention. Clearly she needed a champion. I failed her."

"*I* am her champion," Alexius said. "Forever if she'll have me."

Chapter Eighteen

By the time, the litter arrived at the *ludus,* Alexius's prayers had been answered and Tibi was blessed with oblivion. He told himself he held her to keep her from moving with the sway and occasional bounce of the litter, but the truth was he simply needed her in his arms.

Caros, Quintus, their wives and Tibi's sister were waiting in the outer courtyard when Alexius stepped out of the litter. He knew his friends wanted an accounting of the past day and a half. They and the shrew were going to have to wait. "What?" he dared them to speak. "I'm a farm boy at heart. Your stratagems were too much for me. I simply went and found her."

Alexius reached into the silk-draped litter and lifted Tibi into his arms as though she were the rarest blue glass. With great care, he carried her up the steps and into the chamber she'd used the previous week. He went to the sleeping couch in the corner and eased her onto her stomach.

The three women followed him, gathering around Tibi's bruised form. Even the usually unflappable

Adiona shed tears for the suffering Tiberius had ordered.

Remus, the physician, arrived, casting the men from the chamber. Drying his hands with a towel, he came back a short time later. "As far as I can tell, she has no broken bones. Sadly, there is no way for me to know if she's bleeding within her body. I recommend you keep her bathed and cool, especially until her fever breaks." He reached into his supplies and handed Alexius two black bottles plugged with cork. "This is calendula oil. Spread it gently, yet liberally over her bruises to help them heal. This one is—"

"Mandragora root?"

"It's less addictive than opium and will help her sleep better," Remus said. "A small draught in half a cup of honeyed wine usually does the trick, but then, I expect you remember that."

For the next two days, Alexius refused to leave Tibi's side. He ate his meals by the window, watching his men in the field below. He slept in the chair next to her couch and talked to her until all hours of the night about his farm in Umbria and the progress of the men she'd trained. The only time he left her was when Adiona or Pelonia came to bathe and dress her each morning. They kept her hair washed, brushed and braided. The whole room smelled of the floral calendula oil they rubbed over every patch of abused tissue.

Tibi's fever had eased that first night he'd brought her from Tiberius's *domus,* only to flare again the following day. Last night she'd broken out in a sweat. Alexius hoped the worst was over.

He bowed his head, praying for her health just as he'd done every day since the Lord returned her to him.

"Alexius?" Her voice was a craggy whisper.

"I'm here, Tibi. Are you awake?"

Her eyes were closed. For a moment he thought she was talking in her sleep. "Alexius?"

Afraid he might jostle her, he knelt down on the floor, the cold mosaic tiles biting into his knees.

She opened her eyes. Her beautiful half smile filled him with relief. "I love you," she whispered.

He picked up her hand and kissed each of her fingers. "I love you, too. How are you feeling?"

"The pain. I'm having trouble breathing."

"I know, *agape mou*. I wish I could bear the hurt for you."

"Your ribs?" she asked.

Amazed that she even remembered his wound after all she'd endured, he bent and kissed the top of her head. "My ribs are fine. You need to rest."

Her long lashes fluttered downward. Alexius thought she'd gone back to sleep. He moved to stand. She blinked and looked at him. "Did you say my father… Permission…?"

"Yes, I have the signed contract."

"How?"

He picked a stray piece of linen from her shoulder. "I'll tell you once you recover."

Her eyes slipped shut. "I will."

"I know you will. You're getting better every hour."

"No," she winced when she moved her head. "I will…marry you."

"How is our patient today?"

Tibi looked up to see Adiona walking across the room toward her. As graceful as always in a green *stola* and emerald earrings, Adiona was the most beautiful woman Tibi had ever seen. But despite her kindness and generosity in nursing her back to health, Adiona possessed a natural reserve and sophisticated manner Tibi found intimidating.

"I'm much better. I can take a full breath without pain. I'm going to try to walk today."

"Excellent." Adiona's lovely amber eyes settled on Tibi's face. "But do be careful. I don't want to see you hurt again."

"Thank you. I hope you know how much I appreciate all you've done for me. You certainly didn't need to bother."

"You're no bother, Tibi. You're my friend." Adiona squeezed her hand. "You remind me of myself in many ways. I have a difficult time accepting help, just as you seem to do."

"It's hard to think of you needing aid from anyone," Tibi said honestly. "You seem…perfect. There doesn't appear to be a single flaw in you."

"I'm far from perfect. Ask my husband." Adiona laughed, a lovely sound that invited others to smile.

"Quintus adores you. Anyone can see he does."

"That's because he's adored in return." Adiona sat in the chair Alexius always used and poured a small amount of calendula oil into her palm. "He's my gift from the Lord. Without him I wouldn't be the person I am now. And the person I was before I knew him and the Lord was not a very good or nice one."

Tibi rolled onto her stomach and adjusted her tunic to give Adiona access to her bruises. "Who changed you more? God or Quintus?"

"Quintus is a man, so I'm certain he'd like to think he did." She laughed. "I'm teasing. The truth is I loved Quintus first because I could see and touch him, but the

Lord changed my heart and healed me so that I could have the joyful life I do now."

"You were ill?"

"Not with sickness, but with hate and fear."

Tibi grimaced as Adiona rubbed a particularly sore spot. She turned her head for a glimpse at the beautiful woman who tended her wounds with such care. "I find that so difficult to believe. You're one of the most kind and loving people I know."

"Thank you, but that's the Lord's work, Tibi." She wiped the excess oil off her hands and covered Tibi's back with her tunic and a light cotton covering. "If you don't believe me, ask Pelonia—no, she'll only say nice things. Ask your sister instead. Tiberia will remember me as I was then."

Tibi eased onto her side. Adiona fetched feather-stuffed pillows to prop her up. "Can I ask you a personal question?"

"Adiona sat back in Alexius's chair and rearranged her sea-green *stola*. "Feel free to ask me whatever you wish."

Tibi brushed her fingers across the soft silk pillow. "What did you fear and why did you hate?"

Adiona's gaze dropped to her folded hands in her lap. Certain, she'd offended her new friend, Tibi began to apologize, but Adiona spoke first. "I don't tell many people about myself, but I think the Lord wants me to share with you.

"My father was much like yours—cold and unfeeling," she said. "He thought of me as useless because I wasn't a son."

Adiona's confession grabbed Tibi by the heart.

"When I was twelve years old, he came back from war and sold me into marriage to pay his debts. My first husband was as evil as Quintus is wonderful. I vowed to hate all men because of my father and husband. I didn't realize it, but that hate was the root of much fear. I always had to protect myself and I trusted very few people.

"When Quintus came along, I almost missed him because of my problems. But the Lord put us together in terrible circumstances. Quintus taught me to trust him. Because of his testimony I was able to believe the Lord loved me. He healed my battered heart, became the loving Father I never had and gave me the man and family I always dreamed of."

Tibi blinked tears from her eyes. She noticed there was moisture in Adiona's eyes as well.

A rap on the door frame drew their attention. A nursemaid held Adiona's year-old daughter in her arms. "Forgive me for interrupting, mistress, but this precious darling wants her mama."

Tibi forgotten, Adiona gladly accepted her green-eyed infant, Fabia, with unconditional love. She kissed a blush pink cheek and stroked her baby's soft black ringlets.

Tibi smiled, watching the playful antics of a mother with a daughter who would always be loved. She'd accepted the hole in her heart that was meant to be filled by her parents' affection would stay empty forever. "I envy you."

"There's no need, my friend. Everything I have comes from the Lord and Jesus gives everything He has freely. If you want Him in your life, just ask Him in."

Later, that same afternoon, Tibi was lying on her side leaning on a pillow when Alexius walked in to see her. Freshly shaven, he wore a gray tunic that almost matched his silver eyes. The damp curls of his glossy hair suggested that he'd come directly from a bath.

"You are the handsomest man on this earth."

He kissed her softly and sat in the chair beside her couch. "I think that depends on who's looking at me."

"You're right," she said a little breathless from his kiss. "I imagine everyone else thinks you're ugly."

He chuckled. "Probably."

"Where have you been?" she asked, breathing in his spicy scent.

"On the field, then the bath."

"How are my men?"

"They miss you."

"Really?" Happiness surged through her. She found she liked being appreciated and respected. Her pride in the students' improvement created an affectionate bond she'd rarely experienced. She considered them her friends. "I miss them, too. Tell them so, will you?"

He promised. Velus delivered a tray overflowing with dishes for their midday meal. They ate the poached partridge eggs and smoked ham before Alexius pulled out the board for a game of *latrunculi*. He placed the grid-patterned board on the sleeping couch. Tibi reclined on her side next to the game. Alexius sat in the chair across the board from her. "I will win this time." He placed his blue stones on his side of the grid and looked at her with fierce determination.

"There's always a first time for everything." She laughed as she set up her red stones in front of her.

Tibi tossed her die and moved a piece the allotted three spaces. "Adiona and I spoke of something important today."

His die clacked on the wood board. He moved his first piece four spots. "What was it?"

"Did you know that her father didn't love her, either?"

"I've heard bits and pieces. It's not a pretty story. She doesn't seem to mind her past anymore."

Tibi cast her die and moved another game piece. "How would you feel if *I* became a Christian?"

He stilled, his blue game piece forgotten. His smile cast every shadow from her heart. "I told you I'd win today."

"How so?" she asked, looking at the board and her perfectly set strategy.

"I accepted the Lord as my own the day He brought you back to me."

"What?" The news filled her with more joy than she expected. "Why did you keep such news a secret?"

"I wanted to tell you. You were in such devastating pain. I decided to wait for a better time."

She moved the board, scattering the stones. Surprised by her sudden action, he looked at the red-and-blue pile on the covers, and grinned up her. "What? Was I winning?"

"No," she said, adjusting her pillow. "Forget the game. Tell me everything."

Alexius scooped up a handful of the *latrunculi* stones and slowly filtered them through his fingers. He'd put the dark days of her absence as far out of his mind as possible. "I was frantic when you were missing. I kept reliving Kyra's assault and I knew that if I lost you, I might as well die, too."

"Alexius, no!"

"You know how they are," he continued, referencing their friends. "They were praying all the time and…and

I couldn't help wanting to join them. I told the Lord if He brought you back to me, I'd believe He forgave me. I promised to serve Him the rest of my days if He did."

A breeze blew in the open window, bringing a hint of the honeysuckle blooms on the climbing vines. Concerned that Tibi would catch a draft, he stood and readjusted her covers.

"Pelonia came back a short time later from visiting your sister. They'd been to see your father and he'd barred them from the house. We suspected that he had you. I went later that night and found we were correct."

She frowned, confused. "At night? You brought me home during the day, or so I thought."

"One of your father's servants led me to your window. I found you in your room."

"Wait." Her brow pleated. "My window is on the second floor. What did you do?" She laughed. "Climb the tree outside?"

He scooped the stones again and let silence be his answer.

"You climbed to my window?" A soft, feminine look filled her brown eyes. "How romantic."

"It was an act of desperation. I could have broken my neck."

"I wish I'd known you were there."

"You were crying in your sleep," he said with remembered pain. "That hurt worse than any wound I ever received."

"I'm sorry."

"It wasn't your fault." He stood by the window looking out at the herb garden. He saw Caros holding his two-year-old son, Pelonius, on one arm. The small boy was a black-haired, blue-eyed miniature of his father, minus the scars.

Pelonius picked a leaf off the lemon tree. Caros brushed it across the child's nose, making the boy throw back his head and giggle with innocent abandon.

He couldn't wait until he and Tibi had their own child. She would be the kindest of mothers and he would do his best to be just like his own loving father.

He felt her presence beside him. "What are you doing up?"

"I'm trying to get my strength back." She glanced out the window. "Look at Caros and the baby. How sweet."

Alexius positioned himself behind Tibi, not touching her to cause pain, but ready to catch her if she needed him. He nuzzled her ear, breathing deeply of her natural perfume. "The world is upside down when Caros Viriathos is described as sweet."

She looked back up at him, smiling. "Someday we'll have a child of our own."

"Yes, God willing."

"Why wouldn't He be?"

"Who knows? Maybe I'll be an ogre of a father."

"More like a jokester in your family's finest tradition."

Against her protests, he led her back to the couch and helped her lie down on her side. He tucked pillows all around her.

He decided that there was no point in telling her about the agreement he'd made with Antonius to fight in the senator's name at the Coliseum. He'd already decided the event would be his last as a gladiator. He wanted to start afresh with Tibi and put Rome and the empty years of his life far behind him.

Tibi tugged on his hand. "Where are you?"

"Lost in my thoughts." He sat down in his chair

beside her. "I'd like to leave Rome. What do you think?"

She chewed her bottom lip in contemplation. "I've lived here all my life. Where would we go? Umbria?"

"If you recall, I have a farm there. Our friends live nearby. There are plenty of fields, vineyards, orchards…. You can choose wherever you wish to put up an archery target."

"Well, then, I'm game to go tomorrow." She lowered her lashes and studied her palm. "I don't know if I should ask, but what of your anger? I don't believe you're like my father, but how will you control your wrath if you have nowhere to set it free?"

He sat forward on the chair and clasped her hand. The lines in his face deeper with stress. "Listen to me, *agape mou*. I'm glad you recognize that I'm *not* like your father. He hurts others because he's cruel. I've never done that and I never will. Even so, things have changed in me since the night I prayed. The anger is there, but I feel it dying. Whether it's the Lord healing me, as I've asked, or because you bring me so much happiness that I have no room for anything else, I'm no longer the man I was.

"That night you were caned, when I sat on the floor by your bed, I planned to murder Tiberius—death is what he deserved for hurting you. There was a time when the anger would have overtaken me. I won out because I didn't want to hurt you, and he *is* your father. Plus, I have this new faith in me now that I don't want to dishonor."

She moved the pillow to prop her head. "I'm truly grateful that you didn't kill my father, but a part of me thanks you for wanting to."

"Would you have hated me if I had?"

"No, I don't think it's possible for me to hate you, no matter what you do. I'm glad you didn't harm him for your sake, not his."

"What of your desire to win his approval?"

"I've changed, too." She told him the information her father had given her. "I may not even be his and I'm tired of trying to earn his love. I realized that he's not capable of caring for anyone. That is *his* flaw—not mine."

"Agreed. The old goat's a fool for not treasuring you."

"You helped me to see that I have value. You make me feel more precious than gold."

"Gold is jealous of you, *agape mou.*"

She smiled and caressed his knuckles with her thumb. "As for Umbria, I loved the countryside when I visited my cousins there. It will be good to be near them. I think it will be a wonderful place for us to build a family safe in our new faith and filled with love. But, truth to tell, even if it were a barren wasteland, I'd be happy as long as you were there."

Alexius refused to shed tears in front of her, but he had to choke back the emotion in his throat. "I know other men may think so, but they are wrong. *I* am the luckiest of men because you're mine."

She smiled. "I'll remind you of that the next time you're mad at me."

He chuckled and kissed her palm. "You mentioned our new faith. Have you decided, then, to become a Christian?"

She nodded shyly.

He moved to stand. "Shall I call one of the women to pray with you?"

She shook her head. "If it's all right, I'd rather you were here instead."

He sank back down in his chair. He cleared his throat, realizing that, as her man, he wanted to protect not only her heart and body but her soul as well. "I prayed in Greek when I went to the Lord for myself."

"I can pray in Greek."

"Not with your atrocious accent. He won't understand you."

"Then I'll pray in Latin. Everyone knows it's a better language anyway."

His eyebrow arched and he frowned at her as though she'd committed treason. "Since you're going to the Lord for forgiveness, I think you should start with that remark."

Giggling, she settled deeper into her pillows. She closed her eyes and grew more serious. She opened one eye. "I'm going to begin how I've always heard Pelonia." She closed her eye again. "Dear Heavenly Father, my cousin Pelonia assures me that You already know me, but I'm here before You because I want to know You. I'm sorry I put others before You in my life, but from now on I mean for that to change. My friend Adiona told me You want my trust. I give it freely and I ask You to forgive me for anything else I've done that doesn't please You. And I thank You for Alexius, whom I love with all my heart. In Jesus's name. Amen."

Chapter Nineteen

Tibi sat in the central garden of the *ludus*. Surrounded by fragrant blooms of white, pink, purple and yellow, she rested on her side on one of the blue, padded couches. Her face turned to the warmth of the sun and the cloudless sky, she was thinking of her little black panther. As soon as he came home, she planned to ask Alexius to find out about the cat's welfare.

In the five days since she'd become a Christian, she'd healed rapidly, according to the physician. Her bruises no longer an ugly purple, they'd mellowed to an uglier swirl of deep yellow. She was slow going up and down the stairs, but she was pleased to be walking. Sitting remained out of the question. Otherwise, she would have gone to the Forum with their friends, if for no other reason than to enjoy leaving the house for a few hours.

A pair of birds chased each other through the garden, flying dangerously close to the peristyle's columns.

"My lady," Velus said over the splash of the fountain. He came down the steps, a tray held in his chubby hands. "The day grows warm. I thought you might need some water."

She thanked the steward as he placed the tray on the

table beside her. Ice clinked in a glass pitcher. "Ice? What is the special occasion?"

"You're feeling better."

"How sweet, Velus, thank you."

The older man colored and added gruffly. "Enjoy it. It's from the last reasonably priced barrel until next winter."

Watching him amble back inside the house, she drank deeply, enjoying the cold crispness of the water on her tongue. According to the brass sundial a few flowerbeds away, a half hour passed before Velus returned. "My lady, you have a guest."

"Who is it?"

"Your sister."

"Send her in," she said, intrigued by the unexpected visit. Had she done something that Tiberia felt the need to chastise her?

"Tibi?" Tiberia called from the foot of the garden. "The dwarf said you're out here somewhere. It's important I speak with you."

"I'm here," she called, waving to draw Tiberia's notice instead of going to the painful trouble of standing. "Near the largest fountain."

Tiberia's long shadow reached Tibi first, but eventually her sister stood before her. "What are you doing out here?"

"Taking in some sun. I've been upstairs for the last nine days."

"May I sit?"

"Of course. You're my sister. You needn't be so formal or even have to ask."

Tiberia sank into a nearby chair, her light yellow *stola* flaring across the gravel path. Tiberia fidgeted with the links of her gold belt. Usually, her self-possessed sister was a pillar of haughty calm. "My husband says you plan to wed your gladiator."

"Yes, as soon as I can walk in the procession. I hope you'll come," she said.

"Do you love him or...or is this some sort of silly rebellion against Father?"

Resenting the inability to move without pain, Tibi glared at her sister. "I love Alexius with *all* my heart. If you have any affection for me, you'll be kind to him as well. As for Father, he and I are no longer speaking. He almost crippled me."

Tiberia closed her eyes and hung her head. "I know. I'm sorry I haven't been to see you more often. I came the first day, but you were unconscious. Antonius and I have both felt terribly guilty. I didn't visit...because I didn't know what to say."

"Be at ease, Tiberia. You're not responsible for having me caned."

"We should have been more protective of you. We should have brought you to live with us... Something. Anything. Father's always been hurtful but never like this. You're my little sister. I do love you, even though I haven't always shown it well enough."

"I know. I love you, too. I'm sorry you've been caught between Father and me so often."

Tiberia took a deep breath. "That is why I'm here. Father swore me to secrecy this morning, but I can't stay silent and live with myself."

"What is it?" Tibi tried to maneuver into a semblance of a sitting position. Her sister's anxious expression worried her.

Tiberia wrung her hands. She stood, her pacing crunched across the gravel. "Father...he's planned for your glad... For Alexius to die today."

"*What?* What do you mean?" Ignoring the pain screaming in her back, she struggled to her feet. "Is this a sick joke, Tiberia?"

"No! I swear. If someone schemed against Antonius, you'd tell me."

"Yes. Now tell me what's intended for Alexius!"

"I went to Father's *domus* this morning and over-heard him giving instructions to his steward. It seems there's to be a large contest at the Coliseum today. Did you know of it?"

"No," she replied, determined to stop her father's plans no matter what needed to be done.

"It seems that your gladiator promised to fight in support of my husband's bid for the consul nomination if Antonius secured Father's consent for you and Alexius to marry."

Tears burned the back of Tibi's eyes. Why hadn't she forced Alexius to tell her how he'd secured her father's permission or suspected something sinister when he'd agreed to her marriage with a gladiator?

"Father is against your marriage for several reasons, besides the obvious one that your groom is a former slave. He never would have signed that contract except that Antonius threatened to disavow him publicly if he refused."

Tibi gasped. Her father prized her brother-in-law's name, connections, his very existence. To have Antonius threaten to cut him off so completely must have shattered him.

"Naturally, he felt coerced," Tiberia continued, absently trailing her palm across the top of a fern. "You know that never sits well with him."

"Am I supposed to feel pity?" Tibi asked. "If so, I

can't find any in me after the anguish he's caused. You still haven't told me how he plans to harm my man."

"When your Greek fights today, he'll face three men at once. Nothing too unusual for a champion of his skill, but Father has arranged for poison to be placed on the blades of his opponents. If Alexius gets even one small scratch, he'll be weakened enough for the others to slay him."

Shaking with rage and fear, Tibi hobbled from the garden as rapidly as possible. She yelled Velus's name at the top of her lungs. The steward came running. She quickly told him what Tiberia shared. "Fetch Silo. I'm too slow to go out to the field myself."

Velus returned, his breathing heavy from his run to the barracks. "No good, my lady. Except for the newest recruits, the archers have all gone to the Coliseum. If today's show is typical, they'll participate in group battles. It's a given that most of the game's archers will be killed or wounded by each other."

The faces of Gaidrēs and Ovid filled her mind's eye. She refused to think about losing any of her friends. "Will Alexius be in this battle?"

"No, he'll fight later. He's always the main event."

"We have to get word to him. Velus, you have to hurry. Fetch one or several of the trainers and bring them to me."

Weak and trembling from the effort already spent by her sore legs and back, Tibi leaned against a column along the garden's central path. Afraid to sit down in case she couldn't get back up again, she concentrated on a plan to keep her mind off the pain cramping her strained muscles. Tiberia sat quietly by the fountain, her face downcast.

To Tibi's relief, Sergius arrived. She quickly told

him what had happened and what she needed him to do. "You must take word to the Coliseum. Alexius has to be informed not to allow his opponents to use their contaminated weapons."

"I'll gladly go, my lady," Sergius said. "But what if I don't make it before he enters the field?"

"I considered that. You'll have to use our archers to help him form a distance."

"What if none survive the earlier competition? Who will give him the advantage? I'm no good with a bow and arrows for certain."

"Are *any* of the other men?"

"Those trained have already gone. The new recruits can try, but who knows if they can hit a moving target."

She took a trembling breath, dreading the agony of what she was about to commit to, but convinced nothing was too great a sacrifice to keep Alexius well. "I need you to take me to the Coliseum. And I'll need a litter. One I can lie down in. I won't be able to walk if I have to ride a horse or take a wagon."

"You can take mine," Tiberia said. "I'll have Velus arrange for me to go home another way."

The harried journey to the Coliseum left Tibi breathless and light-headed from pain. Desperate to find Alexius in time, she hurried as fast as her impaired body allowed. The movement required to cover her head with the cowl almost made her scream.

Sergius took hold of her elbow. He guided her to the gladiator entrance and down into the cavernous world filled with the roar of wild animals and the fetid stench of men's fear and humiliation.

Tibi tugged her cloak around her and buried her nose in the thick material. The frenzied cheers of the mob blended with the shouted orders of armed guards herding various troupes of men.

She recognized none of the faces. Her anxiety grew with every unfamiliar set they passed. "Are our men on the field?" she asked Sergius. "I don't see any of them here."

Sergius led her to the *editor*'s office to inspect the roster. Forced to wait in the line outside the door, she fought a doomed battle with impatience. Finally their turn, she followed Sergius into the small, dusty hole. Peeling and ripped parchments from past competitions covered the walls.

"Come in, Sergius. Bring the boy." The *editor* waved them toward a chair and an upturned barrel he used for extra seating. Tibi recognized the rotund man. His name was Spurius, if her memory served from that first day when Alexius spoke with him.

"We're looking for my master or the archery troupe from the *Ludus Maximus*," Sergius said. "Do you know where either of them are or when they're expected to fight?"

A wild cry from the mob filtered through a small window in the upper corner of the office. "The archers are on the field now. They're part of Caesar's army recreating the battle of Alesia."

The crowd exploded with more frenzied shouting. "I haven't seen Alexius. As usual, when he fights he's the draw of the day. He'll go on once Vercingetorix and his Gallic horde fall."

Spurius led her out into the corridor. The press of men had intensified. She flinched from the jolts of pain the constant pushing and shoving inflicted on her back. The stench of unwashed bodies made her gag. How would they ever find Alexius in this crowd?

A burst of crazed shouting and foot-stomping from the mob made the entire amphitheater tremble. Sergius stopped, his head cocked to one side. The human traffic flowed around them like water. "Listen, my lady."

Tibi heard nothing but the roar of the drunken mob above them and the ocean of voices surrounding them.

"They're announcing the master. He begins now!" Sergius started to break into a run. Tibi's cry of pain when he jerked her forward reminded him of her injured state.

"Go on without me," she urged. "Try to speak to him before it's too late."

"No, he's already headed to the field. If I leave you, I fear I'll never find you again."

Frantic, Tibi tried to rush, but her stiff muscles and the pitiless crowd stymied her efforts to reach the platforms that conveyed the gladiators up to the sandy floor of the arena. The closer they came to the staging area, the clearer she heard the announcements above them. The sound of Alexius's name caused a riot of reaction throughout the arena. Feet stomped, sounding like thunder a mere story above her head.

"There!" Sergius pointed to a lift in the center of the staging area that was just sliding into place. "He must have been on that one."

Panic surged through her. "We have to get to him."

"We're too late! There's nothing we can do now."

Unshed tears burned her eyes. "There has to be some way to warn him!"

Sergius gripped her shoulders and forced her to look at him. "Alexius is a great champion. He practically lives in the sand. Three opponents are child's play to him. He'll be fine."

He was trying to help her stay calm, she realized,

but the stress lining his face suggested that concern weighed heavily upon him. Alexius might not be worried about multiple opponents. Most likely he expected injury of one nature or the other, but poisoned blades were a different matter, making it possible for a flesh wound to become a death blow.

Please, God, save him!

"I'll defend him," she shouted frantically over the noise. "I'll need to find a bow and arrows and a way onto the field."

"No, I can't let you," Sergius shouted back. "You've never killed anyone. You wouldn't be able to live with yourself afterward."

"I don't have to kill," she said, aware that she was capable of murder if it meant saving Alexius. "I only have to impair."

Hope lit Sergius's eyes. "The guards won't just allow you to walk into the arena and start shooting. Let me think!"

Alexius rode the lift into the middle of the arena amidst the litany of accolades he'd earned over the years. A sea of golden sand and a tempest of crowd affection encircled him. Too familiar with every aspect of his surroundings, he realized that the only thing different today was his lack of anger.

By this point in the battle, he was usually struggling to contain the thrashing beast within him, but this afternoon the creature seemed quiet. Not certain if he should be glad or concerned for his lack of response, he prayed that he didn't need his fury to propel him to victory.

An expert at most gladiator types, he often chose to fight as a *Mirmillo*. Today, with three opponents to face at once, he set aside the heavy, fish-crested helmet and shield for lighter weapons that were easier to wield. Out of habit, he tightened his grip on the Greek sword he favored and welcomed the impatient throb of blood in his veins.

He removed his helmet and held it in the crook of his arm. A breeze cooled his skin. To the cheers of the mob, he saluted the emperor before turning to offer a similar gesture to Antonius in the first row of senators. A titter of jeers mingled with the thunder of cheers. The emperor nodded to Antonius in approval.

The announcer's voice carried across the throng of fifty thousand on the arena's perfect acoustics. Informed of Alexius's retirement, the mob booed in tandem and jumped to its feet in protest. Sword in hand, Alexius raised his arms, soothing the multitude while he acknowledged their disappointment.

Once the other competitors were named—champions from a rival *ludus*—a door opened in the arena's floor. Alexius strapped on his helmet and checked the placement of the thick leather greave on his arm.

"Please, Lord," he whispered. "I don't know if I can ask for Your help in this matter, but if so, let me be victorious this one last time."

Across the sand, the undertaker, dressed as Charon in a black hood and flowing cape, waited as usual in the shadows of the exit, ready to ferry the dead from the arena.

Amid smoke, blaring trumpets and horns, three heavily armed men appeared. Their swords glinted in the sun. The swarm of buzzing spectators settled in to be entertained.

Without warning, his adversaries attacked. Alexius fended off all three with speed and unmatched skill, although one blade reached close enough to slice a hole in his tunic.

He looked at the gap in the cloth. His anger finally surfaced. He blocked an attack, throwing himself back into the battle. Blow after blow, he defended his title as Rome's premiere champion.

The wild drunken masses cheered his every move and gasped or booed when the others came close to wounding him.

For the crowd's sake, he toyed with his opponents until the ache in his ribs warned him to pick one off. In a single strategic move he sliced an adversary's upper arm, rendering the limb useless for at least a week. Seeing the wounded man fall, the pleased mob cheered louder.

Alexius swiped up the finished man's sword and tested its weight. Now armed as a *Dimachaeri,* he grinned and spun the blades like matched wheels on a chariot.

He advanced. His rivals charged. The incited mob roared. Alexius felt the catch and pull of his blade through the flesh of his prey. He carried through with the blow just as his foe's sword sliced close enough to ruffle his hair.

With a second man down, Alexius faced his last challenger. The day's rising heat and the throb in his ribs annoyed him. Armed as a *Thracian,* the third gladiator wore shin guards and carried a square shield along with his curved sword. The two men squared off like lions.

"Are you ready to die?" the *Thracian* taunted.

"Not particularly," Alexius answered, grateful that he had more to live for than ever.

"Neither am I." The *Thracian* plowed across the

sand. Sword struck sword in a violent clash of sharp, polished steel. Their muscles strained against the power of the other's. Alexius's wounded side began to burn. He felt his six-day-old stitches pull.

The crowd began to chant Alexius's name. His teeth bared as he held back the assault, he saw a *gladius* poised to strike reflected in the *Thracian's* eyes.

Death's cold fingers brushed the back of Alexius's neck. One of the wounded men had awakened. Using all of his reserves to force a turn in their positions, he exposed the *Thracian's* back to the blade instead of his own.

To his amazement, an arrow came from nowhere, piercing the shoulder of the revived attacker. The mob exploded with excitement. The already wounded man dropped his sword and fell to his knees, screaming. Alexius twisted the *Thracian* back around to use as a shield in case of more arrows. Seeing no archers he used his foot to hook the *Thracian's* ankle. With a shove he pushed the man backward, tripping him. Alexius pressed the point of his sword against the fallen man's jugular.

Lusty chants for blood poisoned the air.

"Do it," the fallen man begged. "Just please be quick!"

Breathing heavily, Alexius stepped back, choosing life instead of death. Ignoring the mixed results of the crowd's approval, he glanced over his shoulder, more interested in the archer who'd helped him than he was in killing one of his adversaries.

The undertaker remained an eerie presence near the exit, but there was no one else as far as he could see. His work complete, his agreement with Antonius honored and his marriage to Tibi secured, he saluted the emperor whose nod of approval released him from the field.

With a silent prayer of thanks to God, he stabbed the point of his sword in the sand and turned his back on his old life, satisfied that he no longer needed violence to sustain him.

Ignoring the pain in his side, he stalked to the exit. A glance at the undertaker revealed the thin, wizened face of a man beneath the cowl.

He pushed through the gate, liberated to leave the sand once and for all. He collected Calisto from the stable and headed home, desperate to see Tibi.

When he arrived at the *ludus* the sun was waning. The familiar hint of smoke permeated the air. He climbed the front steps and entered the *domus*. Except for servants cleaning the inner garden, the house seemed empty.

Assuming that Velus had gone to the market or to run some other errand, he took the stairs two at a time and went straight to Tibi's room.

It was empty.

"Tibi?" he called. No reply. Scowling, he headed back downstairs to the servants in the garden. "Where is my lady?" he asked.

The servants' chatter died abruptly. They exchanged puzzled glances. "We don't know, master," a boy called Scipio said.

"What do you mean, you don't know? Where's Velus?"

Scipio shrank back. "I don't know that either, sir."

Old anxiety rose up to taunt him. "What of my guests?"

"They left for the Forum several hours ago," he

said, clearly relieved he had at least that one answer to give him.

Alexius turned and left. Tibi *had* to be with Velus. How like her to push herself when she didn't have to. Her bruises were healing, but to his mind she'd rushed back to walking and now, leaving the house, much sooner than she needed to.

He washed quickly and exchanged his dirty tunic for a clean one.

A commotion on the lower floor sent him running down the stairs. The servants had lit lanterns along the stairwell. In the entry, he found Sergius carrying Tibi in his arms. His first instinct—to break his friend's neck—he checked, noting that not all of his temper had fled yet. "What have you done to her?"

"Nothing. This is all your doing."

"How so?" Stricken with worry, he took her light weight from Sergius with the greatest care.

Sergius turned sheepish. "She swore me to silence."

"Silence? I'll rip out your tongue if you want to stay silent!"

Sergius glared at him. "She went to the arena and saved your wretched hide. The arrow that saved you was her doing. We bribed the undertaker to change places with her. She watched over you. The pain caused from using the bow was more than the poor girl could stand. She lost consciousness in the litter on the way back here."

Remorse filled him. He'd wanted so very much to be her champion. In the end, she'd turned out to be his. "What took you so long to return? I've been worried. I came home to find her gone. To see her this way again is beyond imagining."

"She insisted we check on the health of her men."

How like her. "And?"

"They'll all live, although each of them has some kind of wound or another."

Relieved, Alexius kissed her brow and started back up the stairs.

"She's all right, otherwise," Serguis called to him. "You're a lucky a man to have a woman as brave as that one."

In her room, he placed Tibi on her couch and covered her with the white cotton. He sat down in his usual chair in the dark and waited for her to wake up.

He guessed it was nearly the sixth hour after midday when she began to stir. "Tibi? Can you hear me?"

She nodded gingerly and winced when she turned her head on the pillow to look at him.

"Why did you endanger yourself? Why didn't you stay here where you're safe?" he asked.

She blinked. "Help me turn over."

"No, I rather like you captive if it means you can't run off to the Coliseum behind my back."

Seeing her struggle, he relented and helped her onto her side, a pillow in front of her to balance against. "First, if anyone went behind anyone's back, it was you behind mine. Why didn't you tell me about your agreement with Antonius or that you planned to risk your life to force my father's hand?"

He tugged his fingers through his hair, not used to having to answer to anyone. "I didn't go behind your back. I didn't want to worry you."

"By doing so, you left my sister to carry the tale." Her eyes welled with tears. "I couldn't find you!"

Seeing her tears made him cringe inside. He couldn't even comfort her for fear of hurting her back. "Don't cry, Tibi, please. There was no need for concern."

"No need...?" She wiped the moisture from her cheeks and scrubbed at her reddened eyes. "My father arranged for your opponents' blades to be poisoned. One tiny scratch and you could have been lost to me forever."

Dazed, he sat back in the chair. "Tell me everything."

She did as he asked. "I had to shoot that man," she said nearing the end of the story. The lamplight warmed her tear-streaked face as she unconsciously picked at her fingernail. "I only wounded him, and I know I'm probably wrong to say it, but I would have killed him if it meant saving you."

He slipped to his knees beside the couch and took hold of her nearest hand. "I can't express how grateful I am that you care for me so much."

"I do more than care. I *love* you."

"And I love you. You're mine and I'm yours, no?"

"Yes."

"After today, I owe you my life, not that you didn't own it already."

She leaned forward on her pillows and softly kissed his lips. "You don't owe me anything. Look how many times you've rescued me in the past few weeks alone."

"I didn't mind." He grinned, his shock all but gone. "You keep me from boredom."

She stroked his cheek. "At this rate you'll be the most entertained man alive."

"And once we wed I'll be the most blessed."

Two weeks later, Tibi heard Velus call her name. "I'm here in the garden." A month since she'd been caned, she was almost completely healed. She was preparing for her wedding in two days' time. Adiona and Pelonia were helping her fuss over the details of her first *stola,* what flowers to use and the best meal to serve their wedding guests.

"You have a visitor, my lady," Velus said.

"My sister?"

"No. One of the master's friends. A lady by the name of Dora."

"Dora? Of course, show her in."

Tibi stood and smoothed down her tunic as she followed the paths between the verdant flowerbeds. An older woman appeared with Velus in the arched doorway.

"Finally, I see you," Dora said, her Greek accent similar to that of Alexius, but thicker. "I was so sorry when Alexius told me you were ill."

Tibi welcomed her. She led Dora to a table near the smallest of the garden's three fountains. "I've looked forward to our meeting."

"Not half as much as I have, I promise you. So many rumors about Alexius and his bevy of women, but not once did he bring a woman to the *thermopolium* to meet us or share a meal with him. The day he does..." She clapped her hands. "I *had* to go to the market. That will teach me to stay home, no?"

"He never brought *anyone* before me?"

"Not one."

Tibi smiled, remembering that he'd told her he only brought special women to his Greek oasis.

"I have something for you."

"My panther?"

"Come and see." Dora smiled.

Tibi followed the small woman into the entryway. A cage made of wood slats sat near the wall with a healthy black panther inside it. "He's big, no?" asked Dora. "His eyes opened the day after you left. We think he must be seven or eight weeks old by now. He's bigger than Iris, but she's such a good mama she keeps feeding him."

Tibi sank to her knees on the cool tiles beside the cage. "Is it safe to let him out?"

"Certainly. He's a good boy. He thinks he's a little king to be held, fed and played with all the hours of the day."

Tibi undid the latch and allowed the cub to come to her on his own. "Did you name him?"

"We call him Pest, but you'll find something better, no doubt."

"He thinks he's a little king, you say? Then I think I'll call him Rex."

Dora laughed. "Be careful. Alexius is Greek. Greek men think *they* are the only king in their house."

Dora visited a little longer before having to return to the *thermopolium* to start preparations for the evening guests. Alexius arrived home from the Forum within moments of Dora's departure. "You just missed her," Tibi told him. "She is the kindest lady. She even brought Rex back to me."

"Rex? I'm the only king in my house."

She laughed.

"I'm serious.

She laughed again and told him what Dora said about Greek men. "Come here and see him."

She took Rex from his cage, pleasantly surprised he let her hold him. He hissed at Alexius. Unconcerned, Alexius picked up the cub by the scruff of his neck. "She's mine. Don't forget it…Rex," he sneered. "And we'll get along fine."

Laughing, Tibi wrapped her arms loosely around Alexius and grinned up at him. "She told me something I think will amuse you."

He put Rex on the floor and gathered her close. "What is it?"

"She said I'm the only woman you ever brought to meet them."

He shrugged.

"You said you'd brought a hundred 'special' women there."

"No, you said that."

"You let me think it was true."

"You seemed to want to believe it. I didn't want to disappoint you."

She caressed his cheek. "You've never disappointed me yet."

"Give it time."

She laughed and rolled her eyes. "I'll give you all the days of my life."

He kissed her softly on the lips. "Good. That's exactly how long I need."

Epilogue

A week later, Tibi, Velus, Sergius and Leta awaited
Alexius outside the gladiator entrance of the Coliseum.
Rex was asleep in his cage on the elaborate silk pillow
his aunt Adiona had given him. Because Pelonia and
Adiona insisted their children be kept far away from the
"Den of Torture," as Pelonia referred to the amphithe-
ater, their friends had decided to join Tibi and Alexius's
small band near the city gates.

The roar of the mob signaled the unchanging nature
of Rome, but as far as Tibi and Alexius were concerned,
nothing was the same. In the week since their wedding,
all their wants had fallen into the place.

With a prayer of thanks for all her blessings, Tibi
lifted her face heavenward and relished the sun's
warmth on her face. Today they embarked for Umbria
and the future they'd thought unattainable, but that the
Lord had made possible.

"The task is done." The wagon swayed as Alexius
climbed into the driver's padded seat. He picked up the
reins and released the brake with his foot. "The school's
charter has been returned to the Emperor. My men are

released from their oath, and I'm officially no longer a gladiator *or* a *lanista*."

To Tibi, he seemed free, buoyant even, as the wagon began to move. He wrapped his arm around her shoulders and pulled her close. "Perhaps not," she said, "but no matter what, you'll always be my champion."

He leaned over and pressed a tender kiss to her lips. "And have no doubt, *agape mou, you* will always be my everything."

* * * * *

Dear Reader,

I'm often asked where I get the inspiration for my characters. Most of the time I don't even know myself, but *The Champion* was a little different. Tibi and Alexius's story is similar to the early relationship between my own parents. My mom was raised in a difficult home, and my father was the baby of a big loving family. When they met and married they were happy, but they knew something was missing.

Through the testimony of their friends and family, they realized they needed Christ to forgive their mistakes and make them complete. Though their journey to faith was quiet, it was genuine. They spent the next forty years planting churches, sharing their faith and inspiring others. This month they'll have been married fifty-three years and are closer than ever.

Although I may not usually know where my inspiration to create my characters comes from, I always see them in their later years as similar to my parents, having lived long lives of faith, loving each other and surrounded by their happy families. I pray for these same blessings for you and your loved one.

I hope you've enjoyed Tibi, Alexius and my two other Roman-set stories, *The Gladiator* and *The Protector.*

I love to hear from my readers. Please visit my website, www.carlacapshaw.com, and/or write to me at Carla@carlacapshaw.com.

Be inspired,

Carla Capshaw

Questions for Discussion

1. Due to a childhood filled with pain, Tibi's self-worth is very low. How were you treated as a child and how does that treatment affect you today? If you were damaged, how has Christ made a difference in how you see yourself now?

2. Tibi ran away from her father's threats. Her sister saw her act as rebellious. Alexius views her as courageous. The Bible teaches we're to honor our parents. How do you see Tibi's actions? Was she right to go against her father? What would you have done in her position? Why?

3. When Tibi first went to the Colosseum, she learned the gladiators were different than she believed them to be. Have you ever had preconceived notions about a person based on her occupation or circumstances and later found out she was more like you than you realized?

4. Alexius grew up in a happy, loving home, fairly insulated from tragedy. When tragedy struck, he reacted with violence. After he came to Christ, tragedy struck again, but he was able to react differently because of his new faith. Have you faced tragedy? How did you react? Were you a Christian? If not, do you think you would have acted the same or differently if you'd had Christ in your life?

5. Alexius had given up hope and accepted that his empty existence was all he'd have until the Lord

changed him. How did your life change once you accepted Christ into your heart?

6. Because of her cousin's example, Tibi believes in Christ. She resisted dedicating herself to Him because she knows her father will disapprove. Before you become a Christian, was there a person in your life that kept you from committing yourself to Him? Now that you are a Christian, how has your relationship with that person changed?

7. Alexius had seen the work of the Lord in the lives of his friends, but he feared his anger would keep him from being a true Christian. Once he gave his life to the Lord, he and his needs changed because the Lord was able to work in him. Was there something in your life that kept you from dedicating your heart to the Lord? After you became a Christian, how did that matter change in you?

8. Both Tibi and Alexius came to faith through the examples and testimonies of their friends. Was there someone in your life whose testimony and example helped influence you and bring you to the Lord?

9. Tibi and Alexius both needed acceptance, which they found in each other. But it wasn't until they gave their hearts to Christ that their lives were complete. How did your life change once you accepted Christ? How did your new beliefs affect your relationships with your loved ones?

10. Alexius struggles with anger. All of us have an issue that we struggle against. What is/was your

issue? Have you given your issue to the Lord? Did He help you or is He in the process of helping you overcome it?

11. For legal reasons, Alexius and Tibi believed they'd never be able to marry, but in an answer to prayer, a way appeared. Have you prayed for something you thought was impossible that the Lord helped you accomplish? How did He provide for you?